ROSS MARTIN

The Oxbow

First published by Reelfoot 2020

Book cover by Alexander Hanke:
www.zumheimathafen.com/

First edition

ISBN: 978-1-7349487-0-7

This book was professionally typeset on Reedsy.
Find out more at reedsy.com

For

1

The Coming Flood

I t lay crooked on the water, like a smile on the face of the river. There was no denying its distinctly human proportion, its boomerang-style curve—it was a leg. Rufus watched it float by, as unassuming as a piece of driftwood, but in even less of a hurry to get anywhere.

The Mississippi River had been generous lately, thanks in no small part to the flood. When the river rose, it snuck into places it wasn't supposed to go, picked up things it had no business handling, and deposited them further down river for people like Rufus to scavenge. Mostly it just brought junk, but sometimes he scored big: once there was the velvet portrait of some old singer, another time a propane tank that he was able to return for twenty dollars. But never had he seen anything like this. A smile broke out across his face.

He followed the leg as it bobbed in the current, only a few feet out from the banks. The debris was too thick for him to just wade in and grab it—he'd never reach it without getting himself swept away. Luckily, the rising water had wedged an entire tree against the levee, plucked from the banks upriver like the wind-blown flower-head of a dandelion. It scooped the leg up in its thicket of branches.

With a long, wooden pole—a shovel at one point in its life, now with a horseshoe duct-taped to the end—he stepped up to the edge of the water and reached out. It was far too short. He took a step into the water, but his heel slipped and he plunged butt-first into the mud. Rufus bounced up quickly; the kinds of critters that lingered around the banks this time of year were nothing to be fooled with, as a cottonmouth could lay a person out awful quick.

He sloshed back onto the levee, his boots spilling water with every step. He sat on the grass and pried them off one at a time, dumping a good gallon of dirty river water from each, followed by a fine layer of mud and silt. He looked over at the leg. It hadn't moved—the thing just floated there, toying with him. At one point, Rufus had considered adding the handle of a garden hoe to extend his reach but figured that his grandmother would skin his hide if more garden tools went missing. He cursed himself now for being so cautious. If Rufus didn't bring it in, his brother Gideon would never believe it was there. Or worse, Gideon would find it first.

He wiped some of the mud off his breeches and stomped over to the base of the tree. The water hadn't rotted it out yet, it appeared. Rufus put a foot on it, giving it another shake—the last thing he wanted was to go floating down the river riding a tree. It seemed firm, wedged in place by the ruthless push of the Mississippi. Barefoot, his feet found a grip on the rough bark, and he inched his way up the trunk.

As he climbed out to the far end of the tree he imagined the reactions when people saw what he'd found. They'd likely suspect that his brother, Gideon, had killed the man, Rufus reckoned. Gideon seemed to get blamed for every petty theft, every bit of vandalism in the whole county, and most times they were right. But mostly Rufus just wondered what the paper would say about him. Hell, he might even get a reward. He inched closer to where it floated, parting shriveled leaves still clinging to their branches. He expected a water-logged mass of skin and an acrid punch in the nose. Instead, he saw a fully intact appendage, smooth and well-crafted: the leg was wooden.

Rufus sat back on a branch and let out a sigh. Disappointment swirled with relief. He never really wanted to handle a mangled human limb anyhow. He would have, had the situation called for it—at least that's what he told himself. Looking back down at the appendage, he reckoned a wooden leg was better than no leg at all.

But he needed to act fast. The current was still trying to tease it back out into the river. Cradled in a thin bough of the tree, he stretched for it, hoping to snatch it before the river got too greedy. He moved up the branches to get a better reach. The tips of his fingers only skimmed it. A little stretch and he finally got a grip on the wooden foot. But just as he closed his fingers around it, choppy waves started kicking up against the levee, tossing his tree around violently. On the river, he watched as a strange red fog swept across the surface. Even in the dim light, it was clear something was off. As he looked back down at the water, he pulled his hand away with a shock: The river now ran red as blood.

A sharp crack rang out, the branch giving way. Before Rufus could react, he was in the river. The water stung his eyes and filled his ears. His feet could find no purchase in the mud; the water was too deep. The current dragged him out like an unwilling performer onto a stage. He thrashed about, grasping for anything that might keep him afloat. For all his experience around the river, Rufus couldn't swim a lick.

The current pushed him along swiftly. He fought his way up to take a sharp breath, but then he was back under. A piece of wood bobbed away from him. His head plunged under. He reached again, but again it slipped away from him. This time he went under and was unable to come up.

Rufus sank. The water pressed in on him like walls collapsing. The darkness was deep as his limbs began to feel heavier. The life in him would soon be flickering out.

As he closed his eyes a final time, a feeling took hold of him. It could have been the jaws of death coming to claim him for all he knew, but he felt a surge of energy, a new feeling of control.

He opened his eyes. It was as if he could somehow feel the river itself, like he knew what it was thinking. In seconds, he could feel himself rising to the surface. He was somehow pushing himself to the surface, though he wasn't moving a muscle.

Water streamed down his face as he broke the surface. As he gasped for air, he managed to get one arm over a piece of wood, then another. Rufus heaved breath until his lungs could catch up. He'd swallowed far more filthy water than he'd have liked, but he was alive, and he wasn't sure how.

It was only after he cleared the water from his eyes that he realized that he was tucked in just behind the knee of the wooden leg. He managed to crack a smile. The very thing that nearly killed him was now keeping him afloat. It was smaller than he had expected, almost the size of a child's. Regardless, he was glad he'd managed to find it.

Rufus kicked his legs awkwardly—he was about as graceful

in the water as a cow—and was soon back at the levee, a good distance downriver from where he started. His bare feet found the bottom again, and he pushed the leg into the tall grass lining the banks. He staggered out, landing in a heap. The last of the evening light shone on him as he lay there, trying to catch his breath.

When his breathing had calmed, he looked back to the river. It had gone back to its ugly, turd-brown shade. The fog was gone. He shook his head, having never seen anything like it before. Regardless, he was alive, and that was enough, though he still couldn't figure out how he'd pulled himself out of the water. A strange current maybe, he reckoned, trying to push it from his mind.

He turned back to the leg. It was a solid, weighty piece of work, and old. Chunks of it were missing and there were boreholes from legions of bugs. The straps were broken too. If someone was still using it, then it was time for a new one anyhow. Rufus reckoned he'd fare better on a stump than this rickety thing. It definitely wasn't worth nearly dying over.

Still, he knew that some part of Gideon would be jealous that *he* hadn't found it, and that gave him a bit of comfort. With a breath, he grabbed the leg by the foot and began dragging it down the levee to collect his boots.

But from his perch above the low-lying fields, he could see a set of headlights coming down the service road. The Mississippi was wide and deep here, not a bridge or a town for miles—a person had to have a good reason to come out this far, and Rufus knew one by the name of Gideon. The evening had mostly spilled its darkness into the sky by now, making it hard to see shapes from a distance, but soon the shiny star emblem and the athletic silhouette of a patrol car came into view. It was the law.

Rufus stood poised as the car approached. He had no reason to run—and nowhere to run to even if he had. He crossed his arms and waited.

When the car pulled up in front of him, a spotlight shot out, causing him to cover his eyes. A moment later the light went out and a door opened. Through his light-strained eyes, he could see a woman stepping out—a woman he had never seen before.

"That a leg you got there?" she called out.

"It is," he said reluctantly. "Found it in the river." He studied her silhouette in the dark. "Who are you?"

"Maddox," she said. "New county sheriff. Just started." She was on her way up the levee toward him. Rufus didn't like conceding the higher ground. When she got closer she stuck out a hand. Rufus didn't respond in kind. "Heavens, child," she said. "You take a bath out there or something?"

"No. Fell in."

The sheriff threw her hands up.

"Now, I ain't your momma, but I will say that you need to steer clear of that river—it's like an angry dog in a tiny little cage, just raring to get out." She looked back up at him. She took a deep breath. Her eyes narrowed. It was on to business. "You wouldn't happen to be one of the Pinhook boys, would you?"

"I am," said Rufus defiantly. "Rufus Pinhook."

"Then you probably know why I'm here, I reckon?"

"Yes, ma'am," said Rufus. "Haven't seen Gideon in two days." It was a familiar routine. Law asked for Gideon, Rufus said nothing.

The sheriff studied him, looking for some sign of betrayal—a wince, a twitch, a glance to the ground—that might give him up as a liar. A liar he was, but not one prone to giving it up so easy: Rufus had it down cold.

"Alright then," she said after a few moments, turning to head back down the slope of the levee. "Come on."

"You taking me in? I didn't do nothing."

The sheriff turned around.

"Taking you home, boy," she said. "Unless you want to walk across muddy fields in the dark, sopping wet, and," as she saw his bare feet, "with no boots."

Walking across a pit of cottonmouths sounded better than riding with the law, but Rufus couldn't even remember where he'd dropped his boots. He looked off towards his house, which was nearly a half mile off. She must have seen the hesitation on his face.

"I promise I won't tell anyone that you took a ride with *the law*," she said, putting a hand on her heart. "Now get your butt in the car."

Rufus exhaled and took out after her, knowing full well that Gideon would kill him if he ever found out.

They followed the towering levee for a while before turning off into the field toward his house. The Pinhooks, of course, lived near the river, near enough that they inherited the clouds of river bugs that swarmed every evening.

"Your folks okay with you being out in the river like that?" she asked. He was mildly annoyed at her insistence to make small talk. He gave her a strong glare, but found himself opening up anyway.

"Don't know what they'd think," he said. "Never met 'em. But I don't reckon Grandma Jezebel minds, long as I find something useful."

7

"And just what is it you're looking for, aside from wooden legs?"

"I'm building a boat," he said. "I need pieces for it."

"Okay. And what do you want to do with a boat? Fish?"

He paused before he answered.

"Gonna take it downriver to New Orleans, or maybe even further than that. Maybe South America." He looked around at the barren fields ringed by tall dirt walls that held the river at bay. "Anywhere far from here."

He waited for her to laugh at him like Gideon and other people had, but she didn't even crack a smile. Rufus reckoned her face looked genuinely sad.

They finally came upon Rufus's house. The family home was a houseboat propped up on cinder blocks. The sight of it was confusing, repairs having been done in a piecemeal fashion with whatever materials the river happened to bring their way: sheets of tin, driftwood, even the door of a portable toilet. The Pinhook houseboat only ever set sail on the ocean of cracked concrete slabs where it stood. It was the foundation of some ancient grain elevator or barn, long since decimated by years of creeping river water.

Rufus could already hear the dogs barking as they approached. They were wild critters that howled and yammered at anything that moved; everything, that is, except his Grandma Jezebel. They were utterly devoted to her. Rufus reckoned she liked them more than him or his brother.

"Your place isn't easy to find," she said. "Been driving around here all afternoon. Kept running into water."

"Grandma likes it that way," he said.

She shook her head as she parked the car in a little gravel patch in front of the house.

"Your grandmother keep bottle trees?" she asked, looking at the dogwood tree covered in painted bottles. It was a bit too late in the spring for the tree to bear flowers, but it was bright with colorful bottles that his grandmother popped onto the ends of the branches, a few hanging with wire or twine.

"Only when she's scared of something. She says evil spirits get trapped inside them."

"What's she so scared of?"

Rufus thought about it for a second. The last time she did this was a few days before a small earthquake. She claimed the river told her it was coming. She took all of her nice plates out and boxed them up on the floor. She had it down to the minute, coming in and collecting Rufus and his brother in the middle of the night. They stood in the middle of the field, waiting for "the big one" that everyone always talked about. Sure enough, it came, though it didn't shake any harder than a baby shaking a rattle.

"Who knows? It's always something different." He turned back to the sheriff.

A phantom peeked through the curtain, a phantom Rufus knew to be Grandma Jezebel. The sheriff stopped and scanned the property.

"The boys down at the station say that half the reported thefts in Mingo county could be solved if I just poked around here for a few minutes. Say they've been watching you Pinhooks since you boys were old enough to steal your first bikes." The sheriff smiled. He looked up at his grandmother peeking through the curtains. He was really in for it. When they had almost reached the door, the sheriff stopped. "Think your grandmother is around? I need to talk to her for a moment."

Rufus looked at the window again. The curtain fell. The

sheriff had seen it too.

"She's around," said Rufus. "But she ain't gonna talk to you."

"And why's that?"

"Can't say. She's got her ways, and the rest of the world's got theirs."

His answer somehow seemed enough for her.

"Well. I guess I can tell you then. I'm sure that y'all have noticed that river over there. It's just itchin' to spill over those levees."

"So what?" asked Rufus. This wasn't all that out of the ordinary. Seemed like the river flooded every year or two.

"Well," she said, handing her head a little lower. "It looks like that river is gonna get its chance to roam; they're gonna blow the levee just a little ways from here."

"You mean they're gonna flood us?" asked Rufus.

"That's what I mean. Otherwise half the town will be underwater by the end of the week. Thought it best to flood some fields rather than the whole town."

Rufus let the words sink in. It was like he had touched an electric fence. At that moment Grandma Jezebel erupted from the door of the houseboat.

"Now you listen here," she said as she came down the stairs, her nightgown sweeping the ground. "No one threatens a Pinhook." Her finger was raised in the air as she approached the sheriff. "My people have lived by this river for...well, as long as there's been a river." She pointed at Rufus. "His great great granddaddy, Winslow Pinhook, took a mighty piss and created that river that you see today." She stopped for a moment to collect her breath. "You just try to move us."

With that, she turned and made her way back up the stairs, slamming the metal door behind her. The sheriff looked to Rufus, but he could only shrug. He'd never known his grandmother to listen to anyone. Maybe the river itself would have to carry her away.

"You tell your granny that I'll be back around. We're gonna get you all moved into a shelter soon enough." She turned to walk back to the car. "Rufus," she said, stopping halfway across the yard. "You seem to have a good head on your shoulders," she continued. "Do me a favor and tell Gideon to come see me."

Rufus felt heat swelling around his face and neck. He had to fight back the urge to curse at her, instead kicking the small mound of gravel he'd piled up, scattering it across the overgrown yard.

"You got something to say to Giddy you say it yourself."

The sheriff moved to speak, but held her tongue. She opened the door of her patrol car.

"Reckon I'll be seeing you sooner than I thought," she said as she climbed in. She circled around in the drive, rolling down the window. "And Rufus," she shouted. "Watch yourself. The flood's coming." She drove away, seen off by a chorus of barks from his grandma's dogs.

Rufus gulped as he opened the door of the houseboat.

2

A Pinhook is Never Safe

H is grandmother set on him instantly.

"You making friends with the law, boy?" she said, storming over to him. Her eyes had a way of shrinking down to expose a white ring around them—the effect was that of a cobra flaring out its hood.

"No, Grandma," said Rufus, trying his best to walk past her. He started to head for his room, but she wouldn't relent. She was always hard to deal with when Gideon wasn't home. She'd worn bare spots into the carpet on account of her nervous pacing.

"Where's Gideon?" She was nearly frantic—it was clear who she cared about more in this family.

"I don't know, grandma. He just took off. That's what he tends to do, if you haven't figured it out yet."

For a moment, he thought he could hear the veins popping in her head. He braced himself for a verbal lashing, but instead the old woman stormed into the kitchen where it smelled like she'd been cooking biscuits. She started clanging pots loudly in the sink. He was pretty sure she had no intention of actually washing them, but just liked to hear the metal smashing together. The tiny houseboat was too small for them on good days, but felt especially tight now. He needed air. He walked back to the door.

"Hold on, there," she said. "You ain't going nowhere till Gideon comes home." She fixed him with a stare—a stare from Grandma Jezebel felt physical, like she could wring a person's neck with it. "The river's acting out," she said. "I'm worried about what's going to wash up."

"Just the same old junk that always does," he said. "Why can't I leave?"

"Cause it ain't safe," said Grandma Jezebel. He knew her to be a natural worrier, but this seemed like something entirely new.

"Why ain't it safe?"

She whipped around quickly.

"Because you're a Pinhook, and a Pinhook ain't never safe!" Her words hung in the air for a moment, then she again started her pacing. "When your brother gets back, I don't want neither of you leaving this house." Rufus felt frustration building. The old woman was finally losing it, he reckoned. She turned Rufus, eager for his response. "You hear me, boy?"

"I hear you!" he said. "I also hear those stupid dogs." They'd been barking since he got home. "Can't you shut 'em up?" She looked outside, her brow furrowing. "I'll bet it was that darn cop car," he said.

"No," she said. "It wasn't the cop car…." but her voice trailed off as she caught sight of the leg slung in his arm. Grandma Jezebel dropped the pan she was holding and walked up to Rufus.

"Where'd you get that?" she asked.

13

"Found it in the river."

The old woman looked at it with a flicker of recognition.

"Get in your room," she said, her voice unusually low. She stared down at the leg as if it were a coiled snake. She turned back to Rufus, who hadn't yet moved. "Into your room, Rufus!" "Now!" She snatched the leg from him and shoved him to the bedroom he shared with Gideon. "I don't want you coming out of there until I say." She slammed the door. He heard her moving something in the living room, followed directly by a thud against his door. Rufus tried the handle, but the door wouldn't budge. He tried again with his shoulder. Still nothing—she'd barricaded him in.

Rufus had had enough. He quickly changed from his wet clothes and grabbed a bag off his bed. He threw in the things he thought he would need: clothes, a flashlight, and a pocketknife. He had cans of beans and jars of peanut butter stashed at the boat. He was about to go for the window when he saw his fiddle at the foot of his bed. It was an old thing that he rarely ever played. He picked it up and studied the curved wood. Part of him wanted to bring it along, strap it to his back and play on street corners for money. But mostly it just made him think of his grandmother forcing him to practice. He could find another one when he got settled. He left it on the bed and walked to the window.

Their room opened right up into the dog pen, no doubt by design. The dogs were huddled in the far corner of their pen, noses pointed to the woods. Rufus landed barefoot in the dirt. The beasts didn't even look up. He watched them for a second in disbelief. Under normal circumstances they'd be thrilled at the chance to tear Rufus apart. But they continued barking at something in the nearby tree line.

He hopped the fence. Having left his boots at the levee, he went to the shed to grab his brother's knee-waders. He sat down on the floor of the rickety shed and pulled one of the boots on. It was far too big for him, but better than nothing. He had no more than slipped his foot into the other boot when he noticed what the dogs were focused on. One of the bottles on his grandmother's bottle tree was rattling. He stopped for a moment to watch. The bottle lit up as if a red lightning bug were trapped inside, shaking fiercely.

His feet slid around inside the boots as he walked to the tree. The dogs were motionless, silent, watching the light bounce back and forth inside the bottle. A lightning bug would have to be huge to cause this. Rufus reached for the bottle, but it was hot to the touch. He pulled his hand back quickly, cooling his fingertips on his tongue. With a stick, he poked at it. The bottle continued to buzz louder and faster. As he tried to push the bottle off its branch it shot off like a rocket, slamming into another and shattering into tiny shards. Rufus shielded his eyes. The dogs again erupted. When he looked back up, the light was gone.

The shrill creaking of the front door sent Rufus flying for the shed. Grandma Jezebel appeared in the yard, dragging the leg behind her. The old woman's face—already rutted deep with wrinkles—spilled over with worry. It was like she had aged years in the past couple of days. She immediately noticed the broken glass on the ground, checking the other bottles and murmuring under her breath.

She then walked to the burn barrel in the middle of the yard and tossed the leg in, dousing it with a generous pour from a gas canister. He felt a pang of anger as she tossed in a match, sending flames leaping into the air. She stayed for a moment to make sure the leg was burning, then walked to the dog pen.

But no sooner had she arrived than she screamed out.

"Mutt! Where are you, Mutt?"

Mutt was her favorite; the dog got far more attention than either Rufus or Gideon. She rattled the gate, but it was secure. She spun, manically calling for him. She stared at the shed for a moment. Rufus ducked a little deeper into the shadows. But instead, she took off into the woods, yelling out for the missing dog.

When her hollering had placed Grandma Jezebel a good ways off, Rufus pushed the door open. He ran to the burn barrel and fished out the leg with a garden spade. It was solid black in places, but most of the fuel had burnt off already. It was really no worse for wear.

Leg dragging behind him, Rufus too set off into the woods, though he had no intention of searching for the dog; he had other business that needed tending—his boat.

He had to keep the boat a secret, else his grandmother would have a fit. Plus, it gave him a chance to work on it in peace. He kept it in the woods, not too far from where a large creek drained into the river. This way he wouldn't have to drag it too far when he decided to hightail it out of there.

To the untrained eye, his boat could best be described as a pile of junk: a layer of plywood and sheet metal lashed crudely atop four oil drums, a cabin built from an old kitchen table and a chest-of-drawers, all of it scavenged. It could only be called a boat in a broad sense, as Rufus didn't even know if it would float. He'd find out soon enough though, and then he'd be long gone. But first, he needed a motor, and it was Gideon who would help with that.

He sloshed through the woods for half a mile or so, keeping

a good distance from his grandmother's calls. Recent rains had left the ground muddy, as had the glut of river water with nowhere else to go. Each step was a battle, the mud grabbing hold of his feet, not wanting to loosen its grip. The whirring of cicadas accompanied him as he walked, sprinkled with occasional howls from his grandmother's dogs.

As he came to the clearing where he kept his boat, he noticed right away that something was wrong. It was the oil drums he'd noticed first, and not one of them was attached to his boat. It was soon clear that there was no boat for anything to be attached to. The clearing was cluttered with 2x4s, fragments of ropes, and shattered plywood. The blue tarp that had covered it was now tattered into ribbons strewn across the mud as if a parade had just come through.

"What the..." he started, but then a strong wind blew in from the trees around him. There was a chill to it, strange for this late in the spring. The trees shook back and forth. As he turned back to the levee, a clear, deep splash rang out from the flooded woods. He'd known bullfrogs to make a heavy splash, but this was clearly something more. He strained to see if someone was there, but couldn't see more than a few yards—his flashlight was a cheap plastic thing that had faded down to a sorry glow. He tossed it to the ground amongst the remnants of his boat.

The wind stirred up again, whipping the trees into a chatter. He stopped to look at the woods around him. The thicket formed a wall of darkness. Rufus had been running up and down these fields since he could walk, and liked to pretend that nothing out here scared him, only that wasn't always true. The river could bring strange things with it, bad things.

Another loud *plunk* sounded out, closer than the one before.

17

As he turned back to the levee, a shadow darted behind a tree.

"Come out of there," yelled Rufus. But there was no answer. It couldn't be his grandmother—there was no way she could move that fast.

Rufus decided to get out of there, but only made it about ten feet before he stopped cold. Slinking out of the woods was a man —long and lanky—dressed in old-looking clothes and wearing a wide-brimmed hat, a set of untamed eyes below it. A massive beard sprang from his face like shrubbery.

Rufus took a step back. He couldn't speak. He could only watch as the man bent down to pick something up from behind him. Without wasting a second he heaved the thing. Halfway through the air, it became disturbingly clear what it was—the limp body of a dog. It landed in the water with a heavy *plop*.

3

The Warning

The man stepped forward, moonlight bouncing off his pockmarked face. Rufus's heart flailed around in his ribcage. He was frozen in his tracks. It was like the mud had grabbed hold of his legs and wouldn't let go.

But no sooner had the man taken his second step than a savage cough rang out, as if he'd just taken a big gulp of water right down his windpipe. Rufus watched as the man doubled over, hacking and gasping for breath. He turned to Rufus, a frantic look in his eyes. But there was something else about his eyes that caught Rufus's attention—it looked as if he was crying. Tears poured out of his eyes. But this was more than crying. It was a torrent. The water poured from his nose and mouth like miniature waterfalls. Eventually the man fell backwards, landing roughly in the mud.

Rufus didn't wait to see what was wrong with him and instead took off through the woods.

Thorns tore at him; newly-budded tree branches slapped his ruddy face and eyes. He flung himself through the thickets, his lungs burning so bad that he thought they would burst right through his ribcage. It must have been a mile or better before Rufus stopped against a tree, gasping for air, sure he could cough fire.

It took him a moment to realize he was holding something. Though he'd nearly choked his own heart up, he'd somehow managed to keep hold of the wooden leg. He let out a cuss.

The crack of a twig pulled him back to reality. He pulled the leg up, poised like a baseball bat above his shoulder. He waited, ready to strike. But as he took a step back, a knobby root caught his heel, sending him falling into a pool of knee-high water.

He crawled up onto his hands and knees and pulled himself onto the gnarled roots of an ancient tree. As he caught his breath, he noticed that everything had gone quiet. Nothing disturbed the darkness, not even the bugs. He peeked around him for the wooden leg, but it was nowhere to be found.

As he scanned the woods, a movement caught his attention. A bird, surely. Maybe an owl. His mind willed a big hoot owl to come out and squawk at him before winging it off into the night.

Instead, Rufus saw a figure—human in outline, though clearly not the man from earlier. This figure was no taller than a child. Its face was partly hidden by the brim of a bowler hat, but the legs—short and compact—were all too clear as the figure moseyed towards him with a crooked gait. With a cold smack of awareness, Rufus knew it was the leg he'd been holding, only now it was attached to a body.

"Reckon that feller swallowed a bit too much river water?" asked the figure in a voice deeper than its small stature would have suggested. Rufus pushed himself back against the tree, unable to move. The wooden leg and its wearer stepped into the pool of water that separated them. However, something strange happened: the water parted as if pulled by magnets on either side, leaving him a clear path to creep through. The figure stopped a few feet away and put a hand on his belly. "Doesn't agree with the system, does it?" A cackling laughter rang out, as abrasive as a wheelbarrow of rocks tipping over.

Rufus's tongue had lost all shape and purpose, deflated like a blown tire. He leaned back against a wooden post, stuttering, unable to process what was happening. Finally, a few words managed to slip past his lips.

"Who are you?" he asked, voice shaky and weak.

The laughter stopped, as if turned off at the spigot. The figure put his fingers on his scrunched-up chin. He was dressed in a tattered old suit: a jacket hung down close to his knees and a strange, bunched-up tie was choked up around his thin neck. The color of his skin was somewhere between that of a booger and a fish. His face was a confusing sight. He had a nose, a mouth, eyes—all the makings of a regular old face. But something about their assigned positions rang false. Rufus had heard his friends talk about little demons from their Sunday school lessons and reckoned this had to be one of them.

The figure made a slow circle around him.

"That's a fair question," he said. "Let me be so kind as to provide an answer." He walked to the center of the pool. The water continued to separate for him like curtains being drawn. Finally, with a booming voice and fists thrown to the sky, he began. "I'm God's Last Vomit! The Eighth Day's Calamity! Creation's Castoff! Mongrel of *the Oxbow*!" The figure paused—breathing heavily, having worked himself up into a fit. He looked at Rufus squarely as he spoke again, lowering his voice. "My brother is Death and my sister Malice. I've lived a long time. Seen a lot of things—things you could never imagine. Most have taken to calling me Weego, but that's only because you *thin-bones* can't wrap your filthy tongues around my real name. I'm what you might call an *oxman*."

Rufus tried to move, but he couldn't—wrapped around his arms and feet were the roots that had tripped him, only now they were moving.

Weego surged towards him, stopping only inches from his face. Even though he was no more than four feet tall he lorded over Rufus. He fought to back away from the creature, but the roots would not budge.

Weego reached into the pocket of his raggedy-looking suit coat and produced a glass orb. With the rub of a calloused thumb, a flash sparked from the orb, casting a fractured light throughout the woods. Weego's face came into full view. His eyes were bigger than seemed natural, with red veins cast across them like fishing nets; the nose sat like a dull cherry in the middle of his face; the skin thick and leathery.

The creature's lips slipped over long yellow teeth to reveal a wicked smile.

"Now that you know what I am, let's find out a little more about you." Weego leaned over him. The stench of rot from his mouth was overwhelming. "Right there is the question that needs asking, boy: do you even know what *you* are? Do you know the blood that flows in those veins?" Weego thrust a jagged fingernail at Rufus's wrist and slowly traced up to the pit of his elbow. "Should we find out?" He pressed harder into Rufus's arm.

"What do you want with me!" he managed to shout.

Weego stood and walked a few paces back.

"*Want* with you?" he asked, making a sound as though he'd just swallowed something bitter. "I'd just as soon scrape the eyes out of my sockets and spread them on toast than have to talk with a darned Pinhook." He put a thumb to his right nostril and emptied the contents of the left with a snort. Rufus felt the muscles in his stomach clench. It felt like he'd been given a shot that numbs body parts. Weego began to pace. His hands were clasped together behind his back; his thumbs ran circles around each other.

Rufus worked to calm his breathing. He finally managed another question.

"Did you make the water pour out of that man's face?"

Weego smiled. There was a pride to it.

"You know anyone else't could do it? He's lucky I only had it come out his face." Weego laughed and, as if remembering something important, shone the light from the little orb onto his leg. "You recognize this, don't you?" he said, tapping the wooden appendage. "You tell your granny I don't appreciate her setting fire to it."

"How do you know my grandmother?" asked Rufus, but the creature looked to have no interest in answering him, instead indulging in adjusting his jacket sleeves and straightening his collar, after which he began fishing in his pockets. Rufus was oddly amused at watching this vain little creature. After a moment, he pulled out a long, narrow pipe and packed the chamber with a pinch from his pouch. When the creature lit the pipe, it sparked and let off a fluorescent purple smoke that glowed in the dark. He inhaled slowly, letting the smoke linger in his lungs before releasing the colored vapor from his nostrils. The smoke meandered around them for a while before finally blending into the air.

"I'm here to give you a choice," the creature said. "No, *choice* is too mild. Let's call it a warning." He took another long drag from his pipe. "Leave your home tonight or die a horrible death."

"What do you mean, 'die a horrible death'?" asked Rufus.

"It means not a good death. I can elaborate, but I reckon you're cleverer than that brother of yours." His voice was thick with condescension. "Or maybe the lot of you are idiots. Both of you sure are ugly as sin."

"Listen," said Rufus, but then an eerie foghorn rang out. Weego pointed towards the levee.

"Your boat has arrived," said Weego. In the near distance, a plume of wispy red steam floated above the tree line through which Rufus could just see the ascending decks of an old-fashioned steamboat, tiered like some sort of wedding cake. "What a grand steamer she was in her day. A grand boat indeed. Pride of the Oxbow." He cocked back with his hands on his waist. "That steam is red as blood," said Weego as he turned to look Rufus in the eyes. "But there ain't nothing on that boat that's livin.'"

"How'd it get out there?" Rufus turned back to face Weego. "That's just a creek. No boat that big should be on it."

"Well, that ain't no ordinary boat. That's the Specter Steamer."

"Specter Steamer?"

"Yes, boy, and it's here for you," said Weego, watching the boat with a cocked grin. "The Oxbow has already started to bleed in, and you've felt it, haven't you, boy? How else do you reckon you rose up from the belly of that river out there?" Rufus's mind sank back to that place in the river, tons of water pushing every molecule of oxygen from his body. The creature

24

gave him a nudge to bring him back to reality. It took him a moment to realize that he was breathing heavily. Weego continued. "It was mud magic, boy! And it runs deep in your thin little veins!" He chuckled, but there was nothing of joy in it. "Now that the Oxbow has found you, it'll keep coming until it gobbles you up." At this, the creature brought a hand up to his mouth from which he pretended to eat.

"Is that how you got here?"

"Oh no," said Weego. "Far worse things than me ride on that boat." His eyes narrowed. "And that's saying something. That man you saw earlier, he and his crew followed it. It was them that got a good hit in, knocked off my leg." At this, he tapped his wooden appendage. "But they won't be the only ones, mark my word. Now that they're in, they'll keep coming 'til they bring you back."

"Back where?" asked Rufus.

"Another world." Weego turned to Rufus, genuine excitement radiating from his yellow eyes. "You see, there's a rip in the river, a gash reopened after many years." Weego pulled up the sleeve of his jacket to reveal a jagged lesion on his forearm. "Like any cut, things can get inside, cause it to become infected." At this, Weego put his fingers on either side of the wound and slowly spread the skin apart. It wasn't the sight of it that made Rufus queasy, but the sound of the scab separating. Dark blood ran freely, trickling down his arm. "You Pinhooks, for example. You got in and infected the Oxbow many years ago, brought a whole lot of pain."

"Stop!" yelled Rufus, putting a hand over his mouth. Weego chuckled as he pushed the separated skin back together.

"You'd have to get used to much worse than that in the Oxbow," said Weego as Rufus strained to look away. At that moment, a wail sounded in the distance. It was a terrible scream, not animal, but human. "Ah," said Weego. "That's more like the Oxbow."

When Rufus could again speak, it came out slow and quiet.

"Who was he, and what did he want?" he asked, unsure how the words even escaped his tightly constricted throat.

Weego smiled.

"Our watery-faced friend was just some rough-neck laborer probably, hired by someone more important to bring a Pinhook back to the Oxbow. But, by the sound of it, seems like someone got him instead." Weego shook his head and took his hat off, holding it close to his chest. "Killing that dog was about the stupidest thing that man could have done. He'd have fared better killing *you.*"

Rufus's mind swirled.

"Is Giddy ok?" he said, growing anxious.

"Ha!" shouted Weego, issuing a loud show of laughter. "You actually care about that tick-bite of a brother? How many times has he abandoned you? How many times have you taken the blame for him?"

Rufus shuddered.

"How do you know all that?"

"I've been watching you two since you was old enough to cuss, which was pretty young for that scab-pickin' brother of yours."

"Well then you'll know that I ain't about to leave my brother!" shouted Rufus. "And why have you been watching us?"

Weego's smile faded, his eyes becoming angry slits.

"An old blood bond," he said. "But that ain't no matter now. Hear me, boy. Leave him be. Put some distance between this place and yourself." Rufus's fear had turned to a neatly defined anger which was now aimed at this strange creature. "It's your name, boy!" Weego shouted, shaking his odd little head. "If only you knew." He turned and paced for a moment.

The creature's words piled up in Rufus's head. He couldn't process them. His confusion was making him dizzy. He leaned his head back against the tree trunk.

"Too much for you to handle?" said Weego. "Get smart and cast off that name of yours like the dead weight it is. Be done with it." He crossed his arms and put a finger to his chin. "What name do you reckon you'd choose? I've always been partial to *Hoovis* myself." He seemed pleased with himself, almost lost in thought. But then he turned back to Rufus. "It ain't even that far off from Rufus." He smiled, but it slowly faded. "My point is simple: leave."

"I can't," said Rufus. "I don't even have a boat anymore!"

The creature scoffed.

"Correct me if I'm wrong, but you thin-bones have other means of getting around other than a dirty river, don't you?"

The creature had a knack for tripping Rufus up. His frustration was building.

"I won't go," said Rufus in a low, growling voice. "I ain't gonna change my name, and I ain't leaving my brother."

Weego's face again lost all of its humor as the whine of a boat motor cut through the night air.

"There he is now," said the creature. "Listen to me, boy," Weego said as he leaned in close. "That name will drown you. You go with him tonight and you'll know real pain. Just steal yourself a boat and skedaddle on down the river. Hell, *I'll* steal you a boat, maybe one of them fancy ones that I see those men with big bellies fishing from."

"No! I don't have to listen to some stupid little demon."

Weego took a long, deep breath. Rufus watched as he swept his wooden leg wide to take a step towards him.

"You have no idea what's in store for you." A little smirk popped up on his face. "Allow me to demonstrate."

Water began to seep up from the ground. It rose quickly. The roots that held him tightened around his arms and legs, snaking across him like earthworms on a sidewalk after a hard rain. The tendrils began to constrict his air. He watched the water creep up to his chest, then his neck, his chin. No matter how he struggled, the roots wouldn't relent.

Weego appeared just as the water slipped past Rufus's nose. When he snapped his fingers, the rising water stopped. The water continued to part for the creature as he paced in front of him.

"I should just do the world a favor and kill you dead," he said through gritted teeth. Rufus held his breath as the creature's scowl morphed back into a playful smile. "Pity I can't." At that, the water began receding. Rufus sucked in a breath. "The choice is yours," said Weego. "Though it's only death, I suppose. Sounds pretty nice to me, actually."

The rest of the water receded as the creature turned to walk away. The roots, too, loosened their grip. By the time Rufus made back up to his feet, the creature was gone.

He was left only with the dark silhouettes of trees and ground as dry as if there'd been a drought. A shudder ran through him; he needed to get out of these woods.

4

Brothers

Rufus trudged through the darkness, mud sucking at his boots as he scanned the woods nervously.

The sound of the motor grew louder as the levee came into view. Gideon was close. The creature's strange words swirled around his head as Rufus staggered out of the woods, nervously glancing all around him. He walked up the side of the levee, still trying to wrap his head around what he'd seen, what he'd heard.

He soon saw the boat approaching. However, he could also see that his brother wasn't in it. Driving the boat was his brother's friend, Bear, but Gideon was nowhere to be found.

He didn't have much time to think about it, as something slammed into his back, sending him to the ground. It was the kind of force that could knock the Earth right off its axis. He saw nothing for a moment except a flash of light. Then a weight bore down on his chest. A muffled sound grew louder, clearer. Soon a face came into view.

"That's my brother!" yelled a voice. "Whining like a possum in a trap!"

It was Gideon.

As the world came back to him, Rufus threw an elbow into Gideon's gut as an equalizer. He was thankful that it was his brother and not the wild man, but he still felt the need to match him blow for blow.

Gideon reeled back, allowing Rufus to make his way up. Gideon was buzzing like a wasp trapped under a cup.

"Good hit, brother," he said, letting out a great laugh and pounding a fist to the ground. Gideon was the sort of person who could laugh after taking a punch to the face, so Rufus kept his guard up.

"There's something weird going on out here," said Rufus. "Some guy threw a dead dog at me. And I think that there's some kind of…" he paused for a second, looking for a better word, but there was none to be had. "There's some kind of monster following me."

"Whoa, slow down, numbnuts," said Gideon, now back on his feet.

"Did you see anything following me?" asked Rufus as he scanned the woods.

"Are you serious?" he asked when he could see Rufus wasn't joking. "Dead dogs and monsters?" Gideon let out a chuckle. "You think it might have been one of Grandma's dogs?"

"Could've been."

Gideon's eyes went wide for a moment, but then he attempted a smile, or as near as he knew how to approximate one.

"Well remind me to thank him then," he said. "Stupid dogs." He took off walking back towards the levee. "Now let's go. We've got business."

"What?" shouted Rufus. "Are you not hearing me?"

Gideon turned in a big, inflated gesture.

"I hear you," he said, throwing his arms up. "Some idiot is throwing dead critters at you and you think you're seeing monsters. We've got bigger things to deal with." He took a breath and put a hand on Rufus's shoulder. "There's a motor just brought in to Dyer's Scrap Yard that has my name on it."

Rufus planted himself, crossing his arms. The little creature's warning was like a blinking neon sign in his mind.

"I'm not going," he said decisively.

Gideon turned and glared at him. He had a clear-eyed gaze that could cut to the soul.

"You act like you're in a position to negotiate," said Gideon. "Well, this ain't negotiable, brother."

"Not negotiating. Just telling you that I ain't going with you."

Another wail sounded out through the woods.

"I guess you weren't kidding," said Gideon. "Say hello to the dog man for me. I'm gone." He turned towards the approaching boat.

A shiver tore through Rufus. He turned back to the dark woods. There was no way he was going back in there alone.

"Wait!" he finally yelled. "I want you to promise. I help you out tonight, you get me a boat."

Gideon let out a sharp laugh.

"What, so you can go down to New Orleans, get away from it all?" he said with a scoff. "You'd have as much luck getting Grandma to dance ballet. You'll just end up floating face down, all dead and bloated."

"At least I have a plan to get out of this hell hole," he snapped. "Unlike you."

Rufus had hit his mark. Gideon walked a few quick paces in each direction, a lion circling a cage. He stopped, spit, and

31

looked at Rufus.

"Make your choice now," he said. "It's me or the woods."

Rufus took a breath. There couldn't be a creature. Surely he'd just bumped his head. Still, the thought of trudging through the woods alone was too much.

"Fine," he said. "I'll go."

"Atta boy," said Gideon as he slapped him on the back. "You stand there acting like we ain't even brothers. I knew you'd come around." He put an arm roughly around him, nearly dragging Rufus to the edge of the water. "We may even look for you a real boat tonight."

Rufus was in it now. Whatever Gideon had cooked up, it was now too late to back out.

They stood on the levee near the diversion channel. Normally a little stream that fed into the river, it was now swollen with surplus flood water. Gideon pulled out a flashlight—the kind that police sometimes use to crack a person's skull—and flashed three quick blasts of light. After a moment, two flashes of light appeared from the boat out on the water.

Soon the boat pulled up on the levee. It wasn't much to look at. A dingy metal thing, it was no more than a lackluster fishing boat. Rufus would just as well have floated down river in a cardboard box. But it had a motor, and that was enough.

"You should have seen his face," yelled Gideon to the driver, a squat, toad-like figure sitting at the back end of the boat. A laugh rang out, sounding more like the cluck of an injured chicken. Rufus knew instantly who it was: Bear. He was a true piss-ant of a person. Bear couldn't roar or claw, couldn't really do anything of use. Close as Rufus could reckon, he just chose a name to make all 5 foot 3 inches of him seem bigger and rougher than it actually was. "Nearly wet his drawers when I found him!"

"There'll be no peeing your pants in this boat," said Bear.

"Let's just go," said Rufus, climbing in.

Rufus worked his way to the middle bench, kicking soda cans and bags of chips out of his path. The bottom of the boat was littered with cigarette butts and fishing gear, hooks and plastic floaters, brightly colored worms and jigs. Rufus looked for a life jacket, but there were none to be had.

Bear watched Rufus as he settled himself.

"Always good to have you around, Bear," said Rufus. "Like a snake bite, or diarrhea."

Another cluck of laughter sounded from Bear's weirdly small mouth before he turned and fired up the motor.

Gideon kicked them off the shore, taking his position up front with the spotlight, one leg up on the lip as if he were leading an army into battle. Rufus looked back toward the woods. A chill ran through him. He was glad to have company, even if it was Gideon and his idiot friend. He just hoped the strange little creature had been wrong.

The boat ran a slow jigsaw pattern through the cluttered river. They did their best to avoid driftwood torpedoes, but were still jolted by the occasional log from time to time. The river had stretched out across the land, working its way into every little nook and cranny, picking up anything that wasn't bolted down.

The only real noise came from the low hum of the motor as it struggled to push them inland. Rufus was in no mood to talk anyhow. But then the boat whipped to the left, driving them directly into a wooden projectile. The thud was harsh, like a body hitting pavement. Rufus turned to see the reason for the disturbance: Bear trying to light a cigarette.

33

"You steal that from your parents?" asked Rufus. Bear didn't respond, but kept flicking the lighter, which seemed to have no interest in appeasing him. On closer inspection, the cigarette was bent almost as sharply as a flexed arm. It was pitiful looking, all crumpled up as though it had lived much of its life at the bottom of a handbag.

Gideon finally chimed in.

"Turn us around or I'll put that thing out on your fat forehead," he said.

Bear only grinned.

"Can't put it out if it ain't lit," he said, but then the wheel turned with a harmonious flick and a tiny flame hopped out, giving Bear just enough time to spark the pathetic little thing.

"You all done?" asked Rufus.

Bear looked at him as he sucked in the first puff of smoke. He exhaled, watching Rufus with a cocksure grin.

"You Pinhooks need to live a little." He took another puff, this time coughing violently.

"Just drive the boat, idiot," said Gideon, again taking his position up front.

Bear moved the boat back into the channel. Rufus was eager to continue in silence, but Bear couldn't seem to quit.

"You know, my granddaddy built these levees," said Bear. He spoke slowly, with a smug manner and a drawl that even Rufus and Gideon thought to be backwoods. "Had his own excavating company." Rufus watched him take another drag off the cigarette, this time successfully. Bear then smiled, as if revisiting his glory days. "Reckon y'all boys would be swimming right now if it weren't for him. That little houseboat of yours wouldn't last long in a real flood." Every word seemed to crumble out of his mouth like chewed up gravel. Gideon simply kept the spotlight on the water, ignoring him.

Bear continued.

"I reckon it must be tough never knowing if your house will even be there when you get back. Or if you'll even be in the same place when you wake up in the morning. Don't guess a Pinhook would know what it was like to be proud."

Rufus felt a flash of anger. He picked up a red and white plastic floater from the bottom of the boat and chucked it right at Bear's smug face. It bounced off his forehead with a nice clean pop. Bear was confused at first, but then stood. His weight carried the boat to one side, nearly launching Gideon into the water.

"You done messed up," said Bear, stepping across the boat towards Rufus, who held the sides, desperate not to fall in. Bear grabbed him by the back of the neck. "Can't swim, can you? Let's give you a chance to learn." Again, Bear threw his weight to one side. Water flooded into the lopsided boat. Rufus's head was inches from the water, his shirt already soaked. Bear pushed his nose to the surface, then his mouth. Rufus closed his eyes as his whole face went under.

How many moments passed, Rufus didn't know. But then the boat whipped back in the other direction. Rufus gasped for breath. Bear was no longer on top of him. When he cleared the water from his eyes, he could see that Gideon had Bear held down in the bottom of the boat.

"Bear!" yelled Gideon, right up in his face. "We don't care if your granddaddy pushed dirt around his whole life." His voice got lower. "But all *your* daddy does is sit at the gas station and stare at women. Now shut up and steer the boat."

Bear's head pulsed redder and redder.

"I'll say what I like," he stammered. "This here's my boat."

"And you get the pleasure of sharing it with us," said Gideon, calmly. "But if you ever mock my family again I'll knock the fillings from your rotten, hick teeth."

Gideon released him with a push and stepped to the front of the boat. Bear grimaced as he sat down, reaching around to pluck a fishing hook lodged in his back. After a moment he kicked on the motor, whose whirring did little to conceal the steady stream of curse words pouring from his mouth.

Rufus watched his brother take up his position as though nothing had even happened. Even though Bear was stouter, there was something unpredictable about Gideon, something that commanded respect, or even fear.

As they floated on, the beam of the spotlight revealed trees half submerged, leafless branches sticking out of the water like the quills of a porcupine. With the river so swollen, the whole landscape changed. Roads, train tracks, and whole buildings were underwater. Unless a person was wise to their exact location it was entirely likely they'd find themselves floating many feet above a highway. The tops of electric poles—power long-since cut—marked the only means of navigation.

Rufus was lost in thought when Gideon cut the light.

"What are you doing?" asked Rufus.

"Quiet," he said, looking at the surface of the water. "There's something out there."

Rufus peered over the side. The water was dark. After a moment, however, something disturbed the surface. They were long, narrow slivers approaching them from all sides.

"Snakes!" yelled Gideon.

An icy terror went through Rufus as he grabbed a paddle.

"Get us out of here!" yelled Rufus to Bear, who sat with a stunned look on his face.

But the motor would do them no good; it slowly wound down as if it had been strangled out.

The first snakes approached over the lip of the boat. Gideon smashed his huge flashlight against them, but it did nothing to stop their progress.

It was only after they had begun wrapping around his feet that Rufus realized that they weren't snakes at all, but ropes—ropes that moved of their own volition. When he looked back, Rufus saw that Bear was already on the floor of the boat, completely bound. Gideon fought hard, but the ropes slithered up and around his legs and then his arms.

Soon the ropes had them all completely bound, even wrapping around their mouths. It felt as if he were in a vice grip, frozen on the floor of the boat and completely unable to move. He could barely see through the tightly wound ropes, and even then it was only a sliver of the dark banks.

But then a laughter rang out behind him, followed by a slow, rhythmic tapping from the side of the boat like the tedious countdown of some terrible clock. The boat shifted as someone climbed onto it.

"What about the fat one?" said a raspy voice.

"Boss said we don't need him," answered another. "Toss him over."

Rufus's heart beat rapidly as he heard a bit of struggling, followed by a splash. He couldn't see it, but he knew that Bear was in the water. This is what the creature meant, he realized. This is how he would die.

The only thing he could see was the trunk of an old tree that had washed up on the dark levee. He focused on it as his heart beat wildly. A blue light flittered around it, like the one he'd seen in the bottle. But it was what he saw in the tree that stole his attention. It was the face of a young girl.

Rufus's eyes widened, but a final constriction of the ropes squeezed away the last of his consciousness, and all went black.

5

Shared Blood

"The ropes were too tight, Zell," said a voice in the darkness. "I told you not to use snake ropes unless you had to. You don't know how to charm them."

It took a few attempts for Rufus to open his eyes. Slivers of light found their way past his slowly opening eyelids. It was like being caught between a dream and waking up.

He opened his eyes to the grinning face of an old man. He had a shock of pure white hair combed neatly back over his head.

"Looks like my boys here accidentally choked you out," said the man. "Sorry about that."

They were in a room, he could see, small and lit by a few old-looking lanterns. It smelled like sweat and rot. It was only when he saw out of a doorway that he realized that he was on a boat—an old one by the looks of it. But then he saw a familiar face: his grandma. At seeing her, he tried to stand, but it took only a moment to realize that he was still tied down.

"Grandma!" he yelled.

"Calm down," said the old man. "She's alright."

Rufus looked back to his grandmother. She wore canyon-like wrinkles in her brow. Her bottom lip quivered.

"It found us, Rufus," she said on the brink of tears.

"What found us?" asked Rufus.

"The Oxbow." She looked deathly, a shell of her normal self.

The man walked back in front of Rufus, staring at him from under thick white eyebrows. He was old and slender, well-dressed in a nicely cut vest and fine trousers.

"Who is this?" asked Rufus.

"It's been a while, Rufus," said the man. "Yep," he said as he gave Rufus a once-over. "As I live and breathe. These boys sure do favor their daddy, don't they?" He turned back to Grandma Jezebel. "Shall I tell him, or do you want the honors?"

His grandmother's voice quivered as she spoke.

"Rufus, this is your grandfather."

Rufus felt like his insides had spooled out all across the floor.

The old man walked up to him, a big smile on his face. "Jasper Pinhook," he said.

It was then that Rufus finally saw Gideon sitting to his left, still out cold, but breathing. The incident on the boat came back to him.

"Where's Bear?" asked Rufus. "What did you do with him?"

"Is that the boy that was with you?" asked the old man. He looked at the two men. "What'd you do with him?"

One of the men stepped forward. He was missing many teeth and covered with a patchwork of scars and dirt. Both of the men were dressed similarly to the dog thrower.

"Oh we just laid him down on the banks is all," said the man in a frog-like voice.

"But I heard a splash!" said Rufus.

The man smiled.

"Don't work yourself into a fit, young 'un. These are my connections, Zell and Riggs. Them boys wouldn't hurt a fly—lest I told 'em to." His eyes grew wide and a soft chuckle slid past his lips. "Then they'd mutilate the poor critter, pull its legs out one by one and tear off its wings." The old man stared ahead, almost in a trance. But then he smiled and turned back to Grandma. "Jezzy, I think I'm ready for some cornbread."

Gideon finally snorted. His head bobbed up quickly. He began thrusting so viciously that he pulled himself over.

"Calm down there, boy," said Jasper, kneeling down beside them. He looked up at the two men. "Cut 'em loose," said the old man. "Both of them. I think they'll find that this is right where they want to be."

The man cut Gideon loose first. He popped up on his feet like a prizefighter.

The old man walked over to Gideon and stuck out a hand. "Gideon. I'm your grandfather, Jasper Pinhook," he said.

Gideon looked around, clearly confused. He left Jasper's hand hanging.

"Is this some kind of joke?" he asked. Grandma Jezebel shook her head. He turned back to Jasper. "What are we doing here?"

"I need a reason to visit my grandsons?" said Jasper.

"Enough of this," said Gideon. "I'm out of here." He began making his way to the exit, but both of the henchmen stepped in front of him.

"I wouldn't do that if I were you," said Jasper. "For one thing, we're in the middle of the river. But, most importantly, I'm about to offer you both the chance of a lifetime." He motioned to the chair that Gideon had vacated. "But first, sit down." Gideon reluctantly righted the chair and sat down. The old man took a seat next to Grandma Jezebel. "Before we get started, I'm starving." He turned to Grandma Jezebel, who had a pan sitting in front of her with a towel over it.

Jasper closed his eyes, tilting his head back as he sniffed the pan of cornbread.

"Smells good, darlin'!" he shouted, clapping his hands together. He turned back to Rufus, giving a half-crooked smile. Begrudgingly, Grandma Jezebel pulled the towel from the cornbread and slid it in front of him. The man looked euphoric, years seeming to fade from his face. "Jezzy, Jezzy," he said. "I've missed this."

He took a pocket knife from his belt and opened up the long blade. Grandma Jezebel flinched when she saw it. The man noticed, and paused for a moment. He smiled broadly, and then drove the knife into the bread. He brought up a golden square, still warm. He tossed it hand to hand for a moment before letting it land on the table. He pulled the butter dish over to him and knifed a great hunk, slathering it onto the bread. It was a tense moment, that first bite—the entire boat had gone silent, watching this man get his perfect morsel of cornbread. The crumbling piece landed in his mouth. He closed his eyes, rocked his head back, and melted away.

"Oh, lordy," he said, spitting crumbs that rained down into the butter dish. "You still got it, hon." He picked up another pile of bread and shoved it in his mouth. Grandma Jezebel looked like a child getting scolded, meek and ashamed. This was not the grandmother Rufus knew. The old man plunged his knife back into the cornbread and cut another piece, slow and deliberate. He looked at Rufus, then to Gideon. He motioned back to the pan. "Want some? Mighty fine, this is."

The white-haired man sat there devouring cornbread as if it

were just a regular old Sunday dinner. Rufus looked over to his brother, who showed little emotion. But Rufus couldn't hold back any longer.

"So, did you just come here to eat cornbread after all these years? What do you want?"

The man put his cornbread back down on the table with care, as though he were laying down an injured bird. He took a handkerchief from the breast pocket of his shirt and wiped his lips, folding the cloth carefully before placing it back into his pocket. The tabletop was flecked with crumbs, but the man's shirt was spotless. He smiled as he looked Rufus dead in the eyes.

"This one's got a bit of his mother in him, don't he, Jez?" The old man craned back to look at Grandma Jezebel, who said nothing. He slapped his knee and stood up. "Maybe I should tell you what *you* want first," he said.

"And how are you going to do that?" said Rufus, his voice vinegar sour.

"Shut up and let the man talk," yelled Gideon, his first sound in ages.

Jasper let out an abrasive cackle—his laugh was like a train, rolling to a stop in no hurried fashion.

"You *are* your daddy's sons ain't you?" he said, slapping his knee again. He looked back to Rufus. "I have a good idea of what you want..." he started. "You want to get away from here is what you want." He peeked out the window and made a sour face. "You want to go places, see things—you want to be in control." He drew out each word.

An uneasy ache rumbled through Rufus's stomach. The old man was right, but Rufus wasn't about to let him know it.

"That ain't hard to guess," said Rufus. "Just look around."

"A guess it ain't," said Jasper. "You're Pinhooks. It's in your blood. You can't change the blood." He looked over at a crate. On top of it was Rufus's fiddle. A big grin stretched out across the man's face. "I almost forgot about this. I had Zell bring this along from your house. Which one of you plays?"

"He does," said Gideon, leaning back in his chair and pointing to Rufus. A deep pit formed in Rufus's stomach.

"Well I'll be Moses with a map," he said, thrusting the fiddle in his hands. "Go on, boy," said Jasper, forcing it into his hands. "Play us a ditty—or maybe even a dirge." There was a long, thorny silence. "Let's hear it," he said. "Let's see how much you wasted your grandmother's efforts." He hated playing when he was alone, let alone with an audience like this.

Rufus looked to his grandmother, as if asking permission.

"Go on," she said, the words more mimed than spoken.

He put the fiddle to his shoulder, plucking the strings for a quick tuning. He played the first few notes of the only song that came to mind, one that his grandmother had insisted he learn almost to the point of cruelty. But he wasn't warmed up—his fingers tripped up like a spider walking a tightrope. He stopped, took a deep breath.

"Not exactly a prodigy, is he?" said Jasper.

With new motivation, Rufus put the fiddle back up to his shoulder, gritted his teeth, and pulled the bow across the strings. His fingers pranced across the fingerboard. He pressed the bow against the strings with such force that he thought it would break. His anger worked its way into the neck of the fiddle, and then into the body. He'd played the tune a thousand times before, an old standard, but now it was his.

He ended after only one verse, his point proven. Jasper rocked back in his chair, bringing his hands together to applaud, a long silence between each clap.

"Bravo, boy," he said. "Nice choice of tune, too. *Pinhook Waltz.*" He stood up, slowly, and walked over to Rufus. "May I?" he asked, motioning to the fiddle.

Rufus looked back to Grandma Jezebel, but she was focused only on the table in front of her.

"I guess so," said Rufus, reluctantly handing over the fiddle.

The old man took the instrument, handling it as if it were a fine crystal vase.

"You know this belonged to your daddy?" he asked. Rufus did not. Jasper looked back at Grandma Jezebel. "You remember when Georgie was a young'un, Jezzy? Used to drive us all wild with this thing, playing every song there ever was—and playing them poorly." He smiled as he studied it. Then, without warning, he slammed the fiddle onto the back of a chair, as if swinging an ax. The fiddle smashed into pieces, the strings groaning as they separated from the wood. Grandma Jezebel wailed, raising her hands in the air before sinking even lower into her chair. Rufus stood, raring to take the fiddle strings and wrap them around Jasper's neck. But one of the men caught him and tossed him down to the floor of the boat. Gideon hadn't moved a muscle.

"That's my fiddle!" shouted Rufus.

Jasper lifted one finger, as if he deserved a bit of patience. He sifted through the splintered pieces of wood with the tip of a boot until he found what he was looking for.

"Aha," he said. "I thought something sounded a bit off." He held up an old piece of metal—shaped like a dog whistle—that had been affixed to the inside somehow. "Pretty good hiding spot, Jezzy," said Jasper. "But you should've known I'd find it."

"What do you want!" shouted Rufus, rising again, but the

same man pinned him against the floor.

"Alright, Zell," said Jasper, emerging from behind him. "Let him speak his piece."

"It's more than speak that I want to do," said Rufus, still struggling to stand.

Jasper knocked the man out of the way and got right into Rufus's face.

"Do you want to hit me, boy?" he said. It was like an electrical storm raging behind his glassy blue eyes. He moved closer still, slapping each side of his face again and again. "Because you ought to get it out of your system now. Do you hear me?"

"Let the boy alone!" yelled Grandma Jezebel, pounding on the table.

For all Rufus's rage, the wildness in the man's eyes kept him from lashing out. He could see it now, the resemblance he shared with Gideon—they shared a look that Rufus knew meant things had gone too far.

"I want you to let us go," whimpered Grandma Jezebel. The words started slow at first, but built up in ferocity. "I want you to go back where you came from!" she shouted, hitting the table. Jasper smiled as he watched her. He let her words hang in the air for a moment before he answered.

"Not yet, darlin'," he said, pacing around the table. It seemed like he was plugged into a wall socket, brimming with fighting energy. He tossed the whistle from hand to hand as he walked, until he finally turned and held it up to Rufus and Gideon. "This, boys, is what we needed."

"What's that for?" asked Gideon, finally showing interest.

"This modest bit of metal is going to help us find your daddy." Jasper held it up and studied it, a yearning in his eyes. "A toot on this whistle will summon the most feared boat in the Oxbow, the Specter Steamer. That's how we found you." Rufus thought about the boat he'd seen with the strange creature. The old man clasped his hand tightly around the whistle, then looked back at Rufus and Gideon. "Your granny ever tell you about the Oxbow?"

"She never tells us anything," said Gideon, looking at their grandmother with disgust. "And never a word about our parents neither."

"Jezebel Oxley Pinhook," said Jasper as if scolding a child. "You let these boys go this long without telling them about their home? That's a sin." He shook his head, turning back to them. "That's where we're going, boys. We're going home."

"Where is it?" asked Gideon. Rufus felt a hatred for his brother, something deep in his bones.

"Why do you care, Giddy?" shouted Rufus. "We're not going with this man. He's a lunatic!"

Gideon reached out and knocked Rufus across the head.

"You don't tell me where I go," said Gideon.

Rufus felt a fire run through him, and threw himself on top of Gideon. He grabbed him by the throat, but Gideon was quick to respond with a punch into Rufus's gut. Grandma Jezebel wailed yet again as the old man chuckled. Rufus was rearing back his fist when it was caught by one of Jasper's men. Gideon took advantage and landed one more punch in his unshielded chest.

"Alright, you two," said Jasper. Rufus was thrown back down onto the floor, his stomach and chest throbbing. He had some difficulty breathing, but his adrenaline kept the pain simmering in the background. "But I want to answer your question, Gideon. The Oxbow is the other side of the river."

"I've been over there," said Gideon. "Nothing over there but cottonmouths and rednecks."

Jasper looked Gideon over, smiling before he continued.

"A river changes courses over the years, gets tired of always swimming the same way." His eyes glittered. "Sometimes it'll cut off a whole stretch of river, just move on without it. The Oxbow used to be a part of this river, but not any longer." The man was absolutely beaming. "It's chock full of conjury—*mud magic*, we call it. Strange beasts stalk the banks. Souls wander aimlessly, looking for redemption." The man's eyes got big. "And it's your home. We Pinhooks are destined to lord over the Oxbow like wolves over sheep."

Rufus's first reaction was to laugh at the old man. He couldn't believe what he was hearing. But then the voice of that little demon creature popped into his head, and he remembered the odd things he'd seen—the blood-red steamer, water pouring from the man's face. The creature had used that word as well: *mud magic*.

"It's true ain't it, Grandma?" shouted Gideon. He stood up, irate. Grandma Jezebel could only nod her head. "Why would you hide this from us?" She didn't answer. It was like a slow death, all silence and desperation. Eventually, their grandmother yelled out.

"How did you find us?"

Jasper took a step toward her.

"The Specter Steamer cut the path, darlin'. All we had to do was follow." Jasper looked at Rufus and Gideon. "Listen, I ain't gonna force you boys to go nowhere. But I can't guarantee what'll happen if you stay." He stopped mid-step. "There are those who'd have your throats slit while you slept, those who'd drag you back to Oxalis, our capital, and have you hanged in the square, all on account of your daddy and the name he

passed on to you." He turned to them, sly look on his face.
"Come with me and I'll show you who your father *really* is."

"Don't believe him," shouted Grandma Jezebel. She was
wailing now. "Your daddy's dead and gone." The old man gave
her the wickedest look Rufus had ever seen.

"She would rather forget about her past," shouted Jasper. He
pointed at her. "She'd rather forget about our legacy—forget
about her own son!" He turned back to them. "But I ain't about
to let that happen. Boys, you'll see him. I swear to that."

"That legacy is evil," she said. "Our name burnt to the ground
like the rest of the Oxbow."

"The Pinhook name still sends terror through the Oxbow!"
he shouted, wagging a finger in the air. "You say 'Pinhook'
and the trees will bow down before you, the wind will stop
blowing, people will shrink in fear; they'll actually shrink,
by God!" He turned back to Rufus, panting, trying to calm
his voice. "Your daddy did great things. I fought beside him
proudly." He looked at the whistle in his outstretched hand.
After a deep, controlled breath, he spoke. His words seemed
doused in memory. "Last thing he ever did was to blow this
whistle." He turned to Grandma Jezebel. "You remember that,
Jezzy? You remember that day? The day our son blew this
whistle? Oh he wanted that Specter Steamer. And we were
about to have it all…" He looked like he was tearing up, but
then his face grew stern. "…but then our boy got a knife in the
back." Grandma Jezebel was freely crying. Jasper slammed his
fist down on the table in front of her. "He was your son, too!"
he yelled, aiming hate at her. "You seem to forget that."

"He wasn't my son by then," she said through a wall of tears.
She looked at Rufus and Gideon, gaining some of her spirit
back. "Don't listen to him. He'll use you up and cast you away."

She looked back at the old man, who at some point in life was her husband. "That's what he did to my son. You ruined him, Jasper. You killed him!" She picked up Jasper's knife from the table and launched it at his head. He ducked in the nick of time—reflexes surprisingly quick for a man of his age. It stuck in the wall behind him. The pan of cornbread followed soon after, shattering on the wall behind him and sending cornbread flying. He smiled.

"That's enough, sweetheart," he said in a voice unnaturally tender. He looked back to Rufus and Gideon. He reached into his vest pocket, producing a folded-up piece of paper. He handed it to Gideon. "There he is, boys. The only photo left of him."

Gideon stared at the small photo. Rufus didn't look at the picture. He was instead drawn to his brother's face. There was something in it he'd never seen before: some sort of longing, a sadness. Gideon was completely absorbed by the tiny photo.

Jasper chimed in.

"Let Rufus see him," said Jasper.

Rufus looked to Grandma Jezebel. Her heavy eyes gave him the only answer he needed.

"I don't want to see him," said Rufus flatly.

"No matter," said Jasper. "You'll see him soon enough. Your father wants you in the Oxbow, and I aim to bring you."

He looked at Gideon first.

"I want to go," said Gideon. "I want to find him."

"What about you, Rufus?" asked the old man.

"Rufus is coming too," said Gideon matter-of-factly.

"No!" snapped Rufus, his courage collecting like bugs to a light. He spoke with a firmness he didn't know he had. "You won't be telling me what to do anymore."

"Don't be an idiot, Rufus. Don't you hear what he's saying? We can be respected for once. We can find our dad."

Rufus looked at the shifty old man.

"How can you trust him?" he said. The man's grin was eternally poised, but never quite breaking into a full-on smile. The effect was revulsion. He turned back to Gideon. "I won't go. I won't leave Grandma."

He could see the anger flaring in his brother's face. He was about to tear into him when Jasper stepped in.

"Boys," he said. "We can talk about this on the way. Let's just get a move on."

There was a piece of news that Rufus hadn't told Gideon yet, something that had gotten lost in all the panic. With a deep breath, Rufus spoke.

"Bear is dead."

Gideon's face looked as if it had reset. His eyes blinked a few times, and he looked up to meet Rufus's.

"What did you say?" His voice was shaky.

"Those men…they drowned him."

Gideon grabbed Rufus by the collar.

"Liar!" He looked up to Jasper, who looked exasperated.

Lowering his head, he spoke.

"Your friend is just fine, Gideon," said Jasper. "Now what's it going to be? Come with us or stay here and rot?"

Gideon looked conflicted, his eyes darting back and forth. He took a deep breath and released Rufus's collar.

"You're sure he's alright?" he said.

Jasper put his hand over his chest.

"Cross my heart."

He looked back at Rufus, then to Grandma Jezebel.

"Let's go then," he said.

"No!" shouted Grandma Jezebel.

"That's enough!" shouted Jasper, flipping over a chair. "You were a no-good daughter of a pig-butcher before I married you. You never did have it in you to be anything." He had her backed into a corner, her face defiant, but worried.

Rufus rushed toward them, but Gideon caught him.

"Just sit down," said Gideon, pushing Rufus back down on his chair. "This is all her fault anyway."

Rufus wanted to destroy his brother. He stood up again, trying to step around Gideon, be he continued to block his path. Rufus gave Gideon a hard shove. Gideon looked like an enraged bull ready to charge.

"Let him alone," Jasper said as he moved Gideon to the side.

Rufus had never felt such rage as he stared at the old man. But another feeling consumed him. It felt like water surging through him, as if it were pumping in his veins. The room was suddenly hot, like heat was radiating from the floor.

"There it is!" shouted Jasper. "You're feeling it now, ain't you? Let it out!" He was in Rufus's face, eyes wide and wild. Rufus had sudden clarity. He could see beyond his own body to the river beyond. It was as if he knew every droplet in the river, and that he could control them, could bend them to his will. He felt free; he felt violent.

6

Waves

Dirty brown water began seeping in from the open door, then from the windows, from the crates, splashing everywhere through the boat. Jasper's buzz-saw laugh filled the room. Rufus's thoughts were no longer words. He only knew a control of something far bigger than himself.

The water swept from all sides toward Jasper, pooling at his feet. The old man looked at the water with eagerness, almost glee. One of the henchmen approached Rufus from the side. Pure instinct reacted, and a cannon of water erupted from the floor and flew straight into his chest. The man was flung against the wall like a doll.

"Atta boy!" shouted Jasper. "Take control!"

The water began to climb up the old man's legs—a stream flowing straight up, inch by inch until it was up to his chest.

"What are you going to do, Rufus?" asked the old man. "Now you get to choose whether or not you want to be a Pinhook, a *real* Pinhook."

Rufus's head was swimming. Part of him wanted to strangle

the old man, but then he saw the whistle clutched in his hand. Rufus willed the streams to pry open the man's grip. Jasper's laughter stopped as he tried to keep hold of the whistle. But it was no use. The whistle was free and riding the stream up to Rufus's hand. Rufus took hold of it. He studied it, the water still encasing Jasper like a suit of armor. The whistle was surprisingly heavy for its size, a straight cylinder of silver no bigger around than a pencil and less than half the length.

"You're not ready yet," shouted Jasper, a sliver of fear in his voice. "This ain't the right time."

It was the fear in Jasper's eyes that pushed him to do it. Rufus hadn't wanted to blow the whistle. He wanted to leave this place. He imagined himself on a boat, floating past barges in the sunshine, a fishing line dipped off the side, campfires on the banks at night. But he knew this couldn't end in any other way.

"You say our father wanted this boat," he said. "Well, here it is." Rufus put the whistle to his lips.

"Stop him," yelled Jasper.

Before Rufus could blow the whistle, Jasper's scar-faced henchman leapt towards him, only stopped by a chair crashing down over his head. Rufus looked up to see that his grandmother had inflicted the blow. She looked at him with heavy, sunken eyes.

"I tried to keep you boys safe, Rufus," was all she could manage before the man with giant sideburns grabbed her and threw her to the floor.

Everything stopped. The shouts of Jasper and Gideon faded to nothing. Pure rage ran through him. He knew with clarity that he would destroy the man who had harmed her, and everyone else for that matter. In that a moment, the same feeling he'd known when he'd fallen in the water took hold of him, and the whole river was just another muscle he could flex.

Rufus felt the approaching wave before he saw it. The rumble surged through the boat, rattling through each brittle board. From the window, he saw the water cascading down the river as if a dam had burst. It was on them in seconds.

The hit was savage. Fists of water punching through, soaking everyone and everything, as if the whole force of the river was coming down on them. Every person was on the floor as the boat was lifted off the surface. It groaned under the pressure. They were all now at the whim of the angry river.

"You really done it now, boy!" howled Jasper. Another jolt belted the boat, ripping the roof of the cabin clean off as though a tornado were passing overhead. Everyone clutched whatever they could find to keep steady, but Jasper just sat in front of Rufus, laughing maniacally. "That was a good one!"

Another surge of water smashed into them, pushing the whole vessel into the air and sending the boat rolling to one side. Chairs had toppled and rolled. The thin walls began to break apart. Rufus then saw his grandmother curled up on the floor, tossed by the merciless torrents. He watched helplessly as she rolled toward the edge the boat, the walls having been torn off by the waves. He lunged towards her, but it was too late.

Her legs were first over the edge. She clung to the side, her nails dug in. But her body was frail and would not hold for long.

Rufus reached for her hand as she dangled high above the river, the boat lifted by a tall wave. Their eyes met for only a moment before her strength gave out. His hand just grazed hers before she fell toward the dark water below.

He couldn't even scream. His lungs were empty. His mind buzzed as if electrified, blocking out all other thoughts or noise. As he laid there, the little photo of his father landed face down in front of him. He stared at it, oblivious to everything around him. After a moment, a gust of wind picked it up and blew off into the darkness.

In that very moment, the wave released them. They plummeted back toward the river, hitting the surface of the water as though it were a concrete floor. What was left of the boat broke apart instantly.

For a moment Rufus was weightless, floating through the air as he was flung from the vessel. Debris pummeled him on his trajectory towards the water. Something large struck the side of his head just as he hit the surface. The pain and the cold of the water overwhelmed him. Rufus flung his arms wildly to stay afloat, but there was no fighting. He could only accept his fate in the murky water.

But then a vibrant flash caught his eyes. It was almost like an explosion of light, casting illuminated shrapnel out in all directions. Following the flash was a disturbance near the surface. He soon felt himself being pulled roughly out of the water with an almost unnatural force.

He was cast upon the deck of a boat, landing in a heap. For the second time in a night, he saw the face of a girl before losing consciousness.

7

Enter the Oxbow

Rufus awoke splayed out on a cold metal surface, his bones leaden and too heavy to lift. The air around him was silent, heavy, as if he were in a cotton-padded room. Only the dull, boundless ache inside his head informed him that he could, possibly, still be alive. As he raised himself up, he saw the thick metal bars all around him: He was in a cage.

It was a small cage, barely big enough for a dog. He wrapped his arms around his knees as he looked out on what appeared to be the deck of a boat. There were stacks of crates all around him. It was still night, but a thick red fog had enveloped them, lit up as though a fire were burning all around.

He reached out for the bars, using the little energy he had to try and force them open, but they were solid and unyielding. Frustrated, he sat back down and put his head in his hands. Thoughts of his grandmother quickly consumed him…the look in her eyes before she fell, desperately clinging to the side of the boat. It was like it was happening all over again.

His attention was yanked away by shouting. It was a gruff

voice, low and full of grit.

"Hold on, boys! We're going through!"

The cage began to rattle. It was soft at first, but grew in intensity. Soon, the crates around him shook violently, some of them tumbling to the deck. His view of the river was now clear and he could see that it was bubbling as if they were in a pot on a stove.

The boat began to pick up speed, almost unnaturally so. The water appeared to be sloping at an angle, almost as if their boat had meandered into a log-ride at a theme park.

"This is it!" came the voice. "Brace yourselves!"

Rufus felt his stomach lifting as they fell faster. He grabbed hold of the metal bars just as the boat splashed down. The hit was more like a car accident than a boat ride.

He took a breath. The air quickly turned cool; the sky became black and full of stars. His body still hurt, but he was no worse for the wear. Surveying his surroundings, he noticed a few of the crates had tumbled over the sides; the rest had scattered all over the deck. But then the sound of footsteps caught his attention. A man's voice echoed across the deck.

"Thank heavens we're back in the Oxbow. I was gonna be sick if I had to smell the rotten air of that place for another minute." The man appeared from behind the crates. His hair was long and stringy, reaching down to his shoulders. He wore a tattered old vest and a derby hat. It looked like he hadn't bathed in months.

But Rufus couldn't prepare for what he saw next. Walking behind the man was a giant creature. It had a big, smushed-up nose and deep-set eyes below a brow that arched like the face of a hornet. It moved in giant, lumbering steps. Even though it had a lanky, human-like body, Rufus could see that the creature was something different, some fierce and powerful being—a monster.

Rufus thrust himself against the back of the cage. It felt like millions of tiny icicles were running through his blood. But the commotion only attracted their attention.

The limp-haired man ran over to Rufus's cage.

"Our boy's awake!" he shouted in a weaselly voice. "And I don't think he finds you all that pretty, Sloo."

The hulking creature walked up to the cage and put his thumbs into his suspenders. His shirt was barely big enough for his strangely-formed body, crudely stitched together at his bulging shoulders, which were about as wide as the hood of a car. Its head was huge, but its face seemed squished together and menacing. It sniffed the air.

"He's a young 'un. Don't you think, Murdo?" asked the creature. His voice was otherworldly, octaves deeper than any he'd ever heard.

"Don't get no ideas, Sloo," said the man. "He's bought and paid for." The man leaned in towards Rufus, motioning to the creature. "This one's got him a penchant for eating children." He said this as nonchalantly as if he'd say the creature likes to eat fish. "Couldn't be any more of a *troll* if he tried." At this, the creature snorted. The man raised his hands apologetically. "I forget," he said. "They don't like to be called *trolls*. They prefer *oxmen*, as if that makes them any more respectable."

Rufus was amazed at the man's swagger. The creature could easily have ripped him in half, and yet he continued to ridicule him. The creature snorted again and leaned in closer to the cage. Rufus's throat was too constricted to even swallow.

"Shame I can't eat him," said the creature. His skin matched the yellowish hue of Weego's. They were clearly the same species, though this one was truly monstrous. "What do you think the woman wants with him?" asked the creature. "Could he be a river mage?"

"How else you explain that wave that came and got them?" said the man. "Definitely some nasty stuff going on with him."

A gruff voice sounded from behind them.

"If he was the one who'd called the water, he wouldn't be on the inside of no cage, and we'd all be fish food right now." An old woman stepped out from behind a crate. Both the man and the creature seemed to shrink a bit, clearly intimidated. The woman was short and stocky, draped with layers of tattered cloth. But her steps had confidence; she carried herself with power. She sidled up next to the creature, who had a good two feet on her, and gave Rufus a once over. Even at ten feet away, it was clear that hygiene was not a skill she practiced. Wrinkles draped across her face like old blankets, her squinty eyes were cut deep into them—this was a face that had seen a lot. She began to survey Rufus, looking him up and down.

"This is the reason we had to go to that horrible place?" she asked. She turned back to her boys. "Remind me that I'm never leaving the Oxbow again." She peered in closer. "I don't know what need she'd have for a river rat like him."

It took a few empty tries before Rufus's voice finally appeared.

"Where's my grandma?" he shouted between quick breaths. The woman slowly turned back to him.

"Do you think I care?" she said in a snake-like voice. "Whatever happened I'm sure the old hag had it coming."

He wanted to unleash the river on her. He wanted the whole force of the water to crash down on her round little head.

"You take that back," snapped Rufus.

60

The woman tensed up. A throaty growl began to emanate from her as if she were a pit bull about to be unleashed.

"Ooohweee!" shouted the limp-haired man, slapping his knee. "This one's got a temper!" He leaned in, putting his acne-ridden face next to the metal bars. A smile revealed a few black mounds that Rufus reckoned were, at some point or another, teeth. "Don't you know who this is? This here's Ms. Tatum!"

"I don't care who it is," said Rufus.

Again, he tried to will the water to do his bidding, to capture that feeling he'd had with Jasper and fling these people over the side, but again, nothing happened.

"You should care, boy," she said, throwing the front of her shawl over her shoulder to reveal an array of shiny weapons. They looked like sinister torture implements: gnarled blades, a whip, rows of glowing orbs that Rufus could only imagine did horrible things. "Care to press the issue?"

"Go ahead, boy," shouted the ratty-haired man. "We ain't seen her gut somebody in at least a week!"

At that moment, a girl appeared out of the darkness. It was the face he'd seen before he'd passed out.

"Don't touch him," she said, her voice calm but forceful.

Rufus wondered if he'd dreamt her, or if she were the result of losing oxygen. But there she was, seeming unbothered at being outnumbered by the motley group. She wore a clean dress and stood out aggressively from the dreary surroundings. Indeed, there was a glow about her—an actual glow put off by some sort of radiant blue bug flittering around her head.

"Why you gotta go and spoil our fun?" shouted Murdo.

She gave him a hard stare as a few more of the large, moth-like creatures emerged from her satchel. Upon seeing them,

Murdo's smile faded.

"Leave him be," said the girl.

Tatum smirked, but eventually pulled her shawl back down to cover her weapons.

She took a deep breath.

"It appears you've got a guardian," said the woman. She exhaled loudly. "Well, I'm off to get my beauty sleep."

"And she clearly don't get enough of that!" shouted Murdo.

The woman—like a frog catching a fly—cast a lasso from her sleeve. It looped around Murdo's neck quicker than he could blink, taking him down like a rodeo steer. He grasped his neck as his eyes went bulbous. But after a few seconds she released him, turning back to Rufus.

"I'll be watching you, boy," she said.

The man, rubbing his neck, stood up and staggered over to Rufus. He put his ugly, smiling face next to the bars.

"Better get used to that new cage, son," he said before walking away. The creature lumbered behind him, leaving just him and the girl.

She seemed not to notice him at first, focused instead on the flight path of one of the glowing bugs. After a few mid-air circles, the bug finally flew into the satchel draped across her shoulder. Only after her bug was safely stowed did she turn to approach him, clearly in no big hurry. Rufus swallowed hard and climbed to his knees in his tiny cage.

The girl knelt down to him, giving him a quick look-over. Her eyes were icy blue, her hair dark. Rufus reckoned her to be about his age. After a moment she finally spoke.

"You're ok?" Rufus, unable to find his tongue, nodded. "Ok then," she said, standing up to leave.

"Wait!" Rufus finally managed to squeak. "Who are you?

62

What about my grandma?" The girl turned around, though she didn't look at him. Her mind almost seemed to be elsewhere. She sat in silence as the bug took flight from her shoulder. It was an amazing sight, almost like a lightning bug, though much prettier. Its light shimmered as a cloud of dust floated from its wings and left a trail of glittering light. The girl held her hand out flat, allowing the creature to land on it. Its long antenna stretched out on her palm as it crawled around.

"The men survived," she said as if reading his mind. Her gaze remained on the odd little bug. "Your brother included."

"What about my grandmother?" he said.

She finally met his eyes, though she said nothing. After a moment she disappeared behind a stack of battered crates.

As he sat back in his cage, it felt like a snake was constricting around his throat. He needed to get out of this cage. A frenzied energy blazed through him. He felt like he could snap the metal bars in two. He threw himself against the sides of the small cage, the bars were fixed. A throbbing pain in his shoulder quickly reminded him of his limitations.

But his attention was turned to a dull knocking that came from one of the crates next to him. When he looked over, Rufus saw a finger emerge from a small hole in the crate. There were people in these crates.

"Don't," said a muffled, wavering voice. "Stay quiet or she'll make you sorry." As the voice trailed off, the finger that had emerged from the hole fell out and landed on the deck beside him, looking freshly severed.

Rufus pressed his back against the bars of the cage, getting as far away from the severed digit as he could. After a moment, a rat emerged from between the crates, taking the finger in his teeth and dragging it back into the darkness. A cold nausea ran through Rufus's stomach. If he'd had anything in his belly to throw up, he surely would have.

He heard sounds coming from the crates all around him. It seemed that all of them were filled with people. He tried to take in the rest of his surroundings. The boat was flat and rather narrow, just wide enough for about five or six crates to go across. It was much larger than his own little raft had been.

It took a while for his breathing to calm. As it did, a deep sadness bore into him.

"Hey, boy," whispered the voice from the inside the crate. "You seen my finger? Tatum lopped it off earlier this afternoon."

Rufus looked back to where it had been and shivered.

"A rat got it," said Rufus. "It's gone."

"Darn it."

Rufus could still see no one in the hole, and didn't really want to risk another severed body part emerging, so he looked away. But the voice wouldn't relent.

"Boy," it whispered. "What'd you do?"

"What?" he asked. He could barely hear it.

"I said, 'what did you do?'" The voice was louder this time. It seemed clear enough that it was a man, though he figured no assumptions were safe in the Oxbow.

"I didn't do anything," said Rufus.

There was a knock from a crate across the narrow space from them, followed by an even more muffled voice.

"Yeah, right!" said the newcomer, though Rufus couldn't tell which crate it was coming from.

"Are all of these crates filled with people?" Rufus asked as he started to count them; there were at least twenty.

"Most all of them," said the voice through the hole.

"Why are they doing this?"

"They're bounty hunters!" screamed the muffled voice across the way.

Rufus processed this for a moment. He'd been captured by bounty hunters. Weego had been right—there were others that had come after him, though these people didn't seem to know why they had him. He should have just followed Weego's advice and let his brother go. Gideon was old enough to get himself killed if he wanted to.

But who was the girl on the boat, and why didn't they seem to have any clue who he was?

An eye appeared in the dark hole of the crate. Rufus nearly looked away for fear of it popping out at him, though he felt a bit of relief when it blinked.

"Tatum gets us all in the end," said the voice through the hole. "Can't run from her, I resigned myself to that a while back. I sure tried though, made it a good ways too. Almost clear to the Ice Canyons up north."

"You got the cage, boy," said the man through the hole. "You must be real special. I'll go from this box to a pine one. At least that one will smell better."

"You can't smell it when you're dead!" said the crate across the way, scooting an inch or two across the floor. Rufus was having a full-blown conversation with people he couldn't even see.

"What can we do?" asked Rufus.

There was a short pause.

"We die, boy."

8

Reelfoot

It was too cold to sleep. He wished he'd had a jacket to wear over his T-shirt, but there were bigger concerns. The men in crates had been carrying on for some time now, telling stories and cackling obnoxiously. It was starting to wear on him. Then, from inside their splintered wooden prisons, the men broke out into song.

Rufus buried his head in his knees. He was ready to give up when one of the crates tipped over violently. The singing and laughter went silent. The oxman, Sloo, stood behind it, his humongous foot outstretched and a wicked smile splayed across his ogre-like face. Behind him was the limp-haired man, Murdo, who began kicking all the crates.

"Why are we all so joyous around here?" shouted Murdo, a sadistic grin on his face. "You act like y'all ain't just a few days from dyin.'" He looked to the big creature and pointed at a crate. "I heard this one sniggering, Sloo. Make him sorry."

The creature picked the box up above his head and began wielding it like a cocktail shaker. The man inside groaned and wailed at first, but soon Rufus could only hear the dull thud of a body slapping against the insides of the crate.

"That'll do, Sloo," said Murdo. "Now, I'm ready to play."

The creature brought the crate down directly in front of Rufus, and sat on it. What would have been a normal-sized seat for any human resembled an elephant trying to ride a horse. His knees stuck out and he sat hunched over. He then crossed his lanky legs on top of it, rocking back and forth and pounding each side with his gargantuan fists.

Murdo scooted two other crates over and took a seat. After the man finished picking under his nails, he began spreading a set of playing cards across the top of one of the crates.

"You ever play Reelfoot?" he asked Rufus.

"Don't listen to him," snorted Sloo. "He uses penny magic to cheat us all out of our wages."

"And an oxman like yourself just tears the arms off folks who beat you at a hand," said the man. "And besides, it ain't no penny magic." Murdo smiled as he shuffled a deck of cards. "It's a fine and ancient art form that I practice..." he said, looking up at the creature "...much as you practice grumpiness." He looked at Rufus with a cheeky grin and pointed to the crates littering the deck. "Watch out for that one," he said, pointing to the crate to his left. "He's wanted for burning down Thornside Orphan's House." He shook his head and pointed his knife at yet another, even smaller crate. "That one over there tried to drink a warehouse full of swamp grog and then stole a steamboat."

"I wanna play!" yelled Sloo. His voice was fiery and full-throated, the kind employed by shouty preachers.

"Hold on there," said Murdo. A flicker of a smile appeared on his face. "You played through all your wages already."

"I want to get 'em back!" he said, giving the crate he sat on yet another whack.

"Let's give the boy a try," said Murdo.

"I don't know how."

"Oh, hush," said Murdo. "I'll teach you."

Rufus must have somehow nodded in agreement, as Murdo shouted out, "Atta boy," and began spreading a set of playing cards on the deck between his splayed legs. He had a surgical precision in the placement of each card. They were ornately designed, with images of people and creatures that Rufus had never seen before. Some of them were clearly human, dressed in old-timey military uniforms, holding muskets and rifles. Hideous monsters lined other cards: strange-looking fish with human-like limbs; giant humanoid beasts; a weasel-faced creature with a body like a monkey.

As Murdo began dealing them, something strange happened: they started sorting themselves, as if they knew the place his hands wanted them to go and, as if to save time and fuss, took the liberty of jumping there on their own. It seemed like a simple card trick, but then something even more peculiar happened. The cards—in all of their ragged, faded strangeness—began slipping across the deck of the boat on their own, dispensing themselves into little piles, as if they were being carried on the backs of quick little ants.

Moments later, Rufus had a hand of cards in front of him. He went to pick them up, but Murdo yelled out.

"Don't touch those yet," he said. "You don't know the stakes. We ain't finalized the stakes. You never play a hand of Reelfoot unless you know the stakes, and I never play a hand unless there are stakes."

"I don't have any money if that's what you want," said Rufus.

"I know you ain't got money," said Murdo. "If you did, we'd

have already taken it." The man stood up and, setting his cards down, walked over to Rufus's cage. "But you got plenty to wager," said Murdo. "Let me see your teeth." Rufus kept his mouth shut. Something wild in the man's eyes made him shiver. The man leaned closer to the bars and whispered. "Smile now or I'll have that beast of an oxman over there do it for you. He don't know his own strength. Last fellow he helped smile he tore his jaw clean off."

Rufus opened his mouth, though it was nothing approximating a smile.

"Them's some pretty chompers, Murdo," said Sloo.

Murdo smiled, again revealing his disgusting teeth.

"I could use a new set of those," he said. He crossed his arm and looked at Rufus. "I win, I get those teeth."

"No," said Rufus. "I don't want to play."

"You think you have a choice?" he said, going back to his cards. "I'll deal us up."

"But what if the boy wins?" shouted Sloo.

The man grabbed his bowler had and shifted it up and down his forehead as he thought.

"If the boy wins, I won't cut off one of his ears."

"Fair enough!" shouted the creature.

Rufus was shaking inside. He had been locked up in a cage, and now he was being forced to wager his own teeth.

"Pick 'em up, then," said the man. Rufus, though shaking, did as he was told, picking up the cards. "Alright!" yelled the man. "A boy who'll take a chance."

"Tell him how to play!" yelled Sloo.

"I will!" shouted Murdo. He turned back to Rufus and laid out a complicated set of rules, filled with number cards, spells, boats, and more. He had the enthusiasm of a child. Clearly there wasn't much to do at night in the Oxbow.

"Who starts?" asked Rufus.

"I do," said Murdo. "You play what you're dealt, no redraws."

"Fine." Rufus looked down at his hand of cards. Their ornate designs were striking, even though the cards were tattered from years of use. He thumbed them across, studying his hand until he got to the last card. Written in fancy cursive writing across the top of the card was the name: *Sparpole*. Rufus had to look twice. There was something familiar about the man. It was like he'd seen him before.

"You having a fit, boy?" asked Murdo. Rufus shook his head. "Now try to put together your best combination." Rufus was so stunned that he didn't even know what he was doing. He chose two cards as the man instructed, one being the *Sparpole* card. "Alright," said the man, "I'll go first." He threw down his two cards, a wicked grin on his face. "Good luck beating that. Best hand I've been dealt in a while."

The cards sprung to life as he threw them down; a small army emerged from them, forming a line on the deck with sword-wielding soldiers and cannons that rose from the card. Rufus watched as the small group took aim at him and his cards, waiting to attack. It was an incredible sight, though his own anxiety kept him from fully appreciating it. After running his tongue across the front of his teeth, Rufus closed his eyes and threw down the cards.

The *Sparpole* card rose with viciousness from the smoke. The two small armies faced off in the space between them. In a matter of moments, Rufus's cards had decimated the rest of Murdo's hand. The hand was over. Murdo looked across the smoky battlefield at Rufus.

"Ha!" shouted Sloo. "Boy beat you in his first hand!"

"Fool's luck," said Murdo, spitting. He was angry. "Sparpole in your first hand. By God, that card will go months without showing. What sort of magic you working?"

"I don't work magic," said Rufus.

"The hell you don't."

"I swear it!" yelled Rufus. "I just played what I was dealt."

Murdo watched him for a moment. Rufus felt the beady eyes boring into him. He met the man's glare with one to match. Eventually, Murdo smiled.

"I want a rematch," said Murdo. But as he pointed at Rufus, a few cards slipped from his sleeve. Sloo jumped up.

"Ancient artform my butt," shouted the oxman. "You're a cheat!" He moved on the man quickly.

For his part, Murdo showed little fear of the creature that could have easily torn him limb from limb, and was soon shouting right back at him. The deck of cards was scattered everywhere. Rufus noticed the card he had just played—the one with Sparpole on it—just outside of his cage. He picked it up and quietly slipped it under his leg.

Their bickering eventually required intervention from Tatum, who banished them back to the cabin like scolded school children.

When they were finally out of sight, Rufus slyly flipped the card over and studied the picture. Again, he felt something uneasy in his gut. The figure was striking, a soldier at war, battle-hardened, but proud. It made him feel strangely ill. Rufus leaned back against the cold bars of his cage. It would be a long night.

9

The River Mage

Morning came and went. Their boat chugged along the river steadily, though from what Rufus could see, it didn't look like his river at all. The surroundings were dramatic, high peaks and bluffs, towering trees and thick forests. Of course, Rufus could only see a sliver of it from his cage.

The sun had yet to show its face, as if it were hiding from something—as if it too wanted to be away from all this. By midday, the bit of sky that he could see had become consumed by angry-looking clouds, which soon spilled their innards. Rain drizzled down in an even clatter. Rufus spent the afternoon soaked, curled up in a ball and shivering. However, his mind was a world away, drifting to the boat where he'd last seen his brother and grandmother. Everything was wrecked. What would dying be but a blessing?

It must have been sometime in the evening when the boat's engine finally stopped. Through the stacks of crates he could see that they had landed at a town, though he couldn't see much aside from a few dilapidated boats. The rain, however, had blessedly stopped. Murdo came through banging a pot with a metal spoon.

"Alright, mongrels," he yelled. "Food." He wore an apron smeared with long red streaks and waddled around with a big iron pot. All of the crates around Rufus started to rattle and shake. Even the one that Sloo had jostled so violently—who Rufus thought was surely dead—began to vibrate in excitement. As Murdo placed the pot in the middle of the deck, a brown liquid spilled out. Rufus was engulfed by a foul odor and wished for the return of the rain.

"Cup your hands, you dogs," he shouted. "Those of you with only one hand only get a half portion." Murdo stopped for a moment to enjoy his own joke. "It's cold and it's days old, but it's grub. I don't expect y'all to be too picky."

Sloo undid a small latch on the front of each of the crates, opening up a space just big enough for two cupped hands to stick through. Murdo ladled the stew as he sang a vulgar song about holding up a stagecoach but leaving the gold. He was about to sing the chorus when he finally got to Rufus's cage. The odor so thoroughly disgusted Rufus that he resolved to chew off bits of his own cheeks before taking a bite of it. But the pangs of hunger were overwhelming. The last thing he'd eaten was a candy bar he'd swiped from a gas station near his house. He was reminded of the gas station and its cornucopia of day-old, heat-lamp warmed foods, it's wall-to-wall bags of chips, sugared sodas, and endless chocolates.

A violent strike of the ladle on the bars of his cage brought him back to his senses.

"You hungry or ain't ya?" asked Murdo. He dipped the ladle into the pot and held it aloft.

Rufus lifted his cupped hands, into which the man dished

the soup. The substance was cold and slimy, barely resembling food. It stank of rot—like a mixture of mint and skunk—and had the consistency of thick snot. Hunger pangs or not, Rufus was certain he'd die if he ate this. Still, he didn't know when he'd get another meal.

He brought his cupped hands close to his lips, the stench growing worse with every inch.

"Lung mushroom chowder," said Murdo, smiling. "Found them growing on the carcass of a river fox."

Rufus felt his insides tremor. His hands dropped, sending the soup splattered onto the deck and all over Murdo's pants and boots.

"Yuck!" shouted Murdo. "You got that slop all over me!" He lifted his ladle high, aiming between the bars.

But something flickered in Rufus. It was like some distant memory coming back to him, an itch that he could finally scratch. The river was again his.

The boat rocked, as if a whale were breaching below, tipping it up on one side before dropping it again. Crates rattled and toppled over. The pot of stew dumped onto the deck, on which Murdo swiftly slipped and fell. But Rufus wasn't finished. Murdo was trying to stand when streams of water came up over the side of the boat, climbing around him. It was similar to what Rufus had done to Jasper, only this time it formed four solid walls around the man as if he were inside a fish tank. Murdo panicked and struggled for air. He looked like a drowning mime trying to escape a box.

After a few moments, Rufus started to feel something else taking hold: his conscience. He was watching a man drown, and he was the one causing it. A shudder went through him. The wall of water fell, splashing onto the deck alongside a hacking and coughing Murdo. After a few moments, Murdo looked at Rufus, a deep fear filled his eyes.

"He called the water," Murdo yelled, as he took off toward the cabin. "Tatum! This one's a river mage!"

Tatum and the giant creature rushed over. She looked at him with a mixture of concern and disbelief. She turned to the giant creature.

"Sloo, toss his cage over the river the side."

The creature hoisted the cage high above his head. Rufus's cheekbone felt like it had received a swift punch as he fell hard against the bars. They moved toward the edge of the boat. The river came into view. Panic had overtaken him. A thousand thoughts filled his mind, and none of them gave him any control of the water when he so desperately needed it.

Just as the creature was about to toss the cage into the river, a voice shouted out.

"Don't!" It was the girl, appearing from behind a stack of crates.

Sloo nearly dropped the cage altogether.

"I hate mages," snapped Tatum. "Winesap will get her money back, but I ain't about to let another mage loose in the Oxbow.

From behind the girl, a woman appeared, her brown hair pulled back into a tight bun.

"You don't really have any choice," she said. The woman looked down at the slop at Murdo's feet. "You should be ashamed of feeding that to anyone." She stepped forward. "Are you going to put the boy down?" asked the woman.

"I'll do what I please," snapped Sloo.

Tatum walked right up to the creature and backhanded him across the face.

"You don't want to say things like that to a river mage.

Especially one that's our guest."

The woman turned to the girl.

"I trust they treated you with respect, Josie?"

The girl looked up from her bug for a brief moment.

"Nothing I couldn't handle," she said.

The woman nodded, then turned again to Sloo, who still held Rufus aloft.

"Put him down, idiot," snapped Tatum.

The creature dropped Rufus's cage to the deck. Rufus clung to the bars as he landed violently. He was hurting, but happy not to be drowning.

He looked at the woman who had just saved his life. He could tell by her clothing that she had nothing to do with people of Tatum's sort. That was enough to make her an ally. She was Tatum's polar opposite—clean, wearing a floor-length dress, standing with perfect posture.

"We got the boy," said Tatum. "At no small effort," she added.

The woman walked slowly towards Rufus, her heels clacking with each step. She stopped in front of the cage, studying him, her face expressionless. Rufus did his best to match it. After a moment, the woman turned to Tatum.

"Let him out," she said.

Tatum's face turned up in a twisted scowl, but she finally nodded to Murdo.

"You heard her, you little rat," said Murdo. He pulled open the cage door and took Rufus by the collar. It had been almost a full day since Rufus had stood. His bones cracked in what felt like hundreds of places as he stood and almost fell over from a head rush. There was no time for the dizziness to subside before he was being dragged along toward the cabin. Having been off them so long, his legs were numb. Walking became an exercise in casting his legs out awkwardly in hopes that they'd carry him forward.

"Make way for our guest," Tatum said through a hiss.

They dragged him towards the front of the boat. The elegant woman kept her distance from the three bounty hunters.

The deck was bathed in evening light, the clouds having finally broke. The sun was just beginning to creep behind a sheer bluff that towered above the river. Rufus locked eyes with the girl for a brief second before she turned to follow the woman like an obedient shadow.

The woman stopped in front of a large crate.

"You managed to find the plant as well?" asked Winesap.

"Of course," said Tatum, looking offended at the question. "Sloo had to fight off a pack of swamp trolls for it." At this, Sloo snorted angrily, and made a show of stomping around. Tatum, noticed his displeasure. "Shut up, Sloo," she hissed. "Quit bellyaching and open the crate."

The giant creature huffed, but then went to work sticking his long fingernails under the crate's lid. The nails whined as he pried them out. Knowing the sorts of things that Tatum kept in crates, Rufus was relieved to see that it was just a simple plant inside. It wasn't too dissimilar from a fern, but with closed flower buds that looked like large pieces of red okra.

"This is it," said Winesap. It was the first real emotion he saw on her face; her eyes widened, her mouth opened slightly as she focused on the plant.

Tatum looked back to Winesap, her brow furrowing like an arched caterpillar.

"Don't know what reason you'd have for flame flower," she said. "They're mighty dangerous." Winesap didn't respond. Tatum then rocked back on her heels and crossed her arms.

"Say, you work for the showboat, don't you? The one tied up here in Wagtail?"

"Yes," the woman said calmly.

Tatum shook her head and spit onto the deck.

"You tell that carnival freak, Otto Modest, that he'll get his one day," she said.

"Your business with Otto Modest is your business," said the woman. "Now I'd like to get this underway."

Tatum was quiet for a moment.

"I ought not to even be doing business with you on account of your connection to that man." Tatum stared hard at the woman, who returned her gaze in equal measure.

"That's of no consequence to you."

"The hell it ain't," said Tatum. Rufus looked to the girl to try to get a sense of what was happening, but her eyes were locked on her moth.

"I'll compensate you more than fairly for this plant and the boy," said Winesap.

Tatum looked at her for a moment, considering the proposal, but then grabbed the lid of the crate, tossing it back on.

"Some things ain't worth the money," she said. "Come on boys," she said. "I want to put some distance between us and Otto Modest."

As Sloo made to refasten the lid, the water began to ripple all around their boat. A torrent of water shot out, snatching the lid and flinging it out onto the river. It skidded across the surface like a skipping stone. The big creature looked enraged, but a steady measure of fear hung in his face as well. Tatum took a few steps forward.

"I know you're one of them *Children of Oxum* folks," said Tatum, her face twisted up tightly. "That don't scare me."

"I'm really not concerned whether or not you're scared of me," said the woman, remaining poised. "I want what I've come for. I'll pay your price, with an extra twenty percent. If that's a problem, we can always get the river involved."

The two women engaged in a silent standoff. The tension was as thick as the clouds of bugs.

"You say an extra twenty-five percent?" asked Tatum, putting a finger to her chin. Winesap grimaced at the added charge, but finally nodded. "Very well," said Tatum. "I'll call that your liar's charge."

"You'll get your extra twenty-five percent," said Winesap.

While Winesap reached into a leather sack for the money, Rufus saw Murdo grab something from behind one of the crates. He just happened to see the glint of a blade in the sunlight. Murdo took aim at Winesap.

"Look out!" shouted Rufus.

Winesap turned as the knife was thrown, but the blade only made it a few feet before it turned to a fine mist.

"If you want to test my abilities—and my patience—the results will become a lot more painful," she said, dropping the coins on the deck.

"Alright, your highness," said Tatum, bowing dramatically. "Pleasure doing business with you. Load it up for her, Sloo." Tatum pointed one of her short fingers at Rufus. "I'll be keeping an eye out for you, young 'un," she said. "And when you ain't got this here river mage protecting you, I'll find ya." The woman's voice was throaty and dark. Rufus was sure his nightmares would feature that voice for years to come.

10

Wagtail

They walked the ancient, weather-worn timbers of the docks toward the town. Each step creaked and groaned, especially under the weight of the giant oxman that had come to help Winesap carry the crated plant. A light gust of wind would likely have sent the whole structure collapsing into the river. Rufus couldn't imagine how it supported as much weight as it did, and walked nervously.

High, tree-lined ridges stood in the distance, canceling out any of the day's last sunlight. Dark clouds hung in the space between each bank. The sky edged darker by the minute. The town stood on a great bend of the river, and soon came into full view ahead of them. It was a miserable collection of timber buildings planted in the mud. A number of boats both large and small were moored up along the river, the most noticeable being a large steamboat. The boat was not much better off than the town. It was a classic old steamboat, but with two big paddle wheels on each side instead of at the back. Painted on the side were big faded letters that read "The Otto Modest," below a picture of a wide-faced man smiling menacingly under a bushy mustache. However, a few slats had fallen off which left big gaps where his teeth should have been.

As Tatum's boat disappeared from view, Rufus couldn't help but feel some relief, though he was soon aggravated by an eerie sound floating on the air, almost like a breathy circus organ. The sound cut over the blaring whine of saw blades in the nearby mills. It lilted in and out of tune and played a minor-key dirge that made Rufus apprehensive about following them any further. As he listened to the mournful melody, reality soon wormed its way back in. He needed to find his brother. He needed to make sure that his grandmother was ok. He stopped. The woman waited to turn around, instead gesturing to the lumbering oxman to sit the crate down. When she faced Rufus, there was no confusion or expectation on her face. She simply met his gaze with her fierce blue eyes.

"What do you want with me?" asked Rufus abruptly. "And why were you following me?"

Winesap studied him. After an exaggerated pause, she spoke.

"Josie doesn't know why she was following you," she said. "She just followed my instructions."

"But why?" said Rufus, feeling emboldened.

She cocked her head a bit and began rubbing her right earlobe between her fingers.

"Josie accompanied those louts to make sure they didn't harm you," she said. "As you nearly experienced, people like Tatum can't exactly be trusted to bring someone back in one piece."

"But why were they even after me?"

"You have a gift, in case you didn't notice," she said. "There aren't all that many of us with a gift like yours. When there is, the river tends to tell us about it."

"I'm not even from here," said Rufus, feeling confused. "I don't even know where *here* is."

"That's how we know your gift is great," said Winesap. "It bled through, between the worlds."

The word rang out in Rufus's head. *Worlds*. Could he have indeed passed out of his own and into another? All signs so far pointed to yes. Still, the woman had saved him from those people, even though she had the distinct tone of someone who wanted something. The fact that she'd paid money for him burned in his mind. It was as if he were a dog picked out of a litter. His mind staggered around like a drunkard, further strained by a lack of food and proper sleep. His words slipped past his lips before his mind could catch them.

"So, do you own me now or something?" he asked.

The girl again turned to Rufus, looking somewhat disgusted, but the woman remained poised and even-tempered, almost to the point of annoyance.

"I'm not of the belief that people are property," she said. "I merely paid the price required for your freedom."

"So, I'm free to go?"

"Any person is free to go as they wish," she said, though her look may have hinted otherwise.

"Great then," said Rufus. "I'll be on my way."

The girl, wrapping herself a shawl, finally looked up from the bug in her hand. There was a surprised look on her face.

"You won't want to stay in Wagtail," said Josie. "It's more of a prison than Tatum's boat."

Winesap gave her a stern look. The girl looked embarrassed as she looked back down to her bug.

"Wagtail?" He wasn't sure if it was the name of a town or a command for a dog. He was given no further explanation.

Winesap watched him for another moment.

"I just realized that we don't even know your name," she said.

"Rufus P..." He stopped himself, speaking quietly. "Rufus."

The woman stifled a smile.

"Well, Rufus. Where would you go if you could?"

"I have to find my grandmother and my brother. We got separated."

"Do you think your grandmother is still alive, Rufus?" She asked it matter-of-factly, as though it were a matter of routine. A panic swept over Rufus.

"I don't know," he said, though his voice could only squeak it out, betraying his earlier confidence. "I guess I have a feeling that she is."

"And is this feeling anything like what you just did to that man back there, using the water to do your bidding?"

He hadn't realized she'd seen that.

"No, ma'am," said Rufus, carefully choosing his words. "I don't know what it is."

She studied him a moment longer, but then something shifted. She seemed tired of entertaining his emotions. Her voice snapped back to its business-like tone.

"Tatum is one of the most feared bounty hunters in the Oxbow," she said. "You're lucky that I came along when I did."

Rufus's panic swelled into anger.

"So, you're telling me I owe you something?"

"Rufus," she said in her melodious voice, "nothing in the Oxbow is free."

He wanted to kick through the wooden slats of the docks, but instead took a deep breath; he was somehow still alive, and that was at least partly because of her.

"Well, what do you need?" he asked.

"I'm more interested in what *you* need right now, Rufus."
She pointed to the large steamboat. "I'm in charge of the
performances on that showboat. You need a place to stay.
I can offer you work and a place to lay your head. But, more
importantly, I can also offer you an education." She cupped a
hand over her fist and leaned forward. "All you have to do is
let me help you develop your mud magic."

There was that word again. Rufus felt uneasy at the sound of
it. He didn't know what this so-called *mud magic* was, but he
felt the change it was bringing. He looked back to the woman.
A thousand questions burned in his mind. He only managed
to voice one of them.

"You want to help me?"

She nodded.

"Yes, Rufus. It isn't often I see someone with that kind of
control over the water. This river is very choosy in who it lets
control it, and for some reason, it's letting you."

Rufus thought about the bizarre things he'd been able to
do. They had never felt like they were in his control—it had
all happened whether he'd wanted it to or not. Learning to
control whatever this was would be helpful.

A bead of sweat dripped across his forehead. Winesap
watched it closely as it slipped along his nose and dripped
off. The look on her face was of complete calm; her posture
hadn't slipped even an inch since they'd taken off, and it was
beginning to unsettle him. Another image of his grandmother
flickered in his mind and his frustration sparked.

"But I don't even want mud magic!" he yelled. "I just want
to find my family."

For the first time, the woman's voice rang out; it was sharp and angry.

"Answer this, Rufus: What is it you really want for yourself? What is it you want for you?"

The force of her question was jolting. With sudden clarity, Rufus knew exactly what he had to do.

"I want to leave."

The woman only cracked a subtle smile, barely visible in the diminishing light.

"Very well, Rufus," said Winesap without a trace of emotion. "You're free to go." She stepped aside and motioned for him to pass. It took him a moment to move. Josie looked surprised as he took a step forward. Winesap spoke again. "Josie, accompany Rufus into town."

The girl let out an exaggerated moan, but a single look from Winesap silenced her.

"No, that's alright," he said.

"No," said Winesap. "It isn't. Remember, Rufus, that there are hundreds of people like Tatum out there, and beings much worse." Winesap turned back to the oxman carrying the crate. Before they left, however, she turned back to Rufus. "Good luck," she said before they disappeared into the docks.

"Come on then," said Josie as she stormed down the docks toward town.

"I really don't need your help," he said as he made to catch up with her. She looked at him, shook her head.

"You need a lot more help than you think," she said as she took off toward the town.

Rufus sighed, but followed behind her.

11

Horror Show

After a short time, the town was revealed more fully. Wagtail was a place that had clearly seen better days. The town hugged the water like a crescent moon, built on a great bend in the river. Huge logs collected near the banks, fished out by huge beasts similar to the one on Tatum's boat. They hauled the logs to what looked like sawmills. A tall ridge surrounded the town, stretching upward in a series of steep hills. The hillside had been freshly razed, its trees erased from the landscape, save for the lonely stumps, though a fog-shrouded tree line remained at the top of the ridge.

The sun had by now gone down fully, but the night had yet to consume the sky. As they grew closer, Rufus could see swarms of people gathering along the banks near the boat, where a sort of carnival was going on. Even with the excitement of the showboat, the place seemed somber. It had the look of a frontier town, scrabbled together with wood in a haphazard manner. The townsfolk themselves seemed as worn and tired as the buildings around them, looking unwashed and pitiful, dressed in ratty, old-looking clothes. It was about the most depressing place he'd ever seen; the air was heavy and glum, lit by fires burning in pits along the bank. He was beginning to wish that he'd gone with Winesap.

His attention was again ripped away by the horn-like music that skidded across the air unevenly, almost as if it were hacking and coughing. It was coming from the showboat.

"What is that sound?" asked Rufus.

"It's the calliope," said Josie, disinterested. "They play it before shows to draw people in."

It was not as jolly as he would have expected, but nothing seemed to be jolly in this place. The true size of the showboat was soon revealed. It stood much taller than any of the town's buildings.

They came to the edge of the docks, where a cobblestone road led into the center of the town. Josie pulled a jar from her satchel. It glittered brightly, almost the same shade of blue as her strange bugs.

"What is that?" he asked.

She looked at him; the rolling of her eyes was almost audible.

"Here we are," she said, ignoring his question. "Good luck." She took off towards the dark sawmills near the edge of town.

"Wait!" he said. "Where should I go to get a boat?"

She turned back to him.

"I have no clue," she said. "If I were you I would just worry about not dying." She made to leave, but stopped just short. "And Rufus, don't go to the carnival."

He felt a flicker of annoyance.

"I can handle myself at a carnival," he said.

She smiled.

"No. You can't." Her tone was salty, but he didn't bother replying—hunger had now clouded his brain. She turned and soon disappeared into the dark streets.

He ambled off in the direction of the crowd. However, as he walked out from between a stack of crates, he stepped directly into the path of a horse-drawn cart.

"Watch it, boy!" yelled the driver as the horses made a loud fuss.

Rufus jumped out of the way and allowed it to pass. It barreled on down the cobblestone path. If a strange creature didn't kill him, his own stupidity surely would. He took a breath and continued.

The shrieks of the sawmill battled against the incessant whine of the calliope as he walked towards the showboat. Most folks had collected on the banks near it, where a carnival was going on.

The town was even dingier than he'd imagined. It was covered with mildew and grime, as if it never fully dried out. All the buildings were in various states of decomposition, wooden slats gray and rotting. The sawmills sent a steady rain of sawdust, which mixed with the mud to form mounds of pale muck. It was springy under his feet, covering the boardwalks and leaving footprints of townsfolk streaming down from the surrounding hills. Though all the men wore hats and the women draped scarves over their heads, their efforts at covering were in vain: Every person Rufus passed had slivers of mulch clinging to their hair like un-melting snow. He ran a hand through his to comb out as much of the sawdust as he could, but his hand dropped as his attention was drawn to the carnival.

This was like no other carnival he'd ever seen—the screams of terror told him as much. The showboat was lit in a blue light; the calliope music cast an unsettling mood over everything; townsfolk walked sheepishly amongst the musicians, magicians, and small oxmen floating around on ten-foot-tall stilts.

But the first thing that drew Rufus in was a food stall. Amongst the surplus of foul odors hung the alluring aroma of fried meat. He took out after it, soon arriving at a crude kitchen under a canvas tent. A greedy crowd pushed in around it, but Rufus wouldn't be deterred. He elbowed his way right up to the counter. The sizzle of frying fat sounded like heavenly music. He could have listened to it all night, except that he preferred to eat. But then he noticed what they were cooking.

Splayed out on sticks were strange little creatures—almost like an extra-long squirrel, though with the head of a tiny monkey—deep-fried in a light golden crust. Their whole bodies were still intact, head and all. Rufus was shoved forward, coming face to face with one. Somehow the deep-frying had captured the sheer terror in its eyes.

It was all too much. But as he turned, he again came face to face with one of the cooked creatures, only this time its head was being bitten off by a little girl. Fight as he may, Rufus couldn't break through the crowd and was soon bounced back to the counter.

"What'll you have?" asked one of the gruff cooks, getting right up in his face. Rufus watched as another cook battered a creature, still alive and tied to a stick, readying it for the fryer. Rufus couldn't speak. Everyone groaned with impatience. "What is it then?" snorted the man. Someone behind him gave Rufus a jab in the ribs.

"Do you have anything that doesn't have a face?" he asked.

The two men behind the counter looked at each other.

"Get out of here!" yelled one, pointing to a sign. It read *Fried*

River Lurker. "That's all we got!"

"Go on, git!" screamed the other man, slamming a fist down onto his counter, causing tiny discarded body parts to fly through the air.

Rufus pushed through the crowd. His head felt hot; he struggled to get a fresh breath of air. But he had no sooner escaped the crowd than he was met face-to-face by a monster.

The horrible-looking creature had great bulbous eyes and a giant tongue hanging out of its crooked mouth. It lurched for him. Rufus pulled up his arms in defense, but the creature stopped short and spoke in a muffled voice.

"Help me," it said, grabbing him by the shoulder. As Rufus looked closer, he could see that this was no monster at all, but a tacky costume made to look like an oxman. Its over-exaggerated head was almost offensive, and actually pretty scary. Behind the costumed man was a group of raggedly-dressed children standing cautiously far away, all of them holding sticks and rocks.

"What do you want me to do?" asked Rufus.

The man in the suit turned slowly back to the crowd of children. One of the bigger kids took a few steps forward and, after a measured pause, gave the man a shove. Emboldened by their comrade, the other children descended on him.

"Get him!" came the cry, and they set on the costumed man. The oxman hit the ground to the children's cries of "dirty oxman" and "wicked troll." Rufus watched as the children pummeled him mercilessly. Soon the mask was pulled off, revealing the terrified face of an old man. The mask stole their attention long enough for Rufus to help the old man to his feet. The children kept striking the enormous mask until it cracked like a piñata. The man quickly shed the rest of the costume—down to a pair of dirty long underwear—and ran back towards the boat. A brave child ran up and snatched the suit and in moments the kids were dragging it down the river bank to a chorus of wild shouts.

Queasy and overwhelmed, Rufus put a hand to his forehead. He'd been to his share of carnivals growing up, but this was something entirely different. He then saw a crowd gathering around a small stage. Music played—a mournful fiddle—as younger children and their parents pushed in.

Rufus approached cautiously, making a point of hanging back a good ways from the front. It was a modest stage, about as big as one of those trailers that gets pulled behind a truck. The backdrop was nothing more than a few thick blankets. Flittering blue lights—which Rufus recognized as jars of Josie's bugs—cast an eerie glow over the stage.

It took some time for anything to happen, but there was eventually some movement behind the draped blankets. Finally, the performers arrived on stage, walking out in a solemn, single-file line. They wore elaborate—though tattered—military costumes, most of them with stark white makeup on their faces and dark circles painted under their eyes. It was clear that they were all young folks. Two performers walked to the middle of the stage. They couldn't have been more than Rufus's age. Younger children formed a half-circle behind them.

The actors all put their heads down. At once, the fiddle stopped and, for a moment at least, even the din of the carnival seemed silenced.

Suddenly, blasts erupted from all sides of the stage—even behind where Rufus was standing—forming huge columns of bright green smoke. Rufus nearly choked up his insides, and more than a few of the spectators hit the dirt as if a grenade had been thrown. On the stage, the actors had taken up their positions and were clearly reenacting some great battle. The green vapors had morphed into full-sized soldiers of smoke who walked through the crowd—literally passing through bodies—in their approach to the stage.

"It's mud magic!" spat a man in the audience at seeing the walking smoke. At once, he grabbed his two young boys and pulled them through the crowd, letting out more than one curse as they exited. A few other spectators, similarly disgusted, followed suit.

"Hold steady, men!" yelled one of the taller actors. "Sparpole takes no prisoners, so fight with everything you have!" Amidst the spectacle of it, the name almost didn't register. But then he remembered the playing card.

The actors took positions with play rifles and long, dull-looking swords. But as they readied themselves to battle the soldiers of smoke, an old man began pushing his way through the crowd, fighting the protests of the audience members as he trudged to the stage. After a moment of struggle, he finally stepped onto the stage and looked out over his audience, his eyes wide and fiery. The performers looked perplexed at the invasion but did their best to keep the show going. That is, until the man started screaming. At once, the soldiers of smoke disappeared, like soap bubbles popping in the wind.

"These fools mock us!" he shouted, pointing at the young folks on the stage. "They don't know what it was like during The Sorrows!" The man's lank and wiry arms flung through the air as he spoke. "Mark my words! Sparpole will return!" At this, there were audible gasps from the crowd. An older woman next to Rufus put a hand to her mouth. "These are strange days. Evil watches us from the shadows." He pointed a bony finger at the crowd as if preaching fire and brimstone from a pulpit. "Do *not* let your guard down. They aim to bring him back." He finally stopped for a breath. "He's coming back," he said in a lowered voice, though it began to grow louder, his cadence quicker. "He's coming back! He's coming back!" The man kept shouting it over and over. The actors were dumbfounded. Children in the audience were crying—as were a few adults. Finally, two burly looking men grabbed him and pulled him roughly off the stage. A few in the crowd clapped as one of the men shoved a rag into the man's mouth to silence him. After they dragged him behind the curtain, the actors shrugged and continued with their show.

"Old crank," said a young man standing near Rufus.

"What a loon," said a woman, turning to walk away.

Rufus shook his head. He'd had enough carnival for the rest of his life, he reckoned, but as he began making his way to the docks to find another boat, a tall man in a long dark coat stepped out in front of him.

"Pick a card, boy," said the man in a baritone voice. Rufus could see that he was completely bald underneath his tall top-hat. He had a long face and sad eyes, looking more like an undertaker than a performer. He fanned the cards out.

"No, thanks," said Rufus. He moved to get around him, the man again blocked his path.

"It ain't a choice." The man's long black coat and deep black eyes suggested that this was someone Rufus shouldn't anger.

"Fine." He picked one of the cards.

"Now, watch that card." The man kept his eyes set on Rufus's as the cards shuffled quickly between his hands. Rufus smirked and looked at it. It was just a normal playing card: an ace of diamonds. Nothing happened.

"What am I looking for?" asked Rufus, but no sooner had the words escaped his lips than something began to move inside the card. The printing fell away, revealing an image of his grandmother, holding onto the side of a boat, swirling around in a great vortex of water.

He was unable to move. His eyes were locked on the image. Grandma Jezebel was crying out, but no one was there to help her; no one was there for her.

When Rufus came to he realized that the magician was shaking him. The card was again an ace of diamonds.

"Give me my card back, you vandal." The man was yelling in his face. His eyes were still lazy but had now gone bloodshot. Others around him stared. Rufus swallowed heavily. He gave the card back to the man, turned, and ran back for the docks.

He needed a raft, and he didn't care if he had to steal it. It wasn't long before he found one tied up along the ancient jetty, not much more than a few boards lashed together. He jumped down onto it and began to untie it from the dock. A simple push out into the river would see him away from this horrible town and the freaks that inhabited it.

However, a rustling amongst a stack of crates caught his attention. A squawk of laughter punctured the night air, bringing Rufus to his feet. Something was oddly familiar about that laugh, but he couldn't place it. A small group of men were walking from a boat into an alleyway between two warehouses. Rufus climbed out of the small boat and made his way towards them, stepping over creaky boards with care to try and keep himself undetected. The sounds from the sawmills nearby provided an extra layer of cover.

As he rounded a stack of crates, Rufus saw a man wearing

a long duster jacket that stretched past his boots. A black hat covered his head. He was speaking to someone, though Rufus couldn't see who it was. The glow of a nearby fire was dim, but enough for him to make out another shape, that of a woman. It was Winesap.

Rufus edged his way closer to the side of the building, trying to stay out of sight. A meeting was taking place, though the scream of the blades chewing up old trees drowned out any words. The group was peering into the opened crate. Some were dressed in long, red robes, heads covered with hoods or large hats. The robed figures were clearly excited by what they saw. The top of the crate was opened to show the plant Winesap had collected from Tatum. But it was the figure in in the duster coat that caught his attention. Something about the way he was standing, about the wiry frame and, as he took off his hat, the shock of white hair.

Jasper.

12

Missed Chances

I t wasn't possible. The strangeness of the carnival must have triggered some hallucination. Rufus took a few deep breaths, then poked his head back out. The man he thought was Jasper was no longer there. Winesap was, however, and she turned towards him at that very moment, causing Rufus to throw himself flat against the wall.

If his brother was near, he could end all this and get home. He took a few short breaths, but by the time he'd built up his courage to look again, everyone was gone.

"No!" he shouted. "Gideon!"

He set off down the alleyway, but had only taken a few steps when a huge set of warehouse doors burst open. A behemoth oxman lurched out, hulking shoulders in the yoke of a massive lumber cart. He was a good two feet taller than any man Rufus had ever seen. Long black hair ran over his simple pale face which he kept blowing off with his mouth. The creature and his cart took up the entire alleyway, making it impossible for Rufus to get past.

As the cart shuttled onto the road, a stack of lumber tipped off the side and fell into the mud. The creature didn't seem to notice. A whip cracked loudly from inside the warehouse. The oxman stopped at once. A man stepped out of the shed, whip spooled underneath his arm.

"Plonk!" he yelled. The creature bristled. The man was slight of stature, but strutted like a lion-tamer full of swagger. The gargantuan oxman looked scared as the man approached the cart. The man's tall boots looked far too nice to have actually been worked in. Rufus tried to see beyond the creature and the cart, but there was no way he could get around.

The long spool of the whip unfurled from the man's arms.

"I told you before, Plonk," said the man, a sinister half-grin on his face, "you gotta look at me when I talk to you." The creature still didn't turn, but simply looked straight ahead. The man cracked the whip. It was as loud as any gunshot Rufus ever heard, echoing through the alley. The scream of the saw blades had stopped. The workers from inside the mill—both human and oxfolk—had gathered in the large doorway to see what the ruckus was. A few townsfolk had also come over, forming a barrier that cut off Rufus's other way out. His frustration increased with every beat of his heart. If his brother was here, he was getting away.

All attention was piled squarely on the tiny man yelling at the giant. He cracked the whip again, this time landing it in front of the creature's feet. The oxman jumped as the leather tip scratched the earth before him.

"Atta boy, Plonk," said the man. He looked at the cart, piled high with boards and posts. He ran his hand across their freshly-cut surfaces. Then he began to shake them, sending more boards tumbling into the mud, some being helped along by the man. "You stupid troll." He cracked the whip again.

"Does this seem like a proper load to you?"

The creature looked at the wood lying in the mud, but did not answer.

"Sorry, Plonk," he said. "But I can't hear you. Does it seem like a proper load?"

The creature finally shook his head. The man looked pleased for a moment, but then his demeanor changed. He cracked the whip once more. The creature reared back, trying to clear himself from its reach. The man lurched towards him, sweeping the whip in wide motions, cracking it inches from the beast's uncovered toes. There was a devilish look in his eyes as he drove the creature back against a giant trough of water. Many of the townsfolk laughed as they got out of the way. The man pulled the whip behind his head in a lavish show before sending it flying. The creature lifted both legs, falling back over into the water.

The cackles from the gathered townsfolk were now louder than the whip.

"Let this be a lesson to all you oxfolk," said the man, kicking a mound of muddy sawdust into the creature's face. "I'm tired of your ignorance. I'm tired of your clumsiness." The man got right into the creature's face and spoke in a low, pompous voice. "Your stupidity is no longer acceptable." Rufus waited for the creature to reach up with a powerful arm and tear the man in half, but the creature just sat there in the mud, looking utterly dejected. "Fill the cart right next time, else I won't be so nice."

By this time, a large group of oxmen had come out of the sawmill and were looking on. They were angry, but they didn't dare make a move. All of them were huge, hulking creatures, though none quite as large as the one just accosted. When the man saw them, his eyes lit up. Again, he turned and kicked another pile of sawdust into the creature's face. He looked at the group of oxmen and spoke with all the hate he could muster. "Trolls," he said as if expelling poison from his mouth.

A tremor went through the group, but they didn't dare act. A few men in tattered military uniforms strolled by, touching their rifles as if to issue warning. A tense moment passed, broken by the laughter of the man as he strolled back into the building.

The crowd soon dispersed, smiles on their faces as if they had been watching a grand entertainment. The creature sat in the road, not even attempting to get up. Rufus was sickened by the display and felt bad for the creature. However, he still needed to find his brother, and began to squeeze past the cart.

The oxmen from the sawmill had surrounded the giant and began helping him out of the trough. As Rufus tried to step around them, one of them stepped wide and bumped into him. Something fell from the oxman's belt. It was a jar filled with blue dust—the same blue dust that Josie had. The jar shattered on a rock, causing the blue dust to go flying through the air.

"You little..." shouted the foul-looking creature. He had a gold hoop in his ear and bright red hair spiked up on his head. Before Rufus could blink, he was being lifted into the air, the clenched fist of an angry oxman around his neck.

13

Riot

Rufus wouldn't have breathed even if he could have. He was face to face with the creature, surely even bigger and stronger than the oxman on Tatum's boat. The oxman pulled him close to his face. Rufus could feel the heat of his breath on his cheeks. Seconds later, the creature tossed him as casually as a rag doll.

Rufus landed in the dirt choking and coughing.

"Where you going in such a hurry?" growled the creature.

"Sorry," croaked Rufus, clasping his neck. "I didn't see you."

"You didn't see him!" shouted another of the oxmen. "Clovis there is big as a house!" The other oxmen broke out into laughter.

"We must entertain you, ain't that right, boy?" shouted the creature. He towered over Rufus, who was frozen in place. "Do we make you laugh?" It seemed they were going to work out their frustrations on Rufus.

"No," said Rufus, slowly backing away. "I was just trying to get through." All of Rufus's determination drained out of him as another oxman stepped over to them.

"Let's tear him apart, Clovis. Scatter him all over that carnival," he said with a laugh.

"Let me do it," shouted another oxman.

"Hold on," said the red-headed one. "If anybody gets to tear up a thin-bones, I say it's Plonk." The oxmen turned to the creature still stuck in the trough.

As the oxmen debated amongst themselves about who would get to tear him apart, Rufus happened to see a hand waving from behind a stack of crates—it was Josie. She vigorously waved him over. The oxmen had seemed to forget about him as they began to argue. One of the creatures grabbed a crate and smashed it against the wall, sending splintery bits flying. It gave Rufus the chance to shimmy through the mud undetected.

She forced Rufus to his feet, pulling him down another narrow alleyway. He followed without thought as they emerged onto the docks. They were back to the edge of the carnival before Rufus put his heels into the ground and brought them to an abrupt halt.

"Wait," he said. "I think my brother is here."

"No," said Josie. "We need to get back to the boat, now."

"But I have to see if it was him!" He turned to go back.

"Stop!" yelled Josie, grabbing him roughly by the arm. "Those oxmen were fighting over who would kill you. The one you walked into was Clovis. He's the meanest oxman there is."

"I don't care," said Rufus, shaking his head. "I have to try."

"Getting yourself ripped to pieces by angry oxmen isn't going to help you."

At that moment, the red-haired oxman rampaged through a stack of crates at the edge of the docks. Josie grabbed Rufus's arm and they scrambled towards the showboat. A large explosion sounded from one of the sawmills where a fire had broken out. The carnival-goers took notice of the commotion, turning their attention away from the performers.

"Hurry," she said. "All the boats are pulling up anchor."

Sure enough, Rufus heard the showboat's engines firing up. At the sound, both performers and spectators alike scrambled towards the river. As he ran, thoughts of Gideon overwhelmed him. He stopped and turned back to the docks. They were fully ablaze now, being ripped apart by the raging oxmen.

Josie grabbed him by the shoulders.

"Listen, if you go back there, those oxmen are going to eat you alive. I'm not joking—they'll actually eat you." Rufus took in deep breaths, watching the docks as they were destroyed. "Fine," said Josie. "I'm going. Stay if you want oxmen pulling pieces of you out of their teeth."

She turned and took off for the showboat. The idea flashed in Rufus's mind that he could hide—wait out the riot—until he watched a man get flung out into the river like a skipping stone. The town was being destroyed in front of his eyes. There would be nowhere to hide.

The big oxman, now hooked to his cart, plowed through a building nearby, the limp body of the whip-wielding man slung below his arm. Jasper and Gideon wouldn't be sticking around for this. He muttered a curse and set out after Josie.

They fought through the frenzy of shouting parents and crying children, but as they approached the showboat, a loud horn blew. It was taking off, with or without them.

"Hurry!" yelled Josie as the ramp lifted and the boat lurched forward.

But they weren't the only ones running for the showboat. Some crew members darted in front of them. Two of the men managed to grab ahold of the ramp as it swung back towards the boat. One of them as the man who did the card trick. He smiled as he clambered up onto the stage plank.

There was still time. They could still make it, except another man kept jumping and missing. It was one of the large men from the fried river lurker stand. He was too big for them to simply run around, and the ramp would soon be out of reach.

"Hurry!" shouted Josie, but her yelling seemed to throw him off balance. The man's momentum was soon too much for his squat little legs to keep up with. He tripped violently, tumbling end over end like a snowball rolling down a mountain.

If Rufus had not been so weak from his captivity, he might have made the leap, cascading over the rolling man to climb aboard the showboat and drift down the river to safety. But Rufus's left foot tangled into the man's spinning legs, which pulled him down like a lion taking down a gazelle. Rufus skidded through the mud on his chest. By the time they came to a halt, the man's full weight was squarely on Rufus's back, pinning him to the ground.

The man seemed unable to move. Rufus was unnaturally twisted, his limbs forming a strange human pretzel. Try as he might, he could not get up. Then, he saw Josie running toward them at full speed. She threw a shoulder into the man, which sent him toppling over onto the ground. Rufus had no time to recuperate before Josie hauled him to his feet.

"We have to find another way out of here," she said.

She helped Rufus stagger to the southern edge of town. What few trees remained stood here, hiding a collection of small flatboats and keelboats gathered along the riverbanks. They wasted no time in running out into the shallows, pleading with the boatmen for passage, but each one of them flatly turned them away.

Rufus saw a middle-aged woman struggling to climb aboard a boat.

"Josie!" he shouted, pointing at the woman who looked as if she were about to lose her grip. The two sloshed over to her, helping to boost her up onto the deck. As she turned back around to them, Josie extended a hand.

"Help me up," she said.

However, just as Rufus began to lift Josie onto the boat, the woman grabbed a boat paddle and swung it wildly, narrowly missing his head.

"Back, you animals!" shouted the woman as Josie fell back into the water. Rufus had to dive below the surface to escape the woman's swings.

When he broke the surface again, there were no more boats to be had. Rufus felt helpless as the vessels floated away from them and out into the darkness. Josie finally came to meet him on the riverbank. Her dress was soaked and her eyes held the sting of fresh rejection. The shouts and carnage could still be heard from the town. The night sky now lit up red like a violent aurora borealis.

"They'll find you," said Josie. "Oxmen have a knack for holding grudges. Clovis will be able to track you down."

"Is there no other way out of here?" asked Rufus. She again shook her head. But then another boat came into view. It was a slow-creeping vessel, and dark, with no running lights to speak of. At first it was hard to even tell if it was a boat, as it just looked like a floating pile of junk. It wasn't too far out from the banks, and he reckoned they could easily wade out and catch it. "What about that boat?" he asked.

"Not that boat," she said.

"Why not?"

"Just no."

Rufus looked back to the flaming town. Thoughts of being ripped limb from limb bounced around his head.

"Well I'm going for it," he said. "You said they'd find me, but maybe they won't bother you." With that, Rufus waded out into the water toward the boat.

"Wait," said Josie. Finally, with a deep sigh, she splashed out after him.

The further that Rufus waded out, the more he wasn't sure what he was looking at. It floated lazily down the river, though junk was piled so high that it could have easily been mistaken for some sort of oddly shaped sea monster. Still, there were no other boats; there was no other choice.

The piles of clutter became clearer as they neared the boat. Washbasins, old carts, tools, and countless odd contraptions were strewn about carelessly. The vessel was about as long as a school bus, though a little bit wider. Climbing aboard seemed almost impossible due to all of the extra clutter, but as the boat came by, a clearing presented itself. Rufus gave Josie a boost and then pulled himself up onto the deck.

The boat was eerily quiet. For a moment, Rufus wondered if it had been abandoned in the chaos, but the sound of clanging and the swishing of water soon told him otherwise. Josie gave him a worried look. He took a breath and stepped lightly in the direction of the racket. It was hard to see in the dark; every step had to be considered carefully amongst all the junk. He climbed onto an old, weather-worn armchair and peeked over a mound of rusted farm tools. Rufus saw a small man pulling trash from the river. He was dressed in raggedy, loose-fitting clothes and a droopy hat that made him look like a basset hound. He was in the process of lifting a few large corked bottles when he stopped and looked up.

"No no no!" he shouted. The man darted off like a rat, bounding over his piles of clutter with surprising grace—he seemed to know the location of every piece of junk that the boat held. He disappeared into a doorway, which slammed behind him. The boat's cabin covered the entire back end of the boat and was similarly cluttered with rubbish. Rufus approached and knocked on the door.

"Sir," he said.

"Hold on," said Josie grabbing him by the arm. She spoke in a low, cautious voice. "He's mink."

"What, like the animal?"

"No, like the person. They're a shifty bunch—swamp people, traders; they'll barter you right out of your own skin if you're not careful."

What came to mind when Rufus heard the word "mink" were the horrible smelling creatures that sprayed Grandma Jezebel's dogs.

"Did you see that guy?" asked Rufus. "He's terrified of us."

She breathed heavily. "Just watch yourself."

Rufus knocked again.

"We don't mean to trouble you. We just need a ride if you can spare the room." Rufus looked at the tightly packed spaces around him, instantly regretting his choice of words.

A commotion sounded from inside. A curtain whipped away from behind a small circular window, exposing a bloodshot eye. Rufus shot back a few feet in surprise.

After a moment, the door cracked open.

"Who are you?" he asked. His voice was quick and his accent deep. He was certainly a backwater fellow.

"Sorry, sir," he said. "But we needed to get out of Wagtail.

106

The riot and all."

The man emerged slowly. From under his droopy hat Rufus could see his dark, bloodshot eyes darting back and forth between him and Josie. As he sussed them out, he stepped fully out into the open.

"I know about the riot," he said. "I been pullin' some fine items out of that there river on account of it. Almost as good as a boat wreck for findin' quality goods."

Rufus cast Josie a quick look of confusion. She shrugged her shoulders.

"We were wondering if we could ride with you, just until the next town," said Rufus.

At this, the man's head began to wobble on his neck like a bobble head doll.

"No, no, no," he said, his voice rising in pitch like a kettle beginning to boil. "I don't let nobody ride this here boat." He lifted a large metal stick, a fire poker, into the air and began to wave it at Rufus. "Get on back out into the river. Off this here boat!" His movements were spastic, his voice suddenly shaky. Still, Rufus had to jump to get out of the way.

"Look at that city!" shouted Rufus, pointing towards Wagtail. "There's not going to be anything left of that town! If you send us out there, they'll kill us."

"Ain't my problem," said the man. He swung the poker again, this time it was only inches from Rufus's cheek.

"Listen," said Rufus. "I want to be fair, so let's talk about a deal that works for all of us."

The man perked up at the mention of a deal. He even lowered the fire poker to his side.

"Twenty Oxbow dollars would be a good start," he said.

Josie scoffed behind them.

"We'd both have to work a year to make that much," she spat. The man looked affronted.

"Well, what do you have then?"

Rufus looked to Josie, hoping that there was at least a little bit of money inside her satchel. However, as she opened it, something else appeared: one of her strange bugs. It fluttered into the air around her head, putting on its dazzling light show and leaving a trail of fluorescent dust in its wake.

He pointed at the bug. "You'll get passage for one of those."

"Never!" she yelled, snatching the bug from the air and placing it back in her satchel.

"Good luck then," said the man, raising the fire poker again.

How was it that she couldn't give up a single bug to save their lives? He pointed back at the burning town. Josie looked wary, but slowly reached into her satchel.

"I can give you moxdust," she said, producing a tiny jar of the glittery substance. At the sight of it, the man's eyes lit up.

"Deal." He eagerly snatched the jar and held it up in the air. His dark eyes reflected the dazzling light. He spoke without taking his eyes away. "The name's Remy Moses, and this boat is headed to the Mink Market. If that doesn't please you, then I ain't a bit sorry." He looked at Rufus. "You," he snapped. "Come help me pull a chest of drawers onto the boat. So big I had to tie it to the back." The man trudged over a mound of clutter back to the edge of the water. "Remind me to thank those oxmen if I see 'em."

Rufus turned to Josie. She had a strained look on her face. The city continued to burn behind them, shrieks carrying across the water.

"Just be thankful you're not dead," she said.

"I'm starting to wish I was."

14

Nervous River

The river stretched out ahead of them, darkness so complete that it was hard to know where the river stopped and the deep black of the sky began. Josie had kept her distance. It was Rufus that had caused her to miss her boat; he was the reason they were riding with a mink. Rufus didn't much care what kind of boat he was riding, so long as it was carrying him away from those oxmen.

The chaos of Wagtail was by now some distance behind them, but Rufus could still hear the screams in his head, could somehow still smell the smoke. All the while, the mink kept to his work of pulling discarded implements from the river, things likely scattered by riot. Though exhausted, Rufus was glad to help Remy fish things out of the water. It pushed some of the noisier thoughts from his mind. Remy was quite good at spotting items of value, even at night. After only a few hours, they'd added significantly to the man's piles of bric-a-brac.

Remy leaned out over the edge of the boat and touched the surface of the water.

"Hey, boy," he said. "Feel this water." Rufus knelt down and

109

put a flat palm on the water's dark surface. "You feel that?"

"Feel what?" asked Rufus, more concerned about falling into the river than how it felt.

"The river's nervous," he said. "I been feeling it for the last couple of days. She's got herself all tied up in knots. We might be heading for trouble."

"How can a river be nervous?" Rufus was too exhausted to entertain this strange man's ideas. It felt like the whole sky was sitting squarely on his shoulders.

Remy looked away quickly. His voice grew a little lower, his actions more fidgety.

"I don't know," he said. "But the river has changed." He looked back out over the water. Another dark object was floating their way. "Here we go," he said. "Grab it on *three.*" Rufus readied himself as the man began his count. "*One, two, three,*" he said as they clutched the object and hoisted it onto the boat. It was a small trunk with a big padlock on the front. "Jackpot," he said, rubbing his hands together and tipping up his droopy hat.

"What about the river?" asked Rufus.

"Right," he said as he studied the lock. "The river whispers things to me." He jiggled the lock, which unexpectedly popped open. He turned to Rufus with an excited look in his eyes. He opened the trunk only to find it completely empty. His face turned sour as he nudged the trunk back into the water. He turned back to Rufus. "Expect something big to happen, I'd reckon. Something really big."

Rufus wanted him to elaborate, but the man was already busy dragging an anchor to the side of the boat.

"What are you doing?"

"Dropping anchor."

"You can't do that," shouted Rufus. "We have to keep going." He approached the man, who stepped back quickly, almost cowering in fear. "I have to find my brother!" His voice came out as more of a growl.

"Listen," said Remy, his voice quivering. "Can't nobody bargain with the river. Gotta show it respect."

Rufus could feel his face getting red. He paced back and forth, kicking whatever clutter happened to get in the path of his feet. He turned back to Remy.

"I don't believe you," he said.

"He's right, Rufus." It was Josie, glaring at him from over a pile of rusted-out brass instruments. "Boats don't run the river at night. Only The Otto Modest can, and that's because of the calliope. It soothes the river."

"And I ain't got no calliope," said Remy, tugging anxiously at his hat.

Rufus's breath was quick and deep, like an anxious bull.

"You saying there's no way we can keep going?"

"Not unless you know an all-powerful river mage," said Remy. Rufus and Josie exchanged quick looks. "We minks are blessed with a bit of mud magic, but not enough to carry a boat gingerly enough for the river's liking. River needs its rest like anyone else!"

"Fine then," said Rufus. "But we leave at first light."

"That was my plan all along, boss." Remy looked to the sky as a gentle rain began to fall. He tipped his hat to them. "Good night, folks."

"Wait!" said Rufus. "Do you have any extra room in the cabin?"

Remy's head began to bobble again.

"No one but me goes in my cabin." With that he bounded

over a pile of garbage and disappeared inside. Rufus put his boot through a crate, sending at least a dozen mice scurrying out of the hole in all directions.

Josie looked dry enough, having fashioned a shelter from the pieces of a discarded baby carriage. She seemed to want to have nothing to do with Rufus, and he wasn't really up for talking anyhow. After a bit of digging, Rufus managed to find a tarp which he strung over the legs of an old table. It was poor relief from the rain, but better than nothing. He laid himself down, struggling to find a position where there wasn't a rusty blade poking his back or a stone statue of an oxman threatening to tumble over on him.

He longed for sleep, but his mind flickered with images; his grandmother, his brother, violent scenes from the riot. He was enraged at the man who called himself their grandfather, at Gideon too, for how fully he'd been sucked into their scam. Eventually, however, no distractions could keep the weariness away, and he leaned his head back against the clutter as fatigue took hold of his bones and pulled him down to sleep.

15

A visitor

I t was a single thud at first, not loud enough to wake him. But the knocking soon invaded Rufus's sleep. It was a slow, steady beat, growing louder with each tap. Soon the sound had wrapped itself around his sleeping brain so fiercely he couldn't separate it from his own heartbeat.

A fierce jab to the stomach finally roused him. He sat up quickly, hitting his head on the underside of the table. His first thought was that Remy was pulling more garbage from the river. But the tapping continued, and he soon saw its source. Rufus took a deep, troubled breath.

"Still alive?" said a low voice. A hoarse laugh followed. It was Weego steadily tapping his wooden leg with an ornately designed cane.

"You—" was all Rufus could muster.

"Eager to see me?"

"What are you doing here?" Rufus hissed. His patience had boiled off into the night air, leaving only a simmering anger.

The creature eyed him for a moment.

"I thought I'd give you a proper welcome to the Oxbow,"

he said as he paced the deck. Even with his short legs there was only enough space for about two strides. He took an exaggerated sniff of the air and exhaled deeply. "Smell that air, boy. They don't make air like this where you come from. Smells like dog farts and death back there."

"Where's Gideon?" yelled Rufus. "Where's Grandma?" He rose to his feet, rushing toward the creature. He barely made it a step before a set of watery chains wrapped around him.

"Easy now," said Weego calmly. "Can you play nice?"

Rufus seethed with anger, but managed to nod in agreement. The liquid bonds fell, splashing on the wood deck. Rufus rubbed his wrists. Though made of water, the chains had rubbed his skin raw.

"Aren't you worried about the others hearing you?" asked Rufus, thinking of Josie on the other end of the boat.

"Nope," he said. "I put a water barrier around the mink and that little gal pal of yours. They won't hear a thing." He smiled.

"Where is my family?" snapped Rufus.

"*Family*," he said, putting a finger to his chin. "That's an interesting word. You see, here in the Oxbow, your family is somewhat revered. Not exactly in the good way neither." He looked out at the darkness. "You'll see evidence of your brother soon enough," said Weego. "That boy's been busy."

"What about Grandma Jezebel?" Rufus felt his hands trembling. "Is she alright?" The words tumbled out of his mouth in awkward chunks.

Weego made no effort to speak at first. He cleared his throat and emptied the chamber of his pipe. For once, his wicked smile had faded. Every second was an eternity.

"I don't know," said Weego. "I didn't see." He looked back at Rufus. "But she was always a tough one." His words were about as helpful as a bandage on a slit throat. Rufus thought about how he'd left her. This was all his fault. He waited for the creature to elaborate, but Weego left it at that. "Wait a second," said Weego, as if just remembering the purpose of his visit. The creature began to fish around in his pocket, bringing up a slim piece of metal. "You almost lost this, you fool." It was the whistle, now attached to a strip of leather. Weego held it forward and jiggled it.

"I don't want it," said Rufus, remembering what had happened the last time he'd seen it.

"You don't have a choice, son," said Weego. "I put a string on there to keep your sorry butt from losing it. Just don't let it slip into the wrong hands." At this, Weego paused. "Though I reckon your hands are just as wrong as anyone's." He looked genuinely conflicted for a moment as he mulled over his options, but finally tossed the whistle to Rufus.

Rufus ran a finger over the smooth metal cylinder. It was such a tiny piece of metal. How could it be worth causing such a fuss over? He begrudgingly put it around his neck as Weego lit his pipe. "Keep that whistle close," said Weego. "It might just keep you alive for a tiny bit longer. Not likely, but there's always a chance." Weego released a puff of bright purple smoke into the air. "Say, boy, I saw you call the water back there. Jasper and his boys didn't know what hit 'em."

"What did you see?" asked Rufus.

"You're feeling it, ain't you?" Weego's sinister look came creeping back. "That mud magic—it runs strong in you Pinhooks." He took another drag from the pipe. "There's an anger to yours though. Caused all that mess back there." He began laughing. "Impressive display!" He walked towards Rufus—wooden leg clanking against the planks of the deck.

"And what you did is just a little glimpse of what you're capable of." He paused for a second, nodding assuredly. "You could know real power in this place."

"I don't care," said Rufus. "I just want to find Grandma and Gideon. I don't care about controlling some stupid river."

At that, the river around him began to ripple. Weego smiled as he again spoke.

"Young Pinhook, you can't control squat right now. You'll need some help to get there. But know this: mud magic can just as easily control you." He looked at Rufus dismissively. "But you'll likely be killed and eaten long before you have to worry about that."

"If I'm so doomed, then why the heck are you even here? All you've done since you got here was say I'm good as dead."

Weego let out a full-bodied laugh.

"I warned you, didn't I?" He spun around on his wooden leg, though the leg stayed planted in the same direction. "I told you to run away. Adding another Pinhook to the Oxbow was never going to do anyone a darned bit of good."

The silence was thick as caked mud. Finally, Rufus spoke.

"I couldn't let them take Gideon."

"And did that work?" The words were like pinpricks. Weego put a hand to his chin. "But it's not all your fault I suppose. They had that boy the moment he fell from the womb. He was built for this place." He looked Rufus up and down. "You weren't."

Rufus felt his face reddening, as if the blood were backed up behind a dam, ready to burst.

"What do they want with Giddy?"

"They're going to make him into a proper Pinhook, a real monster. They're a pretty good ways along too."

Rufus stood up.

"I won't let them turn Gideon into a monster."

Weego's eyes got narrow.

"We all have it in us to be monsters, Rufus Pinhook. Especially you."

"Then I have to find him!" His voice echoed across the water. Weego looked like he had to hold back laughter.

"And are you responsible for what Gideon does?" The question echoed in Rufus's brain. "Would that skid-mark do the same for you?" he asked calmly. "You just can't seem to get out of his shadow, can you?" It felt as though he'd cut Rufus all over and thrown him into a salt pit. He seemed to notice Rufus's building anger. "I'll bet you could call the water now, couldn't you?" he yelled.

Rufus let out a grunt.

"So, what am I supposed to do then?"

Weego picked up a dented trumpet from one of Remy's piles and studied it for a moment before casually tossing it back down.

"Oh, I'm sure you'll probably have to kill him."

Weego said it so casually that it took a moment for the words to register.

"No!" he shouted.

Weego simply smiled.

"With any luck, you'll be strong enough to kill when the time comes. Especially me."

"Wait. Kill you?" asked Rufus. "You're a speck. A little worm. Why would you even be worth my time?"

"One day soon you'll know why." He looked off into the night sky, putting his hands on his hips and raring back to take a deep breath. "Looky here," he said, pointing to a red light hovering in the distance. "The Specter Steamer is still following you." Weego smiled and leaned down to the surface of the water. He touched his hand to the water. "That mink fella could feel it. Yes, sir," he said. "A change is on the way." His smile stretched from ear to ear. "And you're it."

"No I'm not," said Rufus. "I'm getting out of here soon."

Weego's face turned sharp and indignant.

"I was mistaken then," he spat in a low voice.

"Mistaken how?"

Weego looked him dead in the eye.

"For believing that you might be better than common river trash."

Something bubbled up inside of Rufus. The word *trash* sizzled in his brain.

Rufus picked up things from the boat—pipes, broken picture frames, old boots—and flung them at the creature. One by one, however, the projectiles evaporated into a fine mist. Rufus, panting and seething, squeezed his eyes shut. He felt the swish of blood running through his body. When he opened his eyes, Weego was stock still, a ring of rain surrounding him like a cage, though it wasn't falling on him.

"That's it!" Weego yelled. "A fine start. But we need more." He charged through the circle of rain which parted like a beaded door. "You have some anger. Use it!"

"I don't want this!" Rufus shouted. "I don't want mud magic!"

Weego stopped a few feet from him, lowering his voice.

"You're a river mage, boy. That doesn't up and leave because you want it to. Let me demonstrate."

Weego moved back to the edge of the boat. He watched the water for a moment with an intense focus. As he lifted his hand, the coiled outline of a snake rose from the surface of the water, like a cobra rising from a snake charmer's basket. For a moment, the two stood looking at each other as if in a standoff. But as Weego lowered his hand, the snake lunged at Rufus. Its fangs met his forearm before he could pull away. His blood went cold at the realization he'd been bitten.

Instead of the pain of fangs puncturing his skin, he felt only wetness. It was not blood, but simply water. Rufus watched in confusion as the snake disappeared into a puddle on the deck, splashing his feet.

"What was that?" asked Rufus, shaking.

"What did it look like?"

"A snake, but it was made out of water."

Weego nodded.

"Maybe you ain't the dumbest of the bunch."

Rufus looked back to the puddle of water.

"You want me to control a snake made out of water?"

"You ain't understanding me, son. You shouldn't be able to control it." He lingered for a moment before finishing. "You *are* it."

Weego's upper lip attempted something of a smile as water rushed over the boat from all sides and swished around Rufus's feet. From the water formed dozens of similar snakes. The creatures writhed and twisted their translucent bodies into knots, hissing at his feet. Every surface was covered by a watery viper waiting to strike. He lifted his leg just in time to dodge one's fluid fangs.

Standing on one leg, he looked at Weego, whose face carried that same wicked grin, that same expectation. Rufus's fear veered back towards anger. He looked back down at the snakes. They were just water. His foot crashed down onto one of the creature's heads. It splashed into a puddle. As if to avenge their fallen brother, the others set upon him.

Rufus swung his fists and legs, but the creatures kept snapping. He could feel the coldness of the watery fangs on his skin. The weight of the creatures, the sheer strength, was surprising as they wrapped their bodies around him. Soon he was covered with dozens of them. They slithered around his neck, then his face. His eyes were squeezed shut by their vice-grip strength. Rufus dropped to his knees. The mass of writhing reptiles worked themselves into ever deeper knots, like a deadly Chinese finger trap.

He managed one last breath as the snakes overwhelmed him.

After a moment of quiet, a loud hiss sounded from deep within the ball of snakes. Soon others joined in, forming an angry chorus. Just as the hiss reached a brutal, assaulting pitch, the snakes exploded into heavy droplets that rained down on the deck.

Rufus emerged unharmed. His fear was gone—something else had taken over. Each movement had a reason to it, a logic unknown to him before, but completely clear to him now. The water below his swirling hand responded, following it almost as if it were magnetized.

Hair hanging wet across his face, Rufus pulled his hand up slowly. Emerging from the water—slowly at first, as if bashful—was one of the water vipers. Rufus pulled it further and the snake emerged fully. The beast felt familiar to him, as if he'd known this water his entire life. He looked back to Weego, who seemed satisfied. However, Rufus wasn't. The viper lunged at Weego, though it barely made it a foot before it was dismissed into a fine mist.

"You're starting to get it," said Weego.

Rufus's patience cracked.

"Every problem in my life is because of this stupid 'gift' you say I have." He looked Weego dead in the eye. "Well, I call it a curse."

It felt as if he'd let out a good deal of pressure, like a steam valve released. There was a moment of abrasive quiet. Finally, Weego smiled and again spoke.

"A *curse*?" He let the word hand in the air a moment. "Listen, if you want to blame your name for every problem in your life, be my guest. They ain't done you no favors, all the way back to Old Winslow Pinhook, whose had his blood fused with water from the river's heart. That's the same blood that you carry in you today." He took a deep breath and shook his head "You just don't see it though. I'm giving you every opportunity to change your station, but you're an ungrateful little rascal. You want to get out of your family's shadow? This is the way."

Rufus sat with the creature's words, annoyed by the truth in them.

Weego walked to the edge of the boat.

"Do what you will with your *curse*, but I'm done." He took a deep breath. "Now if you'll excuse me, I'm still getting reacquainted with my river." He paused, adjusting the cuffs of his frayed jacket. "One last thing…don't go telling anyone you're a Pinhook." "That name's a sandbag tied 'round your legs. Ain't many folks gonna be sympathetic to you with that name." His lips curled over his yellowed teeth, forming a sly, knowing grin. "Not after what your daddy did."

"Wait!" yelled Rufus. "What did my father do?" There was no answer from Weego, only a small ripple as he hopped into the dark river. "Tell me about my father!" shouted Rufus as he ran to the boat's edge. Weego was gone.

"Who are you talking to?" asked a voice from behind him. It

was Josie.

"Sorry," said Rufus. "I think I was dreaming. Did you hear much of that?"

"Just you yelling about your dad." Her face bore the look of someone freshly woken up. Weego's water barriers had clearly disappeared with him.

"Sorry," he said. She shook her head, huffed, and walked back to her shelter.

Rufus laid back down under his tarp. The creature's visit had done little to settle him—the last thing he needed was another mention of how his family was no good. Still, a new energy buzzed within him, raw and untamed. When he was sure Josie wasn't watching, he held a hand out to the river. The water began to swirl at his command. He pulled shapes out of the water with ease. It was like he suddenly knew another language. But as he looked out at the red smoke of the Specter Steamer in the distance, he couldn't help but shudder.

16

The Fiddle

S leep did not return to Rufus that night. He lay on the boat watching the palette of colors wash across the sky, from deepest black to the milky-blue of morning. It was just before sun-up that Remy staggered out of his cabin, all fidgety and nervous. He seemed to be going around taking stock of his possessions, clearly searching for the items that Weego had turned to water.

Rufus had no time for it.

"Can we go now?" he asked, startling the man.

"We'll leave directly," he said, but soon his gaze went beyond Rufus and out onto the river.

Rufus looked out onto the water. A gargantuan creature was wading out from the shore, coming to meet their boat. Though he was already far out into the river, the water only came a little past his waist. The creature had bulbous eyes and a bumpy, nearly-bald head.

"What is that?" asked Rufus.

"Never seen a Dortha giant before?" asked Remy. Rufus shook his head. "Count yourself lucky," he said. "Foul creatures, dumbest of all the oxmen." He got quiet as the creature approached. "Guess I better gather up a few pennies." The creature was holding something, and as it plunged toward them, Rufus finally saw what it was: three dead rabbits dangling by their ears. When it was close to the boat—water still only up to its thick neck—Remy tossed the creature a few pennies, which it caught with its other giant hand, almost the size of a school lunch tray. Rufus watched, awestruck, as the creature tossed the rabbits onto the deck.

"Any news on the river?" asked Remy.

The big creature snorted heavily, emitting snot like a cannon into the water.

"Trouble in Wagtail," he said in short, simple words. "No Wagtail left."

"I hear it was oxmen that done it. They catch 'em?"

"Got away," said the creature with a big, chest shaking laugh. "Clovis never gets caught." With that, the big creature turned and waded back toward the shore.

"What do you reckon?" asked Remy. He held up a rabbit by the ears, giving it a sniff. "Them rabbits worth eating? I think they're only a couple days dead. Better than the last time I came through," he continued. "They were selling corpses dug out of the local cemetery. I had to buy an old deputy. Darn trolls will sell anything they can find."

"You bought a dead body?" asked Rufus. "Why?"

Remy's eyes widened.

"Because they'd have been selling *my* dead body if I hadn't, piece by piece." Remy turned his attention from the rabbits to the surface of the water. He dipped a finger inside and swirled it around. "River's ready for us now," he said. "I'm itchin' to get to the market." With that, he reached into a pouch on his hip and pulled out what looked to be tobacco.

"What are you doing?"

"Just a little offering to the river for good luck." He sprinkled the brown strands of tobacco into the water. As he stood he turned to Rufus. "We should reach Brisco's Outpost today," he said. "I have some business to attend to there, and then we'll be on our way." With that, he quickly disappeared over a mound of junk.

As the boat got underway, Rufus saw that Josie was awake, but it appeared she had no interest in speaking to him.

Boredom entrenched itself so deeply that Rufus took to counting the bristles of an old brush he'd found. He'd nearly passed one thousand when a stray thought torpedoed his count. Frustrated, he tossed the brush into the river. It was clear that he would not be patient enough for river travel.

Rufus took a deep breath and began to dig through the mountains of junk. He thought back to his own collections of trash accumulated from the river. Some of his favorite times were spent searching for materials for the boat. But then he remembered that it was all gone now. The boat, his family, his former life.

As he moved an old chair, he saw the head of what looked to be an old fiddle. It had somehow survived intact. He carefully pulled if from the pile, happy to see that the bow sitting next to it. It wasn't the prettiest of instruments, the body covered with scratches and chips, but it had four strings, and that was enough. A quick pluck of the strings told him that it was in relatively good tune.

It was a small comfort to do something so familiar as to place a fiddle on his shoulder. He pulled the bow over the strings. It was wanting for a bit of resin, but the sound was passable. As he began to play in earnest, the anxiety trickled off him like sweat. It was nice having an action to smooth out the rough edges of the mind. He went through a short medley of songs, mostly just simple tunes that made his grandmother smile.

After a while, he looked up to see that he had an audience: both Remy and Josie were watching him.

"Don't you get no ideas about throwing that off the edge," said Remy. I saw you throw my brush.

"I'd treat a fiddle better than I would most people," said Rufus. Remy didn't respond, but simply slinked back to the far edges of his boat. Josie, however, stayed.

"You play well," she said, stepping over to him.

Rufus nodded.

"Are you talking to me again?"

"Not if you're going to be a jackass," she snapped. Rufus smiled. "Where did you learn?"

"My grandma taught me." He plucked the strings and adjusted the tuning. "Hated every minute of it too."

"Why'd you keep doing it?"

He looked at her and laughed.

"If you knew my grandma you'd know not to say no." Josie still hadn't cracked a smile, but she seemed somehow more relaxed. She took a seat next to him on the deck and watched expectantly. "You want me to keep playing?"

"Do what you want," she replied.

He looked at the fiddle.

"It's funny," said Rufus. "I never wanted to play this stupid instrument while I was a kid, but now that I can't find Grandma, this is the only thing that's made me feel better." Josie didn't say anything, but she also didn't look bored. "Before all this mess started my plan was to build a boat and run away from home, play the fiddle for money on the streets of New Orleans. Know where that is?" Josie shook her head. "Oh well."

There was a moment a silence before she again spoke.

"Do you think you're a person Rufus?"

Rufus couldn't help but let out a laugh at the boldness of the question. Still, there was genuine interest in her eyes, and not an ounce of judgement, which put him at ease.

"I don't know," he finally said. He thought about it a moment. "I don't think I'm bad, but I don't know about good. I mean, people took every opportunity they could to tell me and my brother that we were bad."

"Do you believe them?"

"Listen," he said, realizing he didn't have an answer. He took a deep breath. "I try," he said. "I think trying counts." She looked on. She didn't smile or take her eyes off him. Rufus finally broke her gaze and looked around the messy boat. "I wasn't all that much different from Remy with all the junk I collected." He turned back to her. "Why is it that you don't like minks?"

Josie wasted no time in responding.

"They sided with Sparpole," she said, seemingly unconcerned about Remy hearing her. "He killed a lot of people, and they helped him. At least in the beginning."

"Wait," said Rufus, remembering the name. He fished into his pocket and pulled out the card he'd stolen from Murdo. It was wet and tattered, but still readable. "Is this Sparpole?"

"Why do you have that?" she asked, a suspicious look in her eyes.

"Murdo dropped it," he said. "I just kept it."

She grabbed the card from Rufus.

127

"He was a devil in person form," Josie said. "A river mage who tried to take control of the Oxbow. They called that time The Sorrows. I was just a baby, so I don't remember it." She studied the card as she walked it to the edge of the boat and dropped it into the River. Rufus wanted to protest, but held back. He could see that she would not be willing to talk about it further. He decided it was a good time to pick up the fiddle again. He was uncertain of what to play, so he went to an old standby, a tune his grandma always called *Pinhook Waltz*.

As he finished the first verse, he saw a look of shock on Josie's face. Remy poked his head up from behind a crate.

"Boy, you better be glad I'm mink. That tune is outlawed!"

"What?" said Rufus, though Remy's attention was stolen by something out on the water.

"I'll be," said Remy, taking off his hat to reveal a head of matted brown hair. Rufus couldn't see what he was looking at, but his droopy face had somehow drooped even further. He climbed up to the top of a pile of garbage to see a black plume of smoke rising from the shore. In the near distance, Rufus could see a large plank floating on the water. But it was what was on top of it that made him shudder: a body.

17

Aftermath

They approached in silence. The closer they got to the shore, the thicker the smoke became. It was like a dense fog that canceled out most of the light. Rufus had to pull his shirt over his nose and mouth. Tears formed in his eyes from the sulfur sting.

"Stay sharp," said Remy. Rufus had climbed a ladder to join him at his perch atop his cabin near the rudder. The man steered them in toward the shore. His fidgeting had ceased. In fact, he looked downright brave—braver than Rufus was feeling.

"What is this place?" asked Rufus.

Remy spoke without taking his eyes off the river.

"Used to be a trading post," he said. "Fella by the name of Brisco owns it. It's mostly panners on their way to the Glamorris Highlands. Bunch of scallywags, they are, looking for nuggets of glimmer glass. It ain't the best business though." He turned to Rufus. "He never gets repeat business as no one ever seems to make it back alive." He turned back to the river.

Through the smoke, Rufus could see the orange remnants

of a fire wrapping around the shell of a blackened building. The place sat off the river by a few hundred feet, though it was just a pile of rubble—the roof was gone, most of the walls had fallen in on themselves.

"Are we really going in there?" asked Rufus.

"You're darn right," said Remy. "I got business with Brisco."

The smell intensified, as did the tension twisting up Rufus's insides. The only sound was the boat slicing quietly through the water. The docks came into sight, at least what was left of them; it looked as if a tornado had come through and pried up all the slats.

A voice drifted through the smoke. It caught them off guard at first, but it soon became clear that the voice was singing. Rufus shivered as the voice lilted across the water. It appeared to be singing a child's nursery rhyme. He looked to Remy, but the mink's eyes were focused straight ahead.

"Go drop that anchor," said Remy as they pulled close to the shore. Rufus did as he was told, and climbed down from the cabin. Josie was waiting for him at the bottom of the ladder.

"What is it?" she asked.

"Don't know yet," said Rufus. "But that mink is taking us right to it."

Josie huffed, looking more annoyed than scared. Rufus, however, couldn't help but feel nervous. Something about this scene wasn't right—not that anything in this godforsaken place was right.

No sooner had Rufus thrown down the anchor than Remy splashed out into the shallow water at the edge of the bank. They watched as the man disappeared into the smoke. Seconds ticked by, each one seeming to drag out endlessly. Rufus's eyes were watering from the smoke, but he couldn't seem to take his eyes off the water.

Just when he thought the man wouldn't return, Remy appeared.

"What are you waiting for?" he shouted, waving for them to follow. Rufus and Josie reluctantly plunged themselves into the waist-high water. They followed him to the shore. The singing voice grew louder, causing Rufus's throat to tighten. Finally, they could see an outline in the smoke. Leaning against a post near where the docks had been was a man, legs sprawled as he stared off into the distance. He was covered head to toe in dirt, ash, and a series of cuts. He was alive, though not in good shape.

He continued to sing the same few lines over and over, completely oblivious to their presence. Josie knelt down and put a hand on the man's cheek. Still he did nothing. It was only when one of her bugs lit up in front of his face that his eyes broke their glaze. He let out an ear-piercing scream.

"Calm yourself," yelled Remy, slapping the man across the face. The man curled himself up on the ground, shaking ferociously. "Where's Brisco?"

The man looked up at Remy, trying to speak, but his words seemed chained to his tongue. Finally, with great effort, he spoke.

"They tore him apart," he muttered. "They got him."

"Who got him?" asked Remy. Remy pulled the man back up to a sitting position. His fierceness seemed out of character. The man only drooped again like a limp doll. A slap to the face helped him regain his composure.

"Came in late last night," he said. "They wore robes."

"They wore robes?" he asked eagerly, remembering the robed figures accompanying Jasper and Winesap in Wagtail.

"Who was with them?"

"It was the boy," said the man, eyes growing wide. "He started it."

"What boy?" shouted Rufus, but Remy put a hand up to calm him.

"Let the man speak," he said as he pulled what appeared to be a flask from his jacket and handed it to the man. "Swamp grog," he said. "It'll calm your nerves."

The man took the flask and slowly lifted it to his lips, spilling at least as much as he managed to put into his mouth. After a sip, his breathing approached something almost normal.

"It was the boy," he said. "He came in with the group. Strange looking folks with their red robes—all except a few of them that is: the boy, and old man, and a couple of roughnecks."

"Where did they go?" It was all Rufus could do to keep from shouting.

Remy grabbed Rufus roughly by the collar and pushed him away.

"Hush up," he said as Rufus fell onto his back.

As Rufus picked himself up, Josie eyed him closely. She knew, same as Rufus, who the boy was.

"They come into the restaurant late," the man continued. "We were just cleaning up. A few old-timers had stayed late. They were to take off for the Highlands this morning." He shuddered again.

"Go on," said Remy.

"They come in and the place went quiet," he said. "You never seen these guys go quiet…at least I never had. Anyways they come in and they have a seat. Folks in the robes don't say nothin'. It's the old man who talks. He orders food for the whole crew, and swamp grog—lots of it, but just for him and the roughnecks. We tell him kitchen's closed, but he won't hear it. He was real persuasive."

"Did he say who he was?" asked Remy.

The man shook his head.

"Not a word. He come over to another table and started joking with some of the other old timers. They was havin' a time of it for a while, hootin' and hollerin'. All the while I'm in the back, just cookin' up their food. Everything seems fine, but then I hear one of the men say something that really set him off."

At this, the man looked away. His face was squished up as if he were about to cry.

"What was it he said?" asked Rufus.

Remy shot him a glare, but the man turned to Rufus and spoke.

"He brought up something about Sparpole. I don't know what. I just heard the name and then…"

Josie clapped a hand over her mouth.

"What happened next?" asked Remy.

The man looked him in the eye.

"I don't even know," he said. "Only thing I know is I woke up a hundred feet from the tavern. It was all destroyed. All of 'em dead." He looked Rufus in the eyes. "I think they was Pinhooks. Had to be."

Rufus felt a surge run through his body at hearing his name.

"You two go back to the boat," said Remy. "I'll take care of our friend here." He started to pick the man up.

"Where are you taking him?" asked Josie.

"Just going to get him comfortable is all." He hoisted the man to his feet. The man let out a moan of pain.

"But wouldn't it be better if we took him with us?" she said.

"There's nothing left here."

"He'll be fine," said Remy. "Now unless you plan on staying here with him you ought to hush and climb back on that boat."

Josie looked angry, but turned and trudged back. Rufus was right on her heels. Remy and the man disappeared into the hazy smoke. As he splashed through the water and climbed aboard, Rufus heard the man's lullaby start up again. It was louder this time. The song continued for a time, but then it stopped. It was followed by a sharp whimper, and then nothing.

After a few moments, Remy approached through the shallow water.

"What happened?" asked Rufus.

"He's comfortable," said Remy as he pulled himself up onto the boat. "It's a darn shame about Brisco though," he said. "Fool owed me money."

Rufus felt the urge to stop him, to continue with his questions, but he was close now. Questions would just delay him. He climbed to the top of a garbage pile as they set out on their way. He was unsure what to make of what had just happened. He was close to his brother now, but questions flooded his brain. Was Gideon alright? Or worse, was this his doing?

18

He's Lost Control

"Can't you go any faster?" Rufus asked the mink. They'd been trotting along at the pace of a lethargic sloth for the better part of the day and Rufus was about to blow. He could feel his brother creeping ever further downriver and away from him. Even the fiddle was useless at calming his nerves.

Remy's eyes ping-ponged around in his head as he looked up from mending a busted birdcage.

"No," he said. "Unlike you, I have a bit of respect for the river." Rufus could feel frustration constricting his veins. If the man wouldn't make the boat go any faster, he would.

Rufus felt the water take hold. It felt as if he were holding the river like a rope. All it took was a thought and the boat surged forward. Objects tumbled from their perches as Remy fell face first onto the deck. As the man tried to pick himself up, Rufus noticed something had fallen from Remy's pocket: It was his whistle.

"You thief!" shouted Rufus as his anger spilled over.

"Hold your horses," Remy stammered, but before he could

stand a jet of water sprang from the river, knocking him into a pile of scrap wood. Water lurched up from the sides of the boat. It scooped up the whistle and returned it to Rufus like an obedient dog. A terrified look swept over the man's face as Rufus stormed towards him.

"What were you doing with my whistle?" asked Rufus through tightly clenched teeth.

"I'm sorry!" stuttered Remy. He was dripping wet, his eyes darting back and forth. "I found it. I didn't know it was yours!"

"Liar!" screamed Rufus as he willed the water to rise and form a tight noose around Remy's neck. Rufus felt Remy's fear vibrating through the water, the same way sharks sense blood in the open ocean. With a wave of his hand, the water lifted Remy by the neck. The man struggled to free himself of the water's hold, but there was nothing he could do.

"Stop!" came a scream from behind him.

It was Josie. Rufus turned to see her standing with a look of horror on her face. Rufus's anger crumbled to embarrassment as the water released the man and he fell to the deck.

"River mage!" Remy yelled, clasping a hand to his neck. He scrambled to his cabin, slamming the door fiercely.

Rufus turned back to Josie, whose scorn-filled eyes he was barely able to meet. Before he could say a word, she disappeared to the back of the boat.

Something devious had overtaken him. He'd felt the river's power coursing through him, and for once he enjoyed it.

Still, he felt disgusted with himself. However, this was no time to stop moving. They had to ride through the night no matter what. As he made his way to the front of the boat, Weego's warning rang out in his head. He took a big gulp of the evening air as the boat pushed onward into the open river.

The river seemed to know his intentions and steered them in the direction he wanted to go. The faster the boat moved, the easier Rufus found it to fall asleep that night. But easy sleep did not mean peaceful sleep, as he found himself dreaming of the river. He could feel things he'd never known before: he knew every droplet, every disturbance or ripple, every bug landing on its surface to be consumed by a fish. Down in the depths he also saw something else. It was a face.

Rufus sunk lower and lower, watching the face until it became clear: Gideon. His brother stood at the bottom of the river, lit only by bright moonbeams streaking down from the surface. His face was unnaturally pale as he reached a hand out towards him. Rufus instinctively put his own hand out to meet it. There was an unnatural resistance, as though the water around him was thickening like jelly. With great force, Rufus thrust his hand forward to meet Gideon's.

As their hands met, Rufus suddenly couldn't breathe. His eyes began to sizzle in their sockets; his chest felt as if thousands of bricks were weighing it down. Blackness crept in from the sides of his vision like an old, disintegrating film reel. The last thing he saw was a smile plastered to Gideon's face.

He awoke panting. His hands were wet and cold, but he was alive. He felt thankful for each breath. But there was another unnatural sensation occurring: the feeling of legs crawling through his hair. It was a bug, which he quickly picked from his head and flung across the boat. The creature landed on an old chair cushion, legs up. It was then he saw it was one of Josie's bugs. A pang of remorse shot through him.

"How dare you," said Josie from behind him. She slid down the pile of junk and scooped the little bug into her hands.

"Sorry," said Rufus, though Josie ignored him and began whispering to the bug in her cupped hands. After a few moments, the bug began to shake and buzz. Eventually, it made its way back to its feet. Josie reached into her satchel and produced a jar. As she opened it, a number of bugs emerged, filling the early dawn sky with their bright swarm. The little creature joined the others as they swirled through the air. They left trails of light like miniature fireworks. After a moment, Josie whistled. The swarm promptly flew back to Josie's jar, their glittery dust leaving a glowing cloud in the air around them.

"What do you call them?" asked Rufus.

Josie turned to look at him.

"Moxbugs."

"What's that shiny stuff in the jar?"

But Josie simply huffed and slid the jar back into her satchel. She responded with a question of her own.

"Why do you want to find your brother so badly?"

"Why would you even ask that?" he snapped. He didn't like the question, but realized it had dislodged something. He had to peel back some of the built-up emotion until he got to a feeling he understood. He looked down at his boots. They were his brother's, and they were still too big. He spoke before he realized he'd opened his mouth. "When we were kids, we would always go to the fair when it came to town. It was nothing like that freak show back in Wagtail." He looked back out over the dark water. A light orange color was coming up from the east, breaking the dark of the night. "We looked forward to it all year. We saved up money, or in Gideon's case, stole a little extra. We went down to see what rides they brought along and watched them being built." He turned to

Josie. "Sorry, this is boring."

"No," she said. "Go on."

"Well, even Grandma Jezebel was in a good mood when the fair came to town. She gave us a bit of extra money. When the rides opened we were the first in line. We'd been riding and playing games for hours when Gideon just disappeared. I searched for him for a while. I got nervous. I was looking behind one of the rides when some older boys cornered me. They were just picking on me at first, but then one tried to take my money." Rufus turned to Josie. "I hit him in the gut. First time I ever hit someone other than Gideon, and even him I never hit as hard as I hit this boy. I was scared. I never saw a guy double over like he did. The rest of them laid into me."

"What happened?" asked Josie.

Rufus couldn't help but smile at the memory.

"Gideon found us. He took on five or six of those boys, all a year or two older than him, and left them crying. Not only did he get my money back, but he even made them give up what little money they had. We ate popcorn and corndogs until we barfed." He looked at her, a big smile on his face. "I was Gideon's brother, and in that town, that carried some weight. I never had another person lay a finger on me." The smile began to fade. "Until now."

It seemed like Josie was searching his face for something.

"Do you still live in his shadow?"

Rufus scoffed.

"Listen," he said. "He's family. That's why I'm here." He was eager to change the subject. "Do you have any family?"

"No." It was a harsh and resolute response.

"Well," he said. "I don't know how to explain it." He looked down at his feet. "I made a promise to my grandma. Beyond that I guess I don't really care what Gideon does."

Rufus took off his boots and tossed them in the water. It felt good for a moment, until he realized that now he would have to go barefoot. They sat in silence for another moment until Josie's attention was broken by a boat out on the water.

"Hey," she said, standing up. "That's the Otto Modest."

Rufus looked across the water. A dark silhouette loomed in the distance, punctuated only by a few running lights scattered across it. The commotion on board indicated that they would soon be setting out.

"I guess you'll be going back then?" asked Rufus.

For a moment he thought he saw hesitation in her eyes.

"Yes," she said. "I've been away from my bugs too long."

"You mean you have more?" asked Rufus.

"Of course. Thousands. Even more still in their cocoons." She almost smiled, but then she looked back down to Rufus. "Good luck finding your brother."

"Thanks," he said. "I'll get Remy."

"Can't you just push the boat over there yourself?"

Rufus suddenly felt embarrassed.

"I probably could," he said. "But I'd just as likely drive the boat straight through the side of it. Best to let the captain take over. Plus, it sounds more fun to scare Remy a bit."

She finally smiled and nodded. They climbed over the garbage until they reached Remy's door.

"Remy," said Rufus as he knocked. "We need your help."

A quick flash of eyeball appeared through the window. The door cracked. A low growl emanated from inside—he was angry.

"Need *my* help?" he said. "Thought you had it under control, you heathen."

He slammed the door.

"We need you to drop Josie off," said Rufus. "You'll be losing one of us at least."

The door popped open.

"I'd prefer to lose you, river mage," shouted the man.

"Listen," said Josie, sliding a foot into the door before he could again slam it. "We paid you more than fairly for this ride. I'm getting off early, but you're going to take Rufus to the market with you."

"Why can't the mage just drive the boat himself?"

She looked at Rufus, nodding her head toward Remy.

"I'm sorry I got a little out of control last night."

"You're darn right you did," snapped Remy as he threw the door wide open. "It takes a dark soul indeed to commandeer another man's boat with mud magic. I never heard of an act so vile, so wretched as that. Makes me feel sick at the thought of it." His eyes were wide orbs now.

"So, thievery is just fine for your soul then?"

At this, Remy smiled.

"Thievery is a noble profession," he said. "One of the oldest and most lucrative professions there ever was."

"Are you going to help us or not?" asked Josie impatiently.

The man took a deep breath.

"If it lightens my load, yes. Where am I to deposit you?"

"Over there," she said, pointing. "The Otto Modest."

At this, the man's face went white.

"You didn't say nothin' about dealing with no Otto Modest."

"I didn't say you had to deal with him," she said. "You only need to drop me off."

He studied the steamboat in the distance.

"Why ain't they moving?" he as he walking over to the water

141

and stuck a finger in. His face soured even further. "Steer us away!" he shouted, waving his hands. In seconds he had blown past Rufus and Josie and to the back of the boat where he grabbed hold of the rudder handle. He tried to steer them away from the showboat, but he couldn't break free of the current. "Dang it, boy!" he shouted. "Let us free!"

"Why?" asked Rufus.

"It's a river trap! Hurry, boy! Else we'll get stuck too!"

Rufus looked to Josie.

"Is that real?"

"Yes," she said. "The river traps boats sometimes, but it's never stopped the Otto Modest before."

Rufus tried to will the boat away. It wasn't easy, but he finally managed to loosen the river's grip, though it felt like prying a crocodile's dinner from his jaws. Remy nearly flew off the from the sudden loss of tension on the rudder. Slowly, they peeled away from the showboat. As they passed, people waved and shouted from the decks—trying to get help.

Remy waved back.

"Good luck, fools," he said under his breath. "For their sake I hope it's not too long. I've known a river snare to last for years in some cases. Had to catapult food over to them."

"How did you know it was a river trap?" asked Rufus.

"I told you," he said. "The river talks. You just have to listen." He turned to Josie. "Sorry, missy, but you ain't going back to that boat for a while." Josie didn't respond, but simply stood watching the showboat as the distance grew further away. He turned back to Rufus. "I assume you can handle the steering then," he said as he stormed back to his cabin. "Wake me up when we reach the Mink Market."

With the slam of his door, it was just the two of them.

"I guess you're coming with me after all," said Rufus.

"I guess so," she said, though Rufus could sense the nervousness in her voice.

19

The Mink Market

"You'll want to see this," said Josie.

She shook Rufus vigorously by the shoulders before scampering up a pile of busted musical instruments. He had spent a good portion of the morning just staring at the water, his thoughts circling around like swirling eddies. He had no real interest in following her, but eventually stood up and used a battered old tuba to climb to a good vantage point.

There before him was a gigantic island of flatboats. Hundreds of them huddled on the far side of the river, jigsawed together to form a huge, uneven platform on the water. There were boats of all sizes and shapes, all of them were ridden with junk like Remy's—these were mink boats.

"What is it?" asked Rufus.

"That's the Mink Market," she said. Rufus watched in awe as she continued. "It's a gathering. They usually just travel the river selling their snake oils and mink butter—which is actually pretty good if you haven't ever had it." Rufus hadn't, and even the mention of it brought the subtle taste of vomit

144

to his mouth. "I've seen them even bigger than this before," she said. "So big you could almost walk clear across the river. They're always at the mouth of Dismal Swamp, which is where a lot them had to flee after The Sorrows." The river was wide here, Rufus reckoned, easily able to accommodate the mass of boats and river traffic to pass without much interruption. Still, the island was large enough that a few boats floated near the outer edges of the island holding large pikes with flames burning atop them, directing traffic like makeshift lighthouses.

"What's this all for?"

"Tonight is their celebration," she said. "Night of the Minks." She turned to him. "We'll want to be far away by then." As they watched, Rufus felt something poke him in the ribs. "Here," she said, still watching the Mink Market. It was a pair of dingy old moccasins. "I found them in a pile of junk. Just don't let Remy know that you *stole* them." She smiled.

As Rufus slipped them on his feet, Remy burst through the door of his cabin. He had changed into a new outfit that looked more like a brightly colored patchwork quilt. His mouth was open and his jaw hung slack like a dumb-struck hound. His eyes were wide and full of wonder as he climbed atop his cabin. As he gazed out, he took his hat off and held it to his chest. He almost appeared to be crying. However, when his eyes again passed Rufus and Josie, his face quickly soured.

"I'll be glad to be rid of the both of ya," he spat. He placed the hat back atop his head and made his way to the rudder to steer them in. "Let me take it from here, river mage!" he shouted. Rufus worked his way back into the recesses of his mind. He relinquished control of their little boat back to the river and Remy's rudder.

Remy whipped the boat hard in the direction of the island. It wasn't long until they came alongside a smaller boat puttering its way in. Two mink men—dressed in the similarly shabby garb as Remy—waved big as they passed. One man's smile revealed a massive void where teeth should have been. The other man was dumping a bucket of what looked like fish guts into the river. The smell of rancid intestines rode the wind to smack Rufus square in the nose.

When they were blessedly clear of the tiny mink boat—and the foul smell—Remy kicked the engine on, hurtling them directly toward the island. They were soon surrounded by a handful of vessels that looked to be heading for the exact same spot. Rufus gave Josie a nervous look before turning back to Remy.

"Don't you think you ought to slow down?" he shouted.

But Remy simply snorted and fired their engines further.

As another junk boat came barreling in next to them, Remy tipped his hat and pulled the boat directly into its path. The boat's pilot was luckily nimble enough to jerk the boat out of the way. He stood cursing them as some of his cargo fell off into the river. Remy nearly fell from his stoop from laughter.

They cut off half a dozen other boats as they careened in towards the island at high speed. Josie and Rufus both grabbed hold of anything they could find. Just as it looked like they were going to crash into the island, Remy killed the engine and dropped the anchor. The stop was abrupt and sent Rufus sliding down the pile riding the busted tuba. He landed roughly on the deck. The boat skidded in softly, bumping the island of boats with no more force than a bee landing on a flower.

No sooner had their boat stopped than a few minks dressed in mismatched clothing jumped aboard and began lashing them together. Before their knots were even tied, another vessel knocked into them roughly, and Remy's junk boat was gobbled up into the mass of the man-made island.

The boat turned out to be that of the man that Remy had cut off. He promptly stormed across the boat and forcefully spun Remy around. For a moment, Rufus thought he was about to watch the man actually kill Remy. However, after a moment of hard stares, their expressions changed and the two embraced each other like old family members.

As Rufus untangled himself from the tuba, he noticed similar reunions happening all over. The whole place was crawling with people like it was a disturbed ant hill, people scuttling back and forth.

As Josie descended the pile, Remy approached, crossing his arms and shooting them each as mean a look as he could muster.

"Alright," said Remy, stammering a little. "Unless you two vagabonds are buying something, I want you gone."

"Gladly," said Rufus. Together, he and Josie stepped past Remy and onto another boat. They were quickly swallowed into the mass of activity, swept along into one of the main thoroughfares that illogically crisscrossed the island. The minks all seemed to be in great spirits, hooting and hollering and selling their wares. They all wore brightly colored patchwork outfits similar to Remy's. Some of them wore pointed hats, many wore masks of grossly exaggerated faces.

"Where do we start?" asked Josie.

Rufus looked around. Many of the boats had a tent or a shoddily built lean-to, though they were being modified to look like market stalls. The intense smell of food soon hit him, as did a swirl of loud music. It was enough to make Rufus dizzy. It was barely morning and the place was thronged with people shouting and haggling with each other. He took a deep breath.

"Might as well start here," he said, moving towards the stall nearest to them. Behind the stall sat an old woman. In front of her was a bright assortment of what looked like chili peppers, only these chilies were smoking as if smoldering in a fire. The woman sat with a heavy stoop, her head hanging down near her shoulders. Her face seemed to indicate that she'd had a long, hard life. Her lower lip had somehow risen high above the upper, as if it were consuming everything in its path on the way to her nose. As Rufus approached, she cast furtive glances at them both—she had clearly pegged them as outsiders. Rufus in particular.

"Ain't for sale," she said as she grabbed one of the chilies by the stem and lifted it from the basket. To Rufus's amazement, the chili burst into flame, though it somehow wasn't being consumed by the fire. The woman opened her mouth and began to blow on the chili. A long string of drool slipped down her chin and eventually landed on her chest. After a few more gusts, the chili's flame finally went out. They watched as the woman brought it to her mouth, chomping it between what few teeth she had left. Rufus didn't know whether to be impressed or to throw up.

"Ain't looking to buy anything," he finally said, though he couldn't help but erupt in a coughing fit. Even being this close to the chilies had caused the insides of his nostrils to burn.

"We're looking for someone," said Josie, chiming in.

Rufus, eyes watering, continued.

"A guy who looks kinda like me, but taller. He's with an old white-haired man and maybe some people wearing red robes."

The woman's face didn't change. She continued to eye him

as she picked up another chili and ate it, this time before the flame had even gone out. She spoke as she chewed.

"Ain't seen no one looks as ugly as you," she said. As she spoke, bits of improperly chewed chili fell out of her mouth and sat resolutely on her lip and chin.

Rufus's eyes were drawn to a piece on her lip that screamed out like a bright red exclamation point. He had barely even heard what the woman had said. It was only after Josie grabbed him by the shoulder that he came to his senses.

"She didn't see him, Rufus. Let's go."

They continued walking. Something about the woman's face didn't sit well with Rufus. There was knowledge in it. She was being secretive. He didn't trust her. As he looked around him, he became acutely aware that everyone, no matter how deep they were into their bartering, was watching him.

"What are they looking at," said Rufus.

"They're looking at you," she said, quietly. "Come on." She pulled him roughly by the arm off the main thoroughfare. They hopped across a few boats until they were relatively alone. Josie stopped at a clothesline strewn with the strange quilt-like garments worn by most of the other minks.

"What are you doing?" asked Rufus.

"For whatever reason, they seem to think you're an outsider." Rufus could hear the sarcasm in her voice, but he didn't care. The less unwanted attention he got the better. She pulled down a few of the costumes. "We need to blend in. Put this on." She tossed the costume with force. It was heavier than Rufus expected. It was all one piece, though it seemed to be made out of at least one hundred different scraps of brightly colored fabric.

It took no small effort to find his way in, but eventually the suit consumed him. It hung on him like a blanket. It could have fit him three times over.

Rufus couldn't help but let out a curse as he saw that Josie's costume fit perfectly.

"They seem to recognize you," she said. She eyed him a little more closely. "I'm not sure why."

Rufus didn't know either.

"That must mean that my brother came through here," he said. "I don't know why else they would be looking at me."

"Why would they care about your brother?" she asked, but Rufus was left wondering. He shook his head. "Well, let's see if we can find him so we can get out of here." She began walking back towards the market stalls, but stopped when she found a few of the strange-looking masks discarded behind a crate. She tossed one to him. "Throw this on," she said. "Just to be safe."

Rufus looked at the mask. It was made from an old gray wood that looked like it had sat in the sun too long. Its exaggerated jaw protruded forward aggressively. Beneath two round eye slots was a mouth turned down in a vicious frown. It looked vaguely like one of those giant head statues from Easter Island that he'd seen in a picture, though much more solemn. He reluctantly slid the mask over his face.

He didn't like having his vision partially blocked, and he felt vulnerable as they walked into the crowd. However, Josie was right about them attracting less attention.

Together they walked through the chaos of the market for hours winding their way through the labyrinth of strange music, bizarre foods, and market stalls selling god knows what. The further they made it into the interior, the more crowded it became. Rufus would have forgotten that he was even on the river except for the occasional glimpse of water he spied as they crossed between flatboats.

The market had things for sale that he could have never imagined, including strange fishes and creatures he'd never before seen, some of them having to be products of this strange mud magic. As they passed a stall selling maps, a merchant jumped out in front of them.

"Maps!" he yelled directly in their faces, holding a number of crudely drawn maps of the river. The man pulled up his mask to reveal a blackened smile. "I've got one of Old Tarwater's last moving maps!" he yelled. His costume was as loud as his shouting, a brightly-colored patchwork of designs adorned with what looked like small cowbells dangling from the fringes.

"No thanks," said Josie, trying to pass, but the man slid in front of her.

"Hold on there, miss," he said. "Now you ain't going to come across another map like this in all your life. This here map can tell you every place the river goes, every new branch and subtle change, no matter how small. Hell, it can even tell you when a fish farts if you want it to!"

"No thank you," said Josie.

But as she again tried to step around him, the man grabbed her roughly by the shoulder. Rufus's reaction was immediate. A stream of water shot up from between two of the boats and pummeled him to the ground, soaking all his maps in the process.

The crowd around him went silent. All eyes were again on him. In the excitement, his mask had fallen from his face. Rufus could only hear his blood pulsing through his veins until a shout broke through the din.

"You idiot!" yelled Josie. Her face was full of fury as she

pulled him past the befuddled spectators across the boats away from the thoroughfare.

Rufus didn't know what had come over him. The water had done just what he had wanted, he just didn't know how.

Finally, Josie stopped. There was no one around, but Josie still did her due diligence in searching the boat before she gave him the okay. Rufus panted heavily. Sweat had overwhelmed him, filling the hot, heavy costume he wore. It was a special kind of relief to peel the suit off.

"What are you doing?" said Josie.

"Taking the stupid thing off," he said. "They all saw my face anyhow." Josie didn't respond. It was only after running away from the lights of the thoroughfare that Rufus realized that it was almost evening. "How long have we been searching?"

She hit him with an exhausted look. Their efforts weren't turning up anything but more trouble.

"I want to go back out," he said. "I need to keep looking."

"You just wait here," she said. "Try not to do anything too stupid."

She disappeared back into the crowd.

Rufus slumped down against the cabin. He was tired and hungry, but there was another feeling that overwhelmed him. Somehow, he could feel his brother's presence. It sat like a hard-to-reach itch in his brain. There was something about the energy of the place. It held his aggressiveness in the air like a water-logged cloud waiting to pour.

He sat stewing for some time, long enough that the sun finally disappeared from the sky. He was beginning to think that Josie had abandoned him when she returned holding two bowls of what looked like gumbo. She also had a napkin containing two biscuits. She sat a bowl down in front of him.

The smell of it was incredible enough to send a shiver running through him.

"Here," she said brusquely.

"How'd you pay for these?" he asked.

"Minks aren't the only ones who can deceive." She winked as she sat down.

Rufus didn't know where it came from. He hadn't eaten much in the past few days and it was starting to wear on him. He spooned some of the stew into his mouth. No sooner had it touched his lips than the strong spices began to assault his taste buds. It felt like a snake bite on his tongue.

"Too hot for you?" asked Josie earnestly before she spooned in a huge amount of soup without flinching.

In between quick breaths, Rufus managed to get a question out.

"How are you eating so much at a time?" he asked, starting to sweat.

"I put extra spice in yours," she said. She didn't look as angry as she had before.

Rufus sighed and instead went for the biscuits. He carefully lifted it to his nose and gave it a sniff. With great care, he took a bite. He was relieved to find that it tasted normal, delicious in fact.

"At least this is what I'm used to," he said as he happily gobbled it down.

"Shame I didn't get you some mink butter," she said. "Minks have a lot of faults, but cooking isn't one of them."

He dipped his spoon back into his bowl.

"Was he right about the moving map?" he asked before he put the spoon in his mouth, wincing.

Josie looked up from her bowl.

153

"There are some maps that move with the river," she said. "But there's no way that he has one of them. It's an old mink trick. They charm the ink to move around on the map. Non-minks think it must be an original, so they fork over a small fortune only to find that they may as well have had a toddler draw a map for them. Before they notice the minks are already long gone."

"What a weird place."

"And you'd rather live in a world without magic?"

"Maybe," he said.

"That's sad," she said, sounding genuinely sympathetic.

Rufus eventually worked his way through the bowl, even though he was almost shaking from the scorching spice at the end. Still, he reckoned he needed food in his belly more than he needed taste buds.

They sat quietly for a while. The noise from the market had begun to swell. So, the Night of the Minks had begun.

Josie was looking up at the sky. She hadn't said a word for a while, which wasn't necessarily unusual. However, instead of her typical, near-emotionless face, she had a look of concern.

"What is it?" he asked.

She didn't say anything for a moment, and Rufus didn't want to badger her further. But then she finally spoke.

"It was stupid what you did back there," she said.

"I know," said Rufus. "You don't have to keep telling me."

"Rufus," she said, cutting him off. "Thanks."

It caught Rufus off guard.

"You're welcome."

"I lied to you about my family," she said.

"Oh?" said Rufus.

"I did have a family," she said. "But I don't anymore—except for Winesap." Rufus was surprised by her openness. It wasn't like her, at least not the version he'd been privy to. He wanted to speak, but there was nothing to say. After a moment, she continued. "Sparpole came through our town. I was just a baby. You see, he controlled not only the river, but the spirits that live in the depths as well...the spirits of the departed—*channel ghosts*, they call them. They lurk in the deepest, darkest parts of the river, but Sparpole freed them. When they emerged, no one had ever seen anything like it. Most didn't even believe in them, but they did after they saw them fly."

"Ghosts?" asked Rufus. "Why would he bring them out of the water?"

"Because if they touched you, you became one of them—one of the ghosts. That's what happened to my mother and older sister." Her eyes were sad, but she remained steeled—she knew she wasn't the only person who had to endure such terrible losses. "I was too young to remember it. My father, however..." at this she got a little choked up. He thought he'd gotten all he would from her, but then she conjured up enough willpower to continue. "He had nightmares every day. That I remember. He had the nightmares even when he wasn't sleeping. They said that Sparpole personally tortured him."

A chill went down Rufus's back.

"How did he survive?"

"I don't know," she said. "He lived with it for a while after Sparpole's death, but when I was maybe six or seven, it just became too much for him. He left one day and never came back. Some of the townsfolk said he jumped from the bluffs. I never found out for sure."

"I'm sorry," he said.

"Why are you sorry?" she asked. "It wasn't you that did it."

He felt a tinge of embarrassment, though Josie didn't seem to be accosting him. She seemed clinical about the situation, removed almost. "That's how I came to live with Winesap. She was my live-in caretaker. She raised me when Daddy couldn't. After he died, Winesap took me with her. We've been moving around ever since. Mostly on The Otto Modest."

"I see," he said, trying to wrap his head around everything she'd endured. He began to see his own situation in a different light.

"There's something else I need to tell you," she said. She looked him square in the eyes. For the first time, she looked meek, on the verge of tears. However, as she spoke, the outline of a person came into view a few boats away from them. It was an outline that he knew well.

It was Gideon.

Without a thought, Rufus leapt to his feet.

"Rufus!" shouted Josie, but he was already gone.

20

Night of the Minks

Rufus skipped across the narrow spaces between the boats but couldn't make up the distance.

The figure had made it back to the main thoroughfare, where the full scale of the Night of the Minks became clear. It was like running through a bad dream: the faces of masked beings popping out in front of him; flaming batons being hurled high into the air; warbling music from accordions and fiddles mixing with the shouts of revelers. He jumped over children playing games and ran past fish stalls and adults doing elaborate group dances.

Rufus had nearly caught up to him as the figure peeled away from the main thoroughfare. But as he turned a corner, Rufus came to the large gap between the two boats. He didn't think twice as he made the leap. It was halfway across the open water that he realized he'd undershot the distance. His chest hit the opposing boat, nearly knocking the wind from him. His legs had landed in the water, but he had managed to get his arms onto the deck and pull himself up. As Rufus rose to his feet, he saw his brother walk around a corner.

His chest throbbing from the impact, he staggered across the empty boats until he reached where his brother had turned. There in the darkness was a line of boats moored to a long, floating jetty. It was eerily quiet. The revelry of the market seemed distant. He searched each boat as he walked, all of which were in various states of disarray.

He listened for noise to give away his location, but only heard the occasional knocking of the boats as they drifted against each other. Uncertainty invaded his mind. Was it really his brother he had seen?

A clanging on one of the boats shook the thoughts loose from his head. He zeroed in on the boat in question. It was even grimier than the others, strewn with the carcasses of dead animals and discarded fish guts. He stepped carefully over them as he made his way to the door of the cabin. It was a much larger cabin than Remy's, though the splintered wood around the entrance indicated that the doorway had recently been widened by force.

A curtain hung over the entrance, open just enough that he could see a light on inside. He heard speaking as he leaned against the wall and peeked in.

But as soon as he saw who was inside, he wanted to leave.

Sat around a table, ripping meat from the bones of small animals, was a group of oxmen. As Rufus backed away, a giant hand clenched his throat, lifting him off his feet and throwing him violently onto the deck. It was a scarily familiar feeling.

"Got him," said the hulking creature. The rest of the beasts rushed from the cabin like angry hornets from a disturbed nest.

"See who it is," said another voice crouching down beside him. They turned him over. Their gnarled faces were inches from his. He could smell their rotten breath as they looked him over. Finally, a look of recognition filled the creature's large yellow eyes.

"It's the guppy from back in Wagtail"! he yelled. The one that ran into Clovis!"

"Clovis will be glad to see you," said another creature, snorting loudly.

No sooner had he said it than the fiery-haired oxman stuck his head out of the boat. Rufus remembered him and the ring running through his nostrils. It was the oxman who had started the riot and nearly killed him. The beast was somehow even more muscular, even meaner looking than he had remembered.

"You," he growled, eyes lighting up at the sight of him. "You think you can harm Clovis and survive?" The oxman seemed like a mountain—a mountain ready to crumble down upon him.

Rufus could sense the excitement of the oxmen around him, but all he could feel was pure terror. His stomach seemed to drop to his feet.

"What do we do with him, Clovis?" asked another one of the oxmen.

Clovis looked Rufus up and down for a moment. There was a long pause as the group awaited his orders.

"He ain't gonna be good for nothin' but skinnin' and eatin'," said the creature, almost disgusted. He turned back to the group. "So, let's get down to it!"

As the creatures broke out into a gleeful frenzy, Rufus nearly swallowed his tongue. His throat locked up as he frantically searched for someone to hear the ruckus and put a stop to it. He was completely unable to yell. A blade about the size of his forearm appeared; he was about to end up in the belly of an oxman. Rufus shook violently; his mind flooded with frustration and fear. He couldn't call the water.

But as Clovis reached for Rufus, a torrent of water hit him so hard he was knocked through the wall of a neighboring cabin. The other beasts looked on in confusion. Had Rufus somehow called the water?

His question was answered seconds later when a half a dozen snake-like ropes slithered onto the deck, sending the beasts running like scared dogs into the maze of boats. One by one, the ropes wound around them and they fell to the deck, completely immobile.

Rufus suddenly found himself free, though his freedom was short-lived as another snake rope worked its way around him. As he squirmed on the deck, a few minks emerged from the shadows. They were dressed differently than the others. They wore masks with long squared faces; their costumes were colored black. One of them spoke as they approached.

"What about this one?" asked the man from under his mask.

"Bag him," he said. With that, a cloth sack was slipped over Rufus's head and everything went black.

21

King Mink

They made him walk. Or, more appropriately, they pushed him along. He was unable to see, and the rope was constricting around his body all the way down to his knees, turning his journey into a series of awkward stumbles and near falls. He banged his knees, his shoulders, and his head on sharp corners and blunt walls. His captors showed little interest in guiding him as they shoved him from boat to boat. Still, he was happy not to be torn limb from limb and roasting on a spit.

Eventually, he heard a door creak open. A fierce shove indicated that he was to go inside. He tripped and landed on his stomach. However, he was surprised to find that his fall was broken not by a hard, wooden deck, but by a plush carpeted surface. He was quickly hoisted up and planted firmly in a chair.

"Hold still," barked one of the men.

At that, the bag was pulled from his head. For a moment, he thought he must have been transported off the Mink Market entirely. The room was elaborately decorated, like stepping into an old museum. There were fine, polished wood chairs lined up at the front. In the places that weren't covered with oil paintings, ornate wall paper adorned the upper portions of the walls. The place had the look of a mansion, though they were clearly still on a boat.

After a moment, a door at the far end of the room opened. From it emerged four men, all dressed in old-fashioned vests and nicely cut trousers. They all had grey, neatly-combed hair, though their faces wore wily, untamed beards. After them emerged a woman. She wore a dress of dark red, her shoulders covered by an embroidered black shawl.

The four men took seats in the chairs up front, leaving the chair in the middle for the woman, into which she plopped down unceremoniously.

She eyed Rufus for a moment with a sideways stare, and then up to the guards behind him.

"Cut 'em loose," she said. For all the pomp of her fancy clothing and the luxury of her surroundings, her speech didn't have a lick of formality to it. The men behind Rufus did as they were told. As the snake rope loosened, Rufus took in deep, unrestricted breaths. An awkward silence swept over the room until one of the old men pulled a handkerchief and had a good blow into it. After the noise dissipated, the men looked back to the woman. Her gaze was fierce, and neatly set on Rufus. Finally, she spoke. "So?"

Rufus made to answer, but his throat felt like it was filled with dry dirt. All that came out were a few croaked breaths.

One of the old men grew agitated and stood up as quickly as his frail body would allow.

"The boy disrespects you!" he shouted, pointing a finger at Rufus. "He disrespects all of us by coming on here and workin' his magic out in the open."

"That's enough," snapped the woman. The old man's mouth quivered with anger, but her warning was enough to silence him. She turned back to Rufus. "I'd like to hear from the boy."

Finally, Rufus managed to cough up a response.

"Who are you?" he croaked.

The men turned to each other, but the woman held up a hand.

"It's alright," she said. "I'll answer him." She took a deep breath. "I'm King Mink, and you crashed my party."

"You're a mink?" he asked. "And a king?"

"You've found yourself in a real privileged position, son—an audience with royalty," she said with a knowing smile. "And don't act surprised, son. We minks know the finer things in life, we just have to keep them out of sight is all, else the army would take them away again. We keep our business our own. And yes, I am a king. Most of my own kind don't even know that I'm their leader, and we like to keep it that way." She eyed him closely. "So, why is it that you've come aboard my market and started causing trouble?"

"I didn't mean to," said Rufus. "It's all a big mistake."

"This place is crawling with undercover agents from Oxalis," shouted one of the old men. As he spoke the word *Oxalis*, his lips pursed together as if he were cursing. "She already had to send those big beasts downriver."

The woman continued.

"He's right," she said. "No one brings their trouble to my market. The authorities are itchin' to catch us minks practicing mud magic so they can punish us again. They'll take everything away, and a number of lives to boot. You might've given them good reason tonight."

"I'm sorry," he said. "I was looking for my brother."

"I heard about that too." She paused and let a heavy silence settle over the room. "What business would your brother have had at my market?"

"I don't know, ma'am," he said. "That's what I'm trying to find out."

One of the old men next to her bent down and whispered into her ear. She responded, though Rufus couldn't hear what they were saying.

"Well, young man," she said. "You are correct. Your brother was on this boat. He stood in this very room, on the very spot where your grubby feet are."

Rufus's heart went into double-time.

"What do you mean?" he asked Rufus. "How do you even know who my brother is?"

She smiled a big, sinister smile.

"You don't think I know everything that happens on my river?" She turned to the door she had come through. "Remy, come on out here."

Rufus looked on as Remy emerged. He had cleaned up considerably, so much so that he was hard to recognize. He even wore a nice tailored jacket and had lost his droopy hat.

"What's *he* doing here?" asked Rufus with disgust.

"We all felt the river," she said. "The Specter Steamer passed through just north of Wagtail. I sent Remy to watch out. When we heard about what happened to Wagtail, we knew that Pinhooks had returned," she said, turning to the mink. "What did you find out about this one?"

"He's the real deal alright," Remy said. His eyes went narrow. "And you should've seen what his brother and those river mages did to Brisco's place."

"Were there any witnesses?" asked King Mink.

"One," he said. "But I took care of him." He made a slicing motion across his neck. Rufus felt his blood go cold.

"Good," said King Mink. She turned to Rufus. "Now tell me about this one."

"Well, I thought he was gonna kill me when I took his whistle."

"You *did* take it!" shouted Rufus, taking a step towards him. Remy scrambled behind one of the old men for cover.

"Calm down!" shouted the woman as the two guards grabbed Rufus by the shoulders. After a moment, Remy emerged from behind the chair and spoke again.

"He can call water like no one I ever seen!" he shouted. "He's dangerous!"

The woman looked back to Rufus.

"Interesting," she said. "Your brother didn't seem too impressive at all." She turned to the men. "Do you remember the scowl that boy had," she said as she turned to the men around her all chuckled as she began bunched her face up into a scowl. Even though it was a pretty impressive likeness to Gideon, Rufus was growing frustrated.

"How do you know my brother?" he shouted. Their faces all went straight. The woman cleared her throat and settled herself back into her chair.

"Well," she continued. She looked Rufus dead in the eye. "I mean, we didn't know we had stumbled across the Pinhooks."

Rufus's spine electrified at the mention of the name—his name. It was as if some deep secret had been blown. Rufus felt as if he were on full display.

The woman continued.

"We knew some strange things were going on near Wagtail,

we just didn't know how serious they were." She looked at the men near her. "Your grandaddy came to ask permission." Her voice got lower. "You see, a lot of my people put a lot of faith behind your daddy. And a lot of 'em died. That no-good grandaddy of yours assumed we'd all just be loyal and hitch a cart to his wagon. But his wagon's got busted wheels."

"Where did they go?" shouted Rufus.

The woman grinned. Her red-lipsticked mouth turned up in a genuine smile.

"They asked for permission to enter the Dismal Swamp, which I gave them." Her voice got low. "They think they can bring him back from the dead. But I said that as long as I was in charge of mink kind, we weren't going to be following no Sparpole."

"Wait," he said. "What do you mean, *Sparpole*?" asked Rufus.

The woman's eyes went wide, suddenly filled with pity.

"You don't know?"

Rufus shook his head. An unsteady feeling reverberated through him, rattling his bones like they were tuning forks. She took a breath before turning back to him. "Your daddy was Sparpole."

Though he was indoors, it felt like a great gust of wind had come and knocked him off his balance. It was like he'd left his body as he watched the woman look away from him uncomfortably

"No," he said. "George Pinhook couldn't have been Sparpole."

"He was, boy," said the king. Rufus's head began to spin as she continued. "That boy could slide underneath a door he was so skinny, which I guess accounts for the name. You ever see an actual sparpole? They use 'em on the boats. Slender as all get-out. But your daddy's figure changed, and so did his demeanor."

Rufus's mind was collapsing in on him. He barely heard what she was saying when he loudly interrupted her.

"Did he kill all those people?" he shouted.

The woman looked at him for a moment. Her eyes were big, but sympathetic. One glance at her face was enough—it was true. He could almost see it all reflected back at him: savagery, murder, evil. This was his family legacy. This was Rufus.

"Oh yes, boy. More than you could ever imagine."

He felt dizzy, so he leaned against a bookshelf. The woman watched as Rufus let it all sink in like a balm on his skin. In a way, it was a relief to just know it. But there was anger as well. He stood up.

The woman looked at him. She slowly began to nod. Her face began to lose its softness. She turned to the other men.

"I feel sorry for this kid," she said. "Shame we can't have two Pinhook boys running around in the Oxbow." She looked back to Rufus. "Which is why you'll be taking your leave." At that moment, the snake ropes again came alive, wrapping him up tightly as a hatch in the floor gave way. Rufus plunged into the water.

He fought against the ropes, but it was like fighting against a steel cage. He sank quickly into the murky black water. His chest felt like it was being crushed from all sides, squeezing out the remaining air, the little bubbles floating to the surface. All of his thoughts floated away with them. He could fight no more. The weight of the water had overcome him. With a last glance to the surface, he closed his eyes and stopped kicking. His only thought was the image of his grandmother, fighting to stay on the boat, only to fall away from him. His brother was there too, turning his back on him.

It was a dark, lonely descent to the depths.

But then an energy began to well up deep inside him, a slow flicker at first, but building like a stoked fire. The feeling worked through him. He no longer felt the need for air, no longer felt the constraints of his body. Rufus became something different—something powerful.

The ropes were soon irrelevant. Rufus looked at his hand, which was still there in outline, though it blended with the water around it. He looked back up at the surface. With a simple gesture, a surge of water shot up to King Mink's boat, lifting it from the surface before slamming it down as if thrown by an angry child. The boats lashed to it wrenched as the wave rippled out in an expanding ring. Screams of terrified marketgoers could be heard coursing through the water, but Rufus didn't care. He ascended from the depths with ease, as part of a wave that rose between the narrow spaces between the boats. The column of water deposited Rufus gently on the deck of King Mink's boat. His hand was again solid flesh, but he still felt the power of the river coursing through him.

Part of him wanted to destroy the whole market, tear the boats apart one board at a time. But then, flittering in the back of his head, was the thought of all the suffering he would cause, the death. He thought of the man they called his father. A shame consumed him, so overwhelming that he doubled over and fell to the deck of the boat. His control had vanished, leaving him a shivering mess.

Moments later, he heard footsteps.

"Well," said King Mink. "You're clearly the one with the talent." She eyed him for a time. "I'm going to do something that I may regret, but I'm going to let you live." A flicker of remembrance flashed in her eyes. "Actually…" she began. She turned to the mink men behind her. "Remy, go and get the knife."

At the mention of the word, Rufus tensed up, which she noticed. "Don't worry, idiot. I ain't gonna use it on you. I'm going to give it to you."

Remy returned with a decorative wooden box, which he handed to Rufus.

"He doesn't want the whole box, Remy," she snapped. "Just open it and let him take it out."

Remy did as he was told. Rufus was expecting something as ornate as the box that housed it, but it was just a normal-looking knife: plain wooden handle and a smaller blade that curved slightly upward at the end. However, there was one distinguishing feature: an emblem of a steering wheel and the name *Pinhook* finely etched into the base of the blade.

"Your family used to be something special round these parts," she said. "Special enough to have their names put on their knives. Remy, give him your sheath so the boy doesn't slice himself up." Remy looked flustered, but removed a small knife from a sheath inside his coat and handed it to Rufus.

"Why are you giving me this?" asked Rufus.

"Because, boy. That's the blade that killed your daddy." At the words, Rufus dropped the knife. It landed less than an inch from Remy's foot, sticking straight up out of the wooden deck. "Maybe you need a few lessons on how to hold a knife?"

A new determination swept through him as he looked at the blade.

"No," he said as he reached down and pick it up. He looked at it long and hard. This was the bit of metal that had ended his father's life. He took a deep breath. "I don't want this."

"Too bad, boy," she said. "I don't want it either, so you're stuck with it."

The woman made to turn back to her boat.

"Wait!" shouted Rufus. She turned. "What about Dismal Swamp?"

The woman looked to the old men. They conferred quietly, casting subtle glances at him from time to time. After a moment, they broke.

"Go to Dismal Swamp," she said. "Try and find your brother." Her voice took a sharp turn. "But you won't have any help from us."

"But how do I get there?" Rufus's voice was a bit more pleading than he'd have liked.

The woman sighed. One of the men began to protest, but she dismissed him with a hand.

"Two trappers are leaving for Dismal Swamp tonight," she said. "They asked for permission just before you stumbled in. They're moored at the southern edge of the market," she said, pointing behind her. "If you leave now, you might catch them." She turned back to the men. "Alright, boys. Let's break it up. This market is over." The group turned and began to walk away, but King Mink stopped. "And Rufus," she said. "Watch out for the *red mud*." With that, the minks turned and entered their boat.

As Rufus set off for the trappers, a giant bell rang out. All other noise stopped as the minks began to tear down their stalls. It was only a matter of time before the whole market began breaking into smaller and smaller islands. Rufus would have to hurry if he was going to make it.

As he stepped across to another boat, a voice called out to him.

170

"Where have you been?" yelled Josie. There was a mixture of anger and relief in her voice. Rufus almost couldn't bear to look at her. "I wasn't finished talking to you!"

"I know where Gideon is," he said bluntly.

She froze for a moment, reading the look on his face.

"Well, we should get a move on then."

"No," said Rufus. "I'm going alone."

"That's ridiculous. I'm…"

"Sparpole was my father."

There was a long pause as the words set in. Her face flickered through a dozen expressions as she tried to take in his words.

"Liar," was the first thing she said, her head shaking. Rufus didn't respond at first. There was nothing to say. His family was the reason for the death of hers. She was like a statue crumbling before him. Every part of her began to shake, softly at first, building slowly but surely until she vibrated fiercely.

"I'm sorry," he finally managed just as their section of the island started to separate from the other boats.

Josie turned and leapt across the water to another boat. She stood watching him as their pieces of island drifted further and further apart. With one last, tear-filled look, she turned and ran toward the middle of the disintegrating Mink Market.

It felt as though she had his heart chained to her heels, and that she was dragging it from deck to deck. He wanted to simply roll off into the water and disappear forever. Still, Rufus knew what he had to do—he had to find Gideon.

22

Dismal Swamp

She knew.

His name was out there. It hovered like the charged air before a lightning strike. Part of him wondered if she would tell everyone, but another part didn't care. He just wanted to be freed from this place, from this name.

If he didn't find the trappers soon, he'd be stuck on a random mink boat. Hundreds of torchlights scattered across the surface of the water like a field of lightning bugs. Most of the boats had splintered off from each other by this point, heading out in their various directions. He hopped from one to another in his search. He approached a couple of young men, still dressed in their festive clothing, as they unlashed their boat.

"Excuse me," he said. The men's mouths hung open awkwardly as they looked at Rufus. "I'm looking for a couple of trappers. You seen 'em?" Eyes still locked on Rufus, the young men both pointed in the same direction. He heard shouts ringing out from the boat in question, followed by a wicked growl. He swallowed hard and set out across the last few remaining boats. He managed to step onto the trappers' boat just as it was released from the others.

"Well, well, well," said a voice from behind a stack of crates. It was immediately recognizable. Rufus turned to see a man with limp black hair hanging down to his shoulders, parted down the middle like a curtain over his forehead—it was Murdo. "Get on out here, Sloo!" he shouted. Rufus's heart dropped as the giant creature emerged from inside the cabin. He cursed himself for not realizing that it was Tatum's boat, though Tatum herself was nowhere to be seen.

The creature sniffed the air. His strange, elongated jaw quivered slightly. Rufus wondered briefly if he could make the jump to the other boat, but he'd already missed one such jump tonight. He steeled himself; he was not the same person he was when he'd arrived here. Rufus stepped up to Murdo.

"I need a ride," he said, surprised by the ease in his manner, the confidence in his voice.

Murdo, however, doubled over and slapped his knee as he broke out into laughter. The oxman next to him looked confused for a moment, but eventually issued a few big, awkward chuckles into the night air.

"You hear that, Sloo?" asked Murdo. "This here flea bite says he wants a ride." He paused to laugh for another moment, wiping his eyes of the tears that had formed. "I think we ought to just toss him right over the side, don't you, Sloo?"

The creature stepped forward.

"Don't waste good meat, I say," he barked.

Rufus felt the tingle of the river as water began to creep over the sides of the boat, completely in his control. The creature stopped and Murdo's smile faded.

"You makin' threats, boy?" he said.

"King Mink said you'd take me to Dismal Swamp," said Rufus. "Otherwise your permission to enter would be denied."

Murdo crossed his arms.

"You think I care what a bunch of minks say? We came here for swamp grog." He lifted up a bottle and uncorked it with what few teeth he had left. He put the jug to his mouth and took a swig. After a quick grimace, he smiled. "Ooh!" he shouted, handing the jug to the oxman. "Good batch there, Sloo." The creature also took a swig, though a much bigger one.

"I just need a ride into the swamp, then you can leave me wherever."

Murdo huffed and turned to Sloo, speaking quietly so that Rufus couldn't hear. When he turned, he pointed to the knife hanging from Rufus's belt.

"How about you give me that there knife and we'll call it a deal," said Murdo.

Rufus hesitated, but pulled it from its sheath. As he saw his name etched into the side, shame again washed over him. He almost felt relief as he handed the knife over to the man.

Murdo studied the blade for a moment.

"Well I'll be a marsh wog at a petting zoo." He looked up at Rufus with mild disbelief. "That's a Pinhook blade. Where'd you get it, boy?"

"Took it off a dead guy," said Rufus, leaving it at that.

Murdo turned to Sloo.

"Well, let's get a move on then," he shouted. "No time to waste!" Sloo lumbered over to the back of the boat and fired up the steam engine. Murdo turned to Rufus. "You're just lucky that Tatum's off tracking something of her own," he said, smiling to show his black teeth. "Just remember that we're the nice ones." He gave a wink before making his way up to the pilot house. Rufus heard him exclaim about the blade again as he climbed. He couldn't imagine how such a thing could bring anyone joy. Rufus was just glad to be rid of it.

In moments they were chugging down the dark river. Rufus began walking amongst the crates. His stomach had begun to cramp as he looked at the cage that he'd been confined in only a few days prior. The crates themselves were all empty. They still stank of their former inhabitants—prisoners who surely by now had met their fates.

Rufus noticed a few new boxes too. These were huge, larger than a refrigerator. A chill went over him as he pictured the size of the creatures that would fill such a box. He had half a mind to stick a crate in the water and just float away. Fear fluttered inside him, but he was already so raw with emotion that it barely registered—this was simply one more task piled on the heap of unthinkable things he'd had to do. But he was in this now, for better or worse. His brother was close. He could feel it more now than ever.

"Hey, boy!" yelled Murdo from the pilot house. "Come on up here."

Rufus hesitated. He was not eager to be anywhere near the man.

"No, thanks," he said.

"You'll want to be up here if you can help it," shouted Murdo. "This is Dismal Swamp. Something's liable to snatch you right off the deck. It'd be ear-deep in kid guts before we ever even knew it."

Rufus studied the dark entrance of the swamp. It was thick with sludge and vines where a smaller river cut through, emptying its thick black water into the larger river. The land around them was dark and boggy. It felt like they were at the mouth of something dangerous, something waiting to gobble up all who entered.

Reluctantly, Rufus climbed up to the pilot house. He sat on a stool near Murdo, who looked nervous as their boat moved into the narrow waterway. This offshoot of the river was no more than fifty feet across, or so it seemed. It was so overgrown with weeds and knobby roots that it was hard to say where the river ended and the banks began. Tall cypress trees hanging with Spanish moss formed a ceiling above them. Soon, the canopy of trees canceled out all moonlight. For a moment, they were in near-total darkness, but then Sloo set lit the running lights, which were simply torches that circled the boat.

The boat cut through the thick algae on the water's surface, which collected in large piles on the sides of the boat, looking like giant mounds of lawn mulch. The air had an acrid punch to it, as if everything around him was rotting. The humidity was intense. The temperature seemed to rise the deeper they went into the swamp, and the sweat formed an ever-widening ring around his neck. He now understood how the place had earned its name.

"All kind of strange creatures live here," said Murdo, keeping his eyes on the water ahead of them. "And all of them can kill ya." He turned to Rufus. "You ever hear of a mud walker?" Rufus shook his head. It was just one of the many things about this place he didn't know. "They rise up out of the very ground beneath you. No one's ever caught one, but me and Sloo is about to change that."

"Good luck," said Rufus

"What, you don't think me and Sloo can do it?" said Murdo,

his tone more combative.

"I think you can do whatever the hell you want to do," said Rufus, tired and frustrated. The answer seemed to work for Murdo, as he turned back to the water. It wasn't long, however, before he piped up again.

"So what is it that you're hunting, boy?" he asked.

The last thing Rufus wanted to do was to talk, especially to him.

"Nothing," he said.

Murdo turned from the wheel and gave him a quick look.

"No, boy," he said. "For the minks to let you in, it must be something good. Or were you lying about that?"

"I spoke to King Mink," he said.

"Ha! There ain't no King Mink," he said. "They just shovel that horse manure out there to make everyone scared. Bunch of mongrels." As he spoke, he began blowing his nose into this hand, the contents of which he then smeared across his shirt. "Minks disgust me." He turned back to Rufus. "We're all hunting something. I can see that you've got a plan cooking up right now."

Rufus stood, fed up with the man.

"I'll take my chances on the deck below," he said.

"Suit yourself. But if you get your eyes sucked out by flying leeches don't come running to me. I warned you."

Rufus took a deep breath before walking back out onto the roof of the cabin. He could hear sounds of movement and breathing in the dark, low-hanging boughs above him. Murdo's warning began to make sense, and he decided to make his way back down to the deck.

Calls of wild animals sounded in the distance. They sounded altogether more sinister than the coyote howls and owl hoots he knew. Mostly they sounded like human screams, though somehow louder and more tormented. They also seemed close. He tried to block them out. The gentle hum of insects soon became a comfort.

Rufus found a place near his old cage and leaned back against an empty crate. The last thing he wanted to do was sleep, not when he was so close to finding Gideon. Still, it was late, and Rufus could feel his leaden bones becoming heavier. His eyelids too.

If he slept at all it was only in short, concentrated bursts. He was in the middle of one such burst when a voice pulled him roughly back to consciousness.

"Wake up!"

Rufus opened his eyes to Sloo's huge, lumpy face. He scrambled to get away from him as the big beast rocked back and let out a giant burp of laughter.

"Is he up?" shouted Murdo, descending from the pilot house. "Bout time!"

"What time is it?" asked Rufus, rubbing his eyes. It was still dark, as dark as when they had entered the swamp late last night.

"It's mid-day, you lout," said Murdo. "You just looked so peaceful there we had to let you sleep." Murdo then made a big show of jerky, spastic motions that were clearly meant to mimic Rufus as he slept.

"But it's still so dark," said Rufus, still getting his eyes to adjust.

"It's always night in Dismal Swamp," said Sloo.

"That's lucky for us," said Murdo, his eyes going narrow. "What we're hunting only moves in the dark."

Rufus looked around. The boat was no longer moving.

"Are we setting out soon?" he asked. "I need to keep going."

"But we've just set our traps, boy," said Murdo. "Don't you want to see how they work?"

"I'd rather not," said Rufus, his guard going up.

"But we need your help," said Murdo.

"I don't want to help," said Rufus, moving away from them. He began to feel the call of the water rising from within him.

"Calm down," said Murdo. "I just need you to have a look at this. See if you can identify it." Murdo's hand was clenched shut.

"No," said Rufus, but a shove from Sloo pushed him forward.

Murdo opened his hand to show a dark, gritty substance that looked like a pile of dust.

"I don't know what it is," said Rufus, moving to call the water. But before he could, Murdo blew the dust into Rufus's face. The gritty substance filled his eyes, his nose, his mouth. He reached for his eyes to wipe them, but his arms were too heavy to lift. His head also became unwieldy on his weakened neck. He was awake, but the dust had rendered him all but useless.

Murdo got into his face.

"Fox flower," he said. "Just in case you decided to use that dadburn mud magic on us," he said. "I ain't about to get stuck in no water box again."

Rufus registered the words, was vaguely aware of the ropes being wound around him, though he didn't understand what was happening. Everything went fuzzy, like the sides of his head were being squished in, his field of vision distorting.

Murdo grabbed him by the chin.

"Thanks for your help, boy," he said as the man's face became an unrecognizable swirl of light and color.

23

The Trap

Rufus was vaguely aware that he was swinging. His chin was firmly on his chest. He tried to lift his head, but it felt like a cannonball on a golf tee. As he tried to move his arms, he realized that he was again bound tightly by ropes. His vision was fuzzy, but it soon became clear that he was hanging from a tree.

When he finally managed to look around, there was no sign of the boat. Two torches burned on either side of the banks near him, like beacons in the dark swamp broadcasting his presence. A chill ran down his back as the situation became clear: Rufus was the bait.

He struggled to free himself but stopped when he felt something crawling on his back; something with a lot of legs. He froze. As the little creature climbed around onto his stomach, it became clear what it was: a spider. However, it was unlike any that Rufus had ever seen before, with two clusters of eyes that sat on different sides of his head and a pair of large fangs that glinted in the firelight.

Rufus's muscles tensed. He tried not to move. Beads of

sweat formed on his forehead, running down the bridge of his nose and collecting on the tip. He tried to keep the sweat from dripping, but it was like trying to hold back an avalanche with a snow shovel. A bead fell, landing on the spider. It lurched back and let out a horrible, snake-like hiss, exposing its fangs even more. The hiss grew in intensity as the creature began to climb. He felt each of the arachnid's eight hair-covered legs as they bristled against his chest. Rufus was helpless to stop its slow march towards the exposed skin of his neck.

Just as the first furry leg grazed Rufus's Adam's apple, a gust of wind came out of nowhere. It was a bird, swooping in without warning. His wings were at least the size of a full-grown man end to end. The gusts from each flap were powerful as it grasped the spider in its talons. With another heavy beat of its wings, it was gone as quickly as it came, landing in a nearby tree. The bird was owl-like in most of its features, but with a much larger, blood-covered beak and bulbous, almost human eyes. It screeched at Rufus before it feasted on the spider.

A moment later, the leaves began to sway. It was slight, but noticeable. The temperature felt as though it had dropped ten degrees and the water below him started to ripple. The strange bird looked up from its meal, craning its neck to see the commotion. With a horrid squawk, the creature took off, flying close enough that Rufus could see one of the furry spider's legs hanging from the bird's mouth and what looked like genuine fear in its strange eyes.

Soon other birds and small creatures followed in the same direction as the bird. Something was coming.

The rattling of the leaves and the disturbance of the water abruptly stopped. Everything went still. A shiver ran through

181

Rufus. He closed his eyes and gulped.

When he opened them, he saw the red spots.

At first he thought they were some kind of lightning bugs for the way they glowed, but then he remembered what King Mink had said about avoiding the red mud. More of the glowing spots sprouted up along the bank. They looked like burning hot embers. There were scores of them, paired together like sets of menacing eyes. Not only that, they were moving.

Suddenly, the red mud began to rise. There wasn't much shape to it at first. It was almost like a column of dirt lifting from the banks—a slow motion mud geyser. But then a form started to emerge, more and more defined.

Rufus wriggled and writhed, trying desperately to get free. His efforts, however, only sent him spinning in circles. He tried to call the water, but he was still too woozy from the fox flower Murdo had blown in his face.

His spinning finally stopped. However, it left him facing the opposite direction and unable to see the creature behind him. He could hear it though. The sound was that of a herd of cattle trampling through mud. It sluiced back and forth, growing louder as it approached. Perhaps it was better that he couldn't see the creature coming to end him.

As he listened, Rufus saw the running lights of Tatum's boat in the distance. This was the creature they were going to try and catch.

Rufus was tired and dizzy, but fought against the ropes with everything he had. Still, he only managed to set himself on a slow rotation back towards the creature. Exhausted, he could do nothing but accept his fate. He closed his eyes and let the twisting rope complete its journey. He soon felt the creature's breath, hot like the muggy air of August. It might have been curiosity that drove Rufus to open his eyes, but he found himself face to face with the creature, its glowing red eyes burning like fiery coals.

The creature was a tower of mud, lumbering before him with arms plunged into the water as if still connected to the earth below. It moved with the fluidity of a cat, or a sort of walking mudslide. Not a breath escaped Rufus's lips. His throat clenched shut. His pulse almost came to a halt as if suspended between life and death.

The creature's flame-red eyes were almost hypnotic. It moved slowly and deliberately, inching closer, almost like a dog coming to sniff a new guest. It leaned down to meet him at eye level, close enough that Rufus could see the twigs and stones sticking out from its muddy body. Rufus looked into the red eyes. He became lost in their fiery swirl.

Then, without warning, two large wooden jaws fell from the tree above, snapping together like a beast of prey around the creature. It was Murdo and Sloo's trap.

The box hung suspended from the nearby trees with the mud creature stuck inside, or so Rufus thought. A moment later, a trickle of dirt began to leak through the seams and cracks in the boards. The trickle grew to a stream, until finally the creature began to fully reform outside of the box. It turned back to the box, studying it for a moment before raising a giant fist from the water. Mud splatted everywhere as the blow splintered the box into thousands of tiny shards. He turned back to Rufus, freshly angered.

As it lunged forward, a series of fine mesh nets fell on it, but one by one they failed. When the creature was just a few feet away, it stopped.

The creature opened its mouth like a lion ready to roar. It

was a dark space filled with broken bone, fur, feathers, and blood. It let out a howl unlike anything Rufus had ever heard. He squeezed his eyes shut as the creature moved toward him.

But the move was not at Rufus.

The creature lunged past him like a muddy cross-country skier. It was going for Murdo and Sloo. At once, the scores of eyes began to follow, red streaks coursing through the mud. Soon Rufus heard the steam engine firing. The frantic shouting of Murdo soon followed.

After a moment the boat's engine wretched to a halt. Rufus's insides curdled as the low, howling chorus of the creatures began, followed by the smashing of mud against brittle wood, the breaking and bending of metal, and—worst of all—the tortured screams of Murdo and Sloo. Rufus could not block them out, they soon turned to a single whimper. With the final, sickening splash, the screams stopped.

Only Rufus's thudding heart could be heard in the swamp, floating over the water, canceling out all other noise.

He waited for his turn with the creatures, but they were gone. The swamp beetles were the first to grow so bold with their trills and calls. The sound was a great relief, especially as the chorus of nature started its crescendo towards its noisy din. The mud walkers weren't coming back for him. Somehow, he had managed to live, yet again.

Still, whatever flower Murdo had used on him hadn't worn off, and the water was still as far from his reach as his brother was. He began squirming again, but the knots that they'd used were too tight—those of practiced bounty hunters. He needed to move quickly. If the mud walkers didn't come for him, something else would. He let out a scream of frustration, which was swallowed up by the thick swamp air.

As he spun slowly on his rope, he saw that the bloody-beaked birds had returned, congregating in the trees around him. Their squawks were mild at first, but grew vicious as they quibbled with each other, trying to gain a superior position on a branch near him. And for what, it was becoming unfortunately clear: they were fighting for a chance at Rufus.

One of the birds set out from his limb, passing uncomfortably close. Rufus could hope that they were like buzzards waiting for him to die. But with each fly by, it seemed that they'd be just fine with doing the killing on their own.

As Rufus wriggled and squirmed, he noticed one bird strutting around on a branch above him. The others got out of his way as he made a big show of lifting each one of his feet and squawked in a series of short bursts. He spread his giant wings and let out a grizzled call. He was coming for him.

With one final squawk—more a war cry—the bird set off from his branch. Rufus saw the bloodlust in his eyes as it landed sideways on the rope just above his head. He managed to bob his head out of the way as it began pecking at him, but it was relentless. The bird was aiming for his eyes.

As the bird scooted down the rope to get closer, Rufus noticed a flickering blue light: a moxbug. He'd never been so happy to see a bug in his life. It landed on the bird's neck.

The bird reared back—too close to miss now. But before it landed its blow, it let out a terrible wail. The bug seemed to have stung it. As the bird took off, Rufus saw that thousands of the blue moths had appeared. They set upon the birds, which soon became glowing outlines. They squawked in pure anguish. The devilish birds took flight with the blue swarm chasing them into the night.

However, Rufus was still left hanging, his mind still foggy.

Every attempt to call the water felt like a car with a flooded engine unable to start. He was still no closer to freedom.

But then a single blue light approached from the river, moving slower than the buzzing swarm. Soon the outline of a boat appeared. It was no larger than a typical jon boat, but it had a paddle wheel churning behind it to push it forward. A single figure sat aboard it. Rufus knew it was Josie.

He watched with relief as she approached.

"Josie!" he shouted, but she did not look up. She made no attempt to steer her boat towards him. It appeared that she didn't even see him.

He shouted again, louder. Finally, she turned the boat toward him, cutting its engine just shy of him. She finally looked up, sitting with her arms firmly crossed.

"Are you going to help me down?"

"No," she said matter-of-factly. "You can control the river. Surely you can untie a rope."

"I'm sorry," he said. "I didn't know anything about my father. I only said those things so you wouldn't put yourself in danger."

"I don't need you looking out for me," she said. She turned and made to restart the engine.

"Wait!" he shouted. "You can't leave me here!"

"Why not?" she asked, her voice was disarmingly neutral. Rufus could say nothing. He could see the hurt in her face, though she was good at hiding it. She seemed to honestly be waiting for a response. His own silence stung him.

With that, she started the engine and the boat began paddling away from him. In that instant, he felt more alone than he ever had. He wanted everything to just end right there.

But then he remembered his grandmother. Her words rang out. The pull of the water began to fill the emptiness that had plagued him since he'd reached the Oxbow, and soon he again felt control. The ropes disintegrated into mist, but instead of falling to the water, the water came to him. Like a throne rising out of the river, Rufus was lifted across the surface until he was deposited directly onto the deck of her boat.

She watched him blankly for a second before speaking.

"Don't think I'm impressed."

"I don't," said Rufus. He didn't know how he'd done it—but he was here now, on her boat, and it was hard to be there. For her part, she wouldn't look away from him, though he could tell she wanted to. Finally, he managed a question. "Did you come all this way for me?"

Her head tilted and her eyes squinted.

"No," she said. "Another reason."

Rufus wanted to ask but fought back the urge. One of the little moxbugs floated in from above, landing on the floor of the boat. He looked back to her.

"How did you get the moxbugs to do that?"

"Moxbugs listen to me," she said. "And they're loyal." She looked him dead in the eye. "Unlike humans." There was venom in her voice, but also a sort of resignation, as if she just chalked up his weaknesses as being a part of the greater evil that was humankind.

"Where did you get the boat?" he asked.

"I have ways," she said. Rufus turned to the front of the boat where the fluttering of a few moxbugs lit the way. They had only made it around a grove of tall weeds before they saw it: the remnants of Murdo and Sloo's boat.

24

Signs of Life

The flatboat was wedged upright amongst the reeds, lifted out of the water as if it were a tiny piece of driftwood. What was once cargo floated in the river, utterly destroyed. Nothing disturbed the dark water.

"That's their boat," said Rufus. He didn't want to look, but couldn't pull his eyes away.

"What did this?" she asked.

"Mud walkers," he said. "I saw them…" He went quiet, losing his words as the flame-colored eyes and bone-rattling howls came back to him.

Josie cautiously guided them along the banks as they scanned for signs of life. The moxbugs flitted amongst the crates and other debris strewn haphazardly, providing a welcomed bit of light.

Rufus turned to Josie.

"Do you see anyone?"

"No one living," she said, pointing to a grove of cypress trees.

It was like a smack in the face when he saw what she was pointing at: there, on the banks near the ancient knotty roots of the cypress, were two sets of hands sticking out of the mud, though only from the wrist up—one a man's, one an oxman's. They looked like they had been buried, or perhaps pulled under.

"That's them," said Josie.

The four motionless hands stuck out of the ground, reaching to the sky as if for salvation, as if some other being could have come and plucked them out of their muddy graves. But there was none to be had, and only claw marks in the muck around them signified that they had at any point even been alive.

Rufus had never seen a dead body before, and here were two of them—their arms at least. Nausea coursed through him, but then he caught the glint of something shiny. It was a knife—his knife—still clutched in Murdo's fist.

"Take me over to them," he said.

"What? No way."

"Please," he said

With a deep breath echoing her reluctance, she turned the boat sharply toward the grove. As they approached, Rufus stood and leapt over onto the banks.

"What are you doing?" shouted Josie.

"I have to get something back."

"Those things could still be around."

Rufus carefully studied his surroundings. The overgrowth was thick with a flurry of small bugs and other creatures.

"No," he said. "They're gone."

With a boost of confidence, Rufus walked towards the arms. They stood like birthday candles plunged into a cake. As he stepped off of the roots he expected deep mud, but the ground was mostly dry. The mud beasts had pulled them through solid earth. He felt a pang of sadness for the two, even though they more than likely deserved it.

He knelt down in front of them and began to pry the knife from Murdo's hand. Rufus could see that the blade was muddy. Murdo had at least tried to defend himself. He wiped the mud onto some nearby moss and looked at the blade. The light of a moxbug allowed him to see his family name etched into the metal. He stood, halfway expecting Josie to have gone. However, she was still there, watching him cautiously as he returned.

"We have to keep going," said Rufus as he climbed back in. Josie said nothing, but simply steered them out towards the middle of the river as Rufus stared at the name etched into the blade on his lap. His name.

They floated on until the boat began struggling with the thick, goopy waters of the swamp. The paddlewheel was caked in a mess of green sludge.

"I can help with that," said Rufus.

"I'll manage," snapped Josie, though she sounded less confident than usual.

The engine sounded almost desperate, and soon became a sickly little yelp. Utterly clogged, the motor finally sputtered out. Josie made her way to the back of the boat and tried to clear out the paddlewheel with a stick. Rufus wanted to speak, but got the feeling that she wasn't interested in what he had to say. Eventually, she dropped the stick and let out a long sigh.

Rufus closed his eyes. In seconds, the river was at his fingertips. He willed their little boat forward, cutting through the green sludge without the need for an engine at all. Josie sat back down and folded her arms.

"Do you know where we're going?" he asked.

After a strained pause, she looked up.

"There's only one village. A little place called Fairdealing. At least that's what I heard."

"Then that's where my brother is," he said, and the boat jolted forward, nearly knocking Josie from her seat. She looked up at him, a disgusted look on her face.

"Tell me," she said as she situated herself on her seat. "What do you think is going to happen when you find your brother? Do you think he's going to go back and live with you and your grandma? Where would you even live? Some field? That wave would have destroyed your puny houseboat. And do you think your grandma's still there waiting on the return of her boys?"

Josie was almost out of breath as she finished her assault. Rufus couldn't move, couldn't even think. He felt like the ripped-out guts of a fish. After a moment, she turned around, putting her head in her hands. Rufus did what he could to keep control, but his anger boiled underneath. He hadn't really thought of what would happen after. Just staying alive had been his biggest hurdle. Finding Gideon was the thing that gave him a cause. But Grandma?

"I don't know," he finally managed. "But *when* I find him," he said, saying it slowly and with emphasis, "we'll get home to find Grandma."

He heard the despair in his voice. Josie had too.

Whatever chaos he was feeling inside helped him push the boat along faster between the overgrown riverbanks. They rode quietly, each confined to their own minds. The deeper they got into the swamp, the more ancient the place seemed, almost primordial. It felt like no person had ever stepped a foot in it. The fluorescent green algae that grew on the water's surface gave off a bright glow, as if the lack of light forced it to create its own.

As they rounded a bend in the river, he got the distinct feeling they were being watched. Loud snaps and scrapes could be heard on either side of the banks, forcing him to look over each shoulder nervously. He remembered that people still lived in this god-forsaken place, and that most were still loyal to his father. He thought about all the places he'd followed Gideon, all the trouble it had landed him in—the trouble he was in now. Following a Pinhook was the surest way to land you in a desolate place like this.

As they continued, Rufus was drawn to every splash of a bullfrog, every snap of a twig. It felt like an eternity passing—his nerves had eroded away. There seemed to be a threat concealed behind every tree.

Just when it began to seem he would turn himself inside out, he saw the first signs of civilization. A dock stood at the edge of the water. It was an ancient thing, half consumed by moss and strangling vines. Gnarled tree roots stuck out offensively from the banks. A boat was tied to the dock.

But just as he was about to turn to Josie, he saw the first set of eyes.

His stomach dropped as he looked at Josie.

"It's them," he said, peeking over the lip of the boat.

"Who?" asked Josie.

"Mud walkers."

At that moment, the mud before them rose to form a figure at least ten feet tall. Its head cut a sharp image, twigs sticking out of it like spiked hair. It had an athletic build, but with lanky limbs and large fists still attached to the ground below.

Half a dozen figures rose up behind it, just as many more rising from the water around their boat. The beings formed walls of breathing muck. They moved without taking so much as a step, their bodies slipping across the mud like a plow tilling the earth.

Josie's moths swarmed to her in a protective position, but they would do no good against such beasts.

The creatures moved close, stalking around each other and letting out low growls that shook every cell in Rufus's body.

As he made to turn the boat around, one of the mud walkers lunged at them. Its muddy fist reached out for Josie. She slunk back into the bottom of the boat as her bugs attacked the creature. However, as they landed their stings, the bugs were absorbed into the creature's muddy skin.

"No," she muttered as the giant fist coursed towards her.

Rufus reacted violently, sending a jet of water that wrapped around the creature like an anaconda suffocating its prey. The mud walker let out an ear-shattering wail. The shriek lasted only a second, as the water had cut clean through the creature. It fell to the water in large, dead clumps.

The other creatures scattered back to the banks, though the largest of them stayed in place. Rufus felt a rage burning through him, and was almost eager for the mud walker to give him an excuse to attack. After a moment, the creature approached. However, instead of attacking, it knelt in front of them, lifting an arm as if offering the right of way.

Josie pulled herself back from the edge of the boat and sat down. Her gaze turned from the creature to Rufus.

Rufus stood in the boat.

"Where are the Pinhooks?" he shouted. The mud walker tilted his head towards the dock before his muddy body sunk back into the earth. In seconds, he was gone.

Rufus and Josie exchanged glances before looking at the dock. Rufus moved the boat quickly towards it. His heart was beating wildly now. Rufus leapt onto the dock before the boat even arrived, aided by a walkway of water that rose from the surface.

"Come on," he said, as Josie finally stepped onto the rickety dock. "I know they're close."

They continued along a boardwalk built up above the swamp. Small lanterns hung from posts along the walkways of rotten wood that spread out across the swamp like spider veins, crisscrossing with seemingly no regard for destination. They circled ancient cypress trees—some as wide as a house.

The wood itself didn't even groan under his footfalls—it was too old for that, too water-logged and decomposed. The sound was more of a silent breath, with the occasional tiny squeak. Each footfall was a game of chance. More than once, Rufus had to rethink a step so as not to plunge a foot straight through. The pulverized interior of the boards sprinkled out like sand falling onto the surface of the dark water. Through the gaps in the slats Rufus could see it collect before it sank into the murk.

Thoughts of his brother propelled him along. His heart began to pound faster and faster. They had just passed through a split—more of a tunnel—in a giant tree when the village came into view. It hugged the wide river, which curved in a dramatic arc around it. Large fires burned in cauldrons held high on large wooden pylons, the light from which glinted off the water's surface. There was a surprising number of buildings, all of which stood on stilts or were built directly into the giant trees. They were constructed in a slapdash manner. It seemed that no single design had been agreed upon for each construction, and that whatever materials happened to be available would suit the purpose.

"Fairdealing," said Josie.

They continued on the boardwalk past the stilted houses. Walkways were built up into ancient trees heavy with green moss that hung like tears poised to fall. The walkways connected the elevated buildings, vines used to lash them together. Not one of them looked safe enough to tread upon, though it appeared that no one was around to use them anyhow.

His mind burned with the thoughts of his father. He stopped and turned abruptly to Josie.

"Do you think they're really going to bring him back?" he asked. Perhaps his tone was too eager, as her face sank as though in quicksand. She rushed past him as she spoke.

"I think that's their plan, yes."

He stood for a second, letting the idea wash over him. He'd grown up believing he'd never had parents. Now, one of them was supposedly about to return. As much as he wanted to feel dread, a part of him couldn't help but be interested in seeing the man who'd given him life, even if he'd taken so many more.

They continued to trudge through the desolate village until they arrived at the edge of the graveyard. At a large, menacing tree, Josie came to a sudden halt. There at the edge of a narrow stretch of river was a grave yard. The gravestones looked like crooked teeth sticking up from the ground. A group of people walked into view amongst the tombstones. Most of them wore robes of dark red, holding torches to light their way that cast a hazy glow in the humid air. As his eyes scanned the group, Rufus's attention zeroed in on one figure. Wearing normal clothing and straggling along behind the others was someone he knew all too well.

25

Family Headstone

The blood thickened in his veins. The world around him grew dim. Rufus could only see his brother.

The way Gideon stood was like a silent insult. Defiance infected his posture as he leaned against a large stone monument. It was a declaration that there was no one worth correcting his slouch for. His stooped shoulders and crossed arms were a barricade that no one would ever pass.

Rufus felt the water simmering deep inside of him—he wanted it to consume Gideon for causing all this. But just as quickly came another wave of guilt: it was Rufus, after all, who had caused so much damage. He had caused the wave, and it was because of him that he didn't know if their grandmother was alright.

A jab to his ribs brought him back to reality. Josie was pointing at something else in the graveyard. Gideon was not alone. There among the robed figures was Jasper and his two henchmen. But he was most surprised to see the tall, poised figure of Ms. Winesap emerge from behind a large gravestone.

"What's she doing here?" he whispered.

Josie hushed him, but seemed uncertain of the answer herself. She was, however, eager to move. Rufus followed silently.

They settled in behind a massive tombstone. He could hear the robed figures repeating some garbled chant as they walked toward the slime-topped river, but he couldn't make out the words. Rufus's heart dropped as a tiny moxbug flittered away from them and towards the assembled group. If the bug lit up, they'd be caught.

The creature fluttered in a corkscrew pattern right for the middle of the group. He heard Josie take a sharp breath. It was Winesap who saw it first. Her eyes broke from the chanting group to the buzzing moth. Then, as if on cue, the moth flared up its luminescent behind, commanding everyone's attention. The group watched it flutter for a moment until one of Jasper's henchmen reached up and crushed it in his hands, smearing the fluorescent innards on his pants.

"No!" shouted Josie, rushing from behind the gravestone.

Rufus remained frozen, deciding on whether or not to join her.

"Well, looks like we ain't alone," said Jasper, a big smile on his face. The smile sent a quake of anger through Rufus so volatile that he couldn't stop himself stepping out behind her. At seeing him, Jasper took off his hat and wiped his forehead with a cloth. "Everyone, I'd like you to meet my other grandson, Rufus." He put a hand out in a gesture towards him. "Join us."

In seconds they were being shuffled past the gravestones by Jasper's two henchmen. Each step brought him closer to a reunion he didn't know if he actually wanted. Jasper's eyes floated over to Josie.

"Who's your girlfriend, Rufus?"

Rufus felt his insides burn. He was still unable to speak.

"Her name is Josie," said Winesap, stepping forward. "She's my charge."

Rufus was a bit stunned to see Josie walk right up to her. He could see that she was holding something. It took a moment for Rufus to realize that it was his whistle.

"Wait," said Rufus. Josie turned to him. She looked sad.

"You did a good job, Josie," said Winesap as she studied the whistle. "You even got him here in one piece." She handed the whistle to a robe-wearing man with a scraggly goatee standing near her.

"You tricked me?" asked Rufus. "This whole time you were working for her?"

Josie didn't say anything. For once she didn't meet his eye.

"I could have had you from Wagtail," said Winesap. "But I wanted to see if you were strong enough to survive the Oxbow. Well done." She looked over to Josie. "Josie was my insurance is all."

Rufus felt the world around him start spinning. A tingly sensation lit up all over him: he didn't want to just call the water, he wanted to destroy everything, every bizarre creature, every black-souled person, every blade of grass, in the entire Oxbow. But then, his brother stepped out in front of him.

"Giddy," said Rufus, feeling his pulse climbing. "We need to go." But Gideon just shook his head. His eyes were heavy, strained as he spoke.

"Grandma's dead."

The words rang through the swampy air like the sharp clang of a bell.

Rufus took in a breath. His lips pursed. He looked to Jasper, searching for anything to disprove Gideon's words. The old man looked sad, genuinely so, and took in a deep breath, pulling the hat from his head and crunching it awkwardly in front of him.

"It's true, boy," said Jasper, eyes softened. "She didn't make it out."

Rufus barely had time to process it before Gideon lurched forward, grabbing him by the collar.

"It's your fault," he screamed. The words were laced with venom that stung Rufus even deeper. "You killed her!"

Rufus couldn't speak. He couldn't fight. He just stood there as Gideon snorted like a bull. He wore the look he had when he was raring to hurt someone—and this time it was Rufus.

Jasper stepped between them, his two henchmen each holding one of them. Jasper paced the space between.

"Calm down!" he shouted. His black hat was nearly crushed below his tensed fingers. A tear came to his eye as he looked down. It glinted in the firelight. He looked back to Rufus. His normal, sly demeanor had changed. "Rufus didn't mean to kill her," he said, looking to Gideon. "His rage blinded him so bad that he'd have lashed out at his own reflection if it gave him cause. But the boy's still your brother."

"He ain't my brother no more," said Gideon.

It was like his words had collected around Rufus's throat and begun squeezing.

"No," was all Rufus could choke out. He felt an anger so white-hot that he couldn't recognize it. A torrent of water from the river shot out at his brother, though it never met its mark. Another torrent had risen to meet it, this one controlled by Gideon. He and his brother locked eyes—they were in a battle, though they weren't even touching. The two columns of water were intertwined, held in place like a dead-even arm-wrestling match. As thoughts of his grandmother invaded his brain, Rufus felt his grip on the water begin to slip. The torrents began to tilt towards him, inch by inch, until they were directly in front of his face. He managed to meet Gideon's furious eyes as he was overpowered. Gideon's torrent wrapped itself around Rufus and squeezed tight.

Gideon stepped forward. His lower jaw jutted out the way it always did when he was raring to fight.

"You ain't the only one that learned things, brother."

"That's enough," shouted Jasper, grabbing Gideon by the shoulders. Gideon threw the man's hands away. For a moment it looked as if he might attack him too. Jasper looked Gideon in the eye. "Don't do this now, boy!" he shouted. "Not now! We're too close! Save your pouting for another time."

Gideon's eyes were full of rage. It pulsed through the water that held Rufus.

"It's your fault," he said, his words low and heavy. "She's dead, and that's because of you." The water tightened sharply, cutting off Rufus's breath, but then loosened. Rufus fell as the water retreated back to the river in a snaking trail. It felt as though all his fight had gone with it. The only thing left was the face of his grandmother in those final few moments on the boat. He wanted to let the weight of it crush him.

He turned to see Josie. Tears had formed in her eyes.

Jasper leaned down and touched Rufus's shoulder. Though he desperately wanted to, he didn't even have enough fight to pull away from him. Jasper nodded to his two men, who grabbed Rufus roughly and hoisted him to his feet. He studied Rufus carefully. His face was still somber, but something else had taken over, a glint in his eye gave away his excitement.

"You little piss ant," Jasper said. A bit of a smile finally returned to his face as he put the hat back on his head. "Believe it or not, I'm actually glad you're here." Rufus didn't respond. "I want you to see something," said Jasper. He looked at Gideon. He turned to Winesap, Josie, and the robed figures. "Give us a moment."

With that, he put an arm around Rufus, who was too weary to fight it. Gideon followed a few paces behind as they walked through the graveyard. Rufus could feel his brother's eyes burning into him. His jaw jutted out. His eyes were wide and bloodshot. Something was burning inside him, some new energy, and it frightened Rufus.

The roots of dozens of trees had reduced many of the once-grand monuments to broken slabs of stone, but one stood fully intact. In fact, it was built directly into the trunk of a mighty tree, the roots of which were wrapped around the stone slab as if holding it in an embrace.

The monument was set off from the rest, about ten yards from the edge of the river. Something about it seemed sinister, perhaps the way that there were no other graves nearby, or the way that even the bugs seemed to show quiet reverence in the area around it. The reason for his discomfort soon became clear as Jasper took off towards it.

"This is where he lies," he said, stopping a few feet shy of it. There, chiseled into the stone, was the name he'd been dreading to see, *George Oxley Pinhook*.

26

A Return

The man who had held so much power—who had killed so many thousands—was now buried here, buried under a tree in some backwoods swamp, mourned only by a few fanatics.

Tears filled Jasper's eyes as he ran his fingers through the stone's engraving.

"It's been a long time, boy," he said, patting the monument. He spoke as if whoever was inside could still hear. "Not much longer now."

Gideon walked up to it. The anger in his eyes seemed to soften. Something else was there now. He reached his hand up and touched the stone. He stared at it, unmoving. The curiosity soon became too much for Rufus as well. He shook himself free of the henchmen and walked up to it. He read the name over and over until it became a rhythmic chant in his mind. Still, it did not become natural. It could not be normalized, what his father had done, what his brother and grandfather were doing now.

He turned away.

"Feel however you want about him, boy," said Jasper. "You can't change the blood. Soon you'll meet him and find out what kind of man he is, what kind of man you could be." The words left him feeling raw. He saw that the robed figures, Winesap and Josie included, were now coming back. Winesap was the first to speak.

"Jasper, we don't have time to waste. The flower's potency will start to fade soon enough."

Jasper held up a hand as he turned back Rufus.

"You see, boy. There are others who know that he was a great man."

Winesap interrupted.

"Don't fool yourself, Jasper. George Pinhook was a terrible man. It's his power that made him great, and it's his power that interests me."

Jasper pointed a finger at Rufus.

"Winesap is one of the most powerful river mages there ever was. She's been training up these others, waiting for this day." He grinned big. "Now you get to see it." He turned back to Winesap. "Bring back my boy."

"Wait!" shouted Josie. "I didn't think you would really bring him back." Her voice rose in pitch as she spoke.

"You'll understand soon enough," said Winesap.

"No!" shouted Josie. "You can't do this."

Winesap walked up to her slowly. A stern look formed across her face as a ring of white formed around the irises of her eyes. Josie looked down to the ground, a defeated look on her face. Even after her betrayal, Rufus began to feel a trickle of anger as Winesap turned back to the robed figures.

"Get to work," she snapped.

The group of robed figures placed the plant onto the ground

near the grave. Three of them waded out into the shallow part of the water, each holding a lit candle. The light reflected off the surface, giving their faces an eerie glow. The other three river mages began tearing petals and grinding flower pods. Winesap dropped them into a pile between the gravestone and the river and used a flint to light a fire. As the spark hit the flower, a fire sprang up. It was unnaturally large, burning bright orange at first, but soon turning to a deep green tinged at the tips with dark purple. The flower appeared to not burn up, looking as though it would burn for some time.

"Now we need Pinhook blood," said Winesap. Rufus tensed up. He looked to Josie, who seemed nervous as well. "Bring the boys over." One of Jasper's goons shoved Rufus forward. Gideon walked of his own accord. Winesap sized them up. "Which of you is stronger?"

Gideon wasted no time in answering.

"I am."

Winesap looked him deep in the eyes before speaking.

"Maybe in an arm-wrestling match," she said, but then her eyes turned to Rufus. "But it's Rufus who has stronger magic. Bring him here."

Gideon gave him a look of wrath as two river mages dragged Rufus toward the fire.

"I see you brought your own knife," said Winesap. One of the mages took it from his belt and handed it to her. At seeing the knife, Josie stepped forward, her mouth open, but Winesap hit her with a look that stopped her cold. Winesap's eyes opened wider as she studied the blade. "Where'd you get this, Rufus?"

"King Mink," he said. "They thought maybe I could use it."

Winesap smiled.

"I don't know what to say." She turned to the other river

mages. "How fitting that the same knife that stopped Sparpole before, plunged into his back, will now be the same one that brings about his return?" There was chatter amongst the group, though it quickly fell away to silence. "And did you know who it was that plunged this blade all those years ago?" Rufus shook his head. It didn't matter to him. None of this did. "The answer is closer to home than you might think." Rufus didn't understand what she was trying to say. "It was none other than your very own grandmother who did it."

"No!" shouted Gideon, kicking the ground in anger.

"It's true," she said. "He could only be stopped by someone with his own blood." She reached over and took Rufus's left hand. He fought at first, but hers was a soft touch. "She feared his power," she said, looking at Rufus with sympathetic eyes. "But she didn't kill him. She only released him from his body. He's been a wandering spirit ever since." Winesap's thumb traced the perimeter of his palm. For a moment, he felt himself relax. For a moment, he felt nothing.

But when he looked back down, his hand was covered in red liquid: she'd sliced a gash across his palm.

"No," said Rufus, but two mages forced his hand over the fire. He winced at the pain as one of them squeezed his hand shut. Blood dripped into the flames as if he were wringing out a wet rag. The mages chanted as the fire sputtered and began to swirl. From deep within the flames, images appeared of a man, though they were small and soon puttered out.

"It's not working!" yelled one of the mages, a man with a thin mustache and straggly goatee. "We need more blood."

"Give it time, Thomas," said Winesap.

"We don't have time!" shouted the young man. "We're too close to let this fail! You've dangled this moment in front of us for years. It's now or never." He looked to the other mages. "Bring him back to the fire."

Winesap and Rufus locked eyes. Hers were filled with worry. Rufus could do nothing as one of the men put a hand around his forehead and retched his head back, exposing his neck. His pulse quickened as he struggled to free himself. The water tickled at him, but was just beyond his reach.

"Wait!" shouted Jasper. "What are you doing to him?" His smirk evaporated.

"Sparpole needs a host," said the man. "If you want your son back, this is the only way, else he'll stay a roaming spirit."

Rufus's eyes met Josie's, whose face was tear-streaked. She turned and buried her head into Winesap's side. All sound faded away. Only the whoosh of blood running through his veins remained, blood soon to be spilt.

Rufus could see Gideon standing in the periphery. His mouth was open, but he stood frozen.

"Gideon!" he shouted. "Help me!"

But Gideon only looked on like a meek and helpless child.

The mage lifted the knife. The look on his face was savage. Rufus squeezed his eyes shut—a tear streamed down his cheek. He waited for the cold touch of the blade, the warm gush of his life as it spilled onto the dirt.

The sound of skin puncturing was louder, more pronounced than Rufus had expected. He waited for the pain, though it never came. It was only after he opened his eyes that he realized that it wasn't his skin that had been pierced.

Jasper stood behind Thomas. The mage's eyes were wide in surprise, his mouth open. After a moment, a trickle of blood came from the corner of the mage's lips. That's when Rufus saw a blade lodged in the bottom part of his throat.

The mage dropped the knife at his side as he fell to his knees. He landed in the dirt, lifeless.

Winesap put a hand to her mouth, muffling a small moan. It took the rest of the mages a moment to realize what had happened, but soon they were wailing beside their slain comrade. The mages holding Rufus joined them, and he soon found himself freed and panting heavily on the ground. One of the mages closed the man's eyes before they turned as a group, sights set squarely upon Jasper.

Zell and Riggs each rolled up their sleeves, ready to defend the old man, but they had not even taken a step forward before they were forced to their hands and knees, choking on the water that the mages had summoned to fill their lungs. They put their hands to their throats as they gurgled out their last remaining breaths. Jasper didn't look to his drowned men, but kept his eyes focused on the mages encircling him.

"I ain't gonna let you harm those boys," he said, his voice meek, but defiant. Gideon radiated a nervous energy, bouncing from foot to foot. Josie too, watched in silent horror as the robed figures surrounded Jasper.

"Stop," shouted Winesap. "That's enough."

One of the mages turned to her. It was a young woman, maybe twenty years of age.

"You're right," shouted the young mage. "You should kill him!"

"More death won't bring Thomas back," she shouted, but the mages continued to encircle Jasper.

As they closed in on the old man, Rufus noticed that the flame from the burning flower had leapt to Thomas's robes. Starting near his feet, it quickly began to run over his body. Rufus could also see that his whistle was clenched in the dead man's hand. He grabbed it before the flames could consume it. The heat from the fire was intense, hotter than any fire he'd ever witnessed. He smelled burnt hair and felt that his face had been singed, but he had the whistle.

Just as the mages were about to strike, screams from the river pulled their attention away. The purple fire had leapt from Thomas's body and spread across the surface of the river, quickly surrounding the mages in the water. They dunked themselves below the surface, but it didn't help; the flames burned even underwater. They thrashed about, issuing ear-piercing screams as the fire began consumed them.

Their muffled screams soon faded as they began to blur together like modeling clay being shaped into another form.

From the still-flaming surface rose a single, newly-formed body. It was no longer Thomas or any of the other mages, who had been completely consumed by the flames. This was someone else. The body was somehow vaguely transparent, almost washed free of color. Its whole being shifted buoyantly as if it were a balloon swishing with water. The flame roared around the body, illuminating the image of a man. He wore what appeared to be a military uniform, a thin sword hanging from his belt. The water and fire connected with his lower legs, as if he were wearing a gown made of burning river. The figure touched his chest as if to make sure he was actually there. A grin appeared on his face as he studied his surroundings.

Rufus didn't need to be told who it was—he knew it right down in the marrow of his bones.

It was Sparpole. It was his father.

27

Whistleblower

His appearance was striking. He had a short beard and rugged features, but most remarkable was his eyes. They were so familiar, but somehow distant, like looking into a mirror but not recognizing the image staring back. They carried the same unwieldy fire as Gideon's. Rufus knew then that this man could do evil.

It was Jasper who spoke first.

"Georgie?" he said as he walked towards him, stepping past the robed figures who seconds before had meant to kill him, but who now stood in rapt attention. Jasper walked to the edge of the banks, even took a few steps into the water before he stopped, dropping his hands down to his sides in disbelief. His eyes filled with tears. "Georgie. My boy."

The figure turned to him. There was a moment of confusion, but then the flicker of recognition.

"Pa?"

"It's me," said Jasper, bringing a hand to his mouth. Sparpole smiled before looking to Gideon and then to Rufus. Rufus could not move, could not think.

"Are these my boys?" asked the watery figure.

"That's them," said Jasper.

"Boys," said Sparpole, his voice shaky. He put his hands out toward them, though he did not move from his place on the water. Gideon stepped out onto the surface of the river. He didn't even seem to notice that he was walking on top of the water, as though it had somehow hardened into ice. Rufus could barely give this feat a thought, however, as he too felt the urge to go to the watery figure, as if obeying some parental command. But as he made to take his first step, he caught himself backing away.

"What's wrong with you, boy?" shouted Jasper, but Rufus could only shake his head. "This here's your daddy. Go on."

"No," said Rufus.

"Don't you go doubting him now, Rufus," said Jasper, his voice almost pleading. The old man grabbed him by the shoulders. His fierce blue eyes were wide with excitement. "It's been a long time coming, this moment. I spent over a decade in the frozen north just to bring you here—just to bring our family back where it belongs." As the man pleaded with him, Rufus was struck by how he had never belonged anywhere except the dusty field he'd grown up on. Whatever this was, he knew he didn't belong here either.

"It's alright," said Sparpole. "He probably don't remember me." A loose smile appeared on the figure's face, though with the wavy movements of his skin it was hard to read. The figure lurched forward, almost as if in pain. Clasping his chest, he spoke to Jasper in a weak voice. "I ain't got long, Pa," he said. "I need blood."

"How?" said Jasper. "I don't understand."

Sparpole looked at the three kneeling robed figures.

"You, river mages," said Sparpole. "Step forward." The figures arose without the slightest hesitation. They walked to the edge of the water and stood obediently.

"You want to serve?" he asked.

They couldn't answer quickly enough, each of them swearing their full allegiance to the man.

Sparpole listened to their praise for a moment, then nodded. With the snap of his watery fingers they each fell to the ground, gurgling until they lay motionless. He heard a gasp from Josie as Winesap covered her mouth with a hand. The purple flame quickly spread from the river and began to consume them. As their bodies disappeared, the smoke drifted towards Sparpole, which he breathed in as if taking a long drag off a pipe. The smoke made him fuller, more fleshed out. He saw the look of horror on Winesap's face.

"You killed them!" shouted Rufus.

Jasper rushed forward, grabbing him by the shoulders.

"It's alright," said the old man, though his face said otherwise. "They wanted this. This was their plan all along, to give themselves up so that Georgie...Sparpole could live."

"No!" shouted Rufus. "He'll just keep killing."

Rufus threw an elbow into Jasper's gut and broke free of his grasp. The old man heaved and coughed as he fell to the ground. Seeing him knelt down, struggling to catch his breath, Rufus felt a bit of pity for the old man.

"You're a Pinhook, alright," said Sparpole, but his smile evaporated as he focused in on what Rufus clutched in his left hand. "Is that my whistle?" Rufus had forgotten about it. "Good job, boy!" he shouted. "Give it to me."

Rufus looked down at the cylinder of metal in his hand. He thought about the lengths his grandmother had gone through to keep it hidden. The thought of his grandmother sent a deep sadness reverberating through him.

Jasper, still kneeling, croaked out, "Give it to him, boy."

"I won't." Rufus tossed the whistle into the dark river.

Sparpole let out a loud, raucous laugh as the whistle floated back up to the surface as if being carried on a tray.

"Gideon," he said. "Come do me a favor." Gideon stepped forward without hesitation. "Give that whistle a toot."

The water lifted the whistle to Gideon, still standing on the river's surface.

"Don't do it, Gideon," said Rufus.

Gideon looked almost possessed.

"And why should I listen to you?" he snapped.

He put the whistle to his lips and blew. The ear-piercing screech sent Rufus's hands to his ears. It felt as though molten iron had been poured down them.

When he opened his eyes, the surface of the river was bubbling, a fluorescent steam lifting from it. From the depths, a fiery red light emerged, growing brighter until the outline of a steamboat appeared below the surface. It was the Specter Steamer.

The boat erupted from under the water, coursing through the air before landing with a splash on the surface of the narrow river. By rights, it shouldn't have even been able to float in such a space, but this boat clearly wasn't subject to the laws that governed other steamers.

Sparpole turned back to see the Specter Steamer.

"You did good, Pa," he said as Jasper made his way back up to his feet. "You did real good." He looked again at Rufus. "We've got one last thing to take care of. Come with me, boys."

"No!" said Rufus. "I ain't going anywhere with you."

Sparpole's face seemed to vibrate. For a moment Rufus thought that his watery skin might burst.

"Just come and welcome your daddy home!" shouted Sparpole, tossing a lasso of water to bind Rufus.

"Rufus!" shouted Josie, throwing something in his direction. It caught the glint of the fire as it flew through the air: it was his knife. It stuck in the ground near him. Rufus grabbed it as Sparpole sent another lasso to bind Josie. She screamed as the tendrils of water squeezed around her.

"No!" Winesap shouted, breaking Josie's watery bonds at once. Sparpole sent a torrent of water that blasted Winesap viciously across the graveyard and into the trunk of a tree. Josie yelled as she took off after her. It was then that Rufus finally felt the tickle of the water working through him. His bindings began to loosen, but Sparpole sent another wave crashing into him as if he were being tossed around in a tempest. Rufus choked and coughed as Sparpole pulled him to the water, his bindings so tight he felt they might slice through him. Even in his fragile state, Sparpole was too powerful.

Jasper stepped forward, a wild look ringing his eyes.

"Where are you going with those boys, son?" he asked.

Sparpole set his sights on the Specter Steamer.

"To my boat." With that, he and Gideon set off across the top of the water, dragging Rufus behind them. The force of it was too much, and Rufus lost his grip on the knife. It sank below the surface, his heart sinking with it.

"Don't hurt them boys!" shouted Jasper as he splashed out into the water after them. There was desperation in his voice as he made his way up to his knees, his waist, then his shoulders. "Don't hurt 'em! Don't hurt them boys!"

Jasper's cries disappeared as the red fog enveloped them.

28

The Specter Steamer

The surface of the water felt more like concrete. Every bump jolted him until he felt like his insides had broken loose. With a final hoist, Rufus was tossed onto the deck of the Specter Steamer, landing painfully on his arm. Though his bonds were still wrapped firmly around him, he managed to get up to his knees.

The air was colder on the boat, as if they'd left the swamp and entered a wintry tundra. From his position on the bow, Rufus saw a quick flash of movement on one of the upper decks. A soft chuckle—that of a child's—rang out from somewhere in the fog; it sent a chill down his back. He could feel the presence of far worse beings aboard, things that pulled at the deeper, darker parts of his soul.

Sparpole stood at the foot of a grand set of stairs that led to the upper decks. Every piece of the boat seemed ancient and weather worn, a capsule preserved from another time. A look of awe was splayed across his warped face, a face that seemed to be losing shape quickly.

"This is it, boys," he said.

"What are we doing here?" asked Gideon. There was confusion in his voice, but also an eagerness. Rufus could do little but listen.

"We're here to take what's ours, son." At that, Sparpole glided forward, dragging Rufus along with him. His loose form wobbled and buckled as he ascended the stairs, a trail of water leaking from him as if he were a snail climbing a rock.

They reached the top to find a set of heavy-looking wooden doors. The deck posts around them were covered with snaking vines, though they seemed long dead. Sparpole turned to Gideon, whose face was full of wonder.

"Open them, son." There was an expectant pause as Gideon grabbed the ancient doors and pulled. The hinges let out a horrible creak, seeming agitated at being violated after so many years. With the doors finally open, they entered. It was a grand parlor, a long, ballroom-like space. The air inside was frigid enough that Rufus and Gideon could see their breath. All noise was strangled down to a choked silence. Parts of the walls had been ripped away, exposing some bizarre world beyond, a world far different to the swamp that should have been there. It was a world of stone buildings and fires that burned brightly in the distance. The world was so vivid that Rufus felt as though he could reach out to the fires and singe his fingers. The bits of wall remaining were stained deep crimson, as though splashed by waves of blood.

Rufus was too awestruck, too overwhelmed to struggle. He could only watch as Sparpole circled the gallery. The way the man moved reminded him of Gideon, of how his brother would circle slowly until he'd set on his direction, but then setting out in a burst like a shark attacking his prey. But something else struck him as he looked at the figure. In the eerie light of the steamer, Rufus was disoriented by the likeness he shared with Sparpole. It was as though the figure had come and stolen his face, implanting his own crimes on his cheekbones and in the contours around his eyes, his evil on his prominent chin and the arches of his eyebrows. Rufus found himself trying to will his face to reform in some less sinister shape. The thought of sharing anything with this person almost made him ill.

Sparpole made his way to the far end of the room where there stood another set of doors.

"On the other side of those doors lies the path to the pilot house," he said. "We climb until we meet the pilot, a banished soul and our ancestor, Winslow Pinhook. From him, we take control." He turned to the boys, his watery face now ballooning with excitement. "Then we take this boat to the heart of the river, and from there, it's all ours—this world, and all of the river realms." He turned to them. "But there's something I need first. I need more than just some river mage to really bring me back...I need my own blood."

Gideon wasted no time.

"I'll do it," he said. "Let me help you." The eagerness in his voice was unsettling. It didn't sound like him at all—he was like someone possessed.

"No," said Sparpole. "I've got plans for you yet." He turned to Rufus. "It's you I want to help me come back."

Gideon shot Rufus a look of jealousy.

"I won't," said Rufus, but he had barely finished his sentence before jets of water took slammed him against the floor. The water pinned him down like shackles.

But another voice rang out, stealing his attention.

"Don't be so hard on the boy," said a figure near the entrance.

Rufus needed only to hear the wooden footsteps to know who it was.

"Weego, my old friend," said Sparpole, though there was something cautious in his tone.

Weego began to inspect the room.

"Been a while since I've been aboard this old boat," he said. He walked leisurely, as if this were just another day. He finally turned to Sparpole. "Been a while since I've seen you, George."

Sparpole's whole body shook like a gelatin mold.

"You've come at a good time," he said. His voice took on a more suspicious tone. "So long as you're aiming to help."

"I ain't really aiming for anything, George." Weego leaned on his wooden cane. "I think my time is up. I don't really have much of a…what do you call it? A desire to live anymore."

Sparpole let out a loud, awkward laugh.

"Weego, old buddy, I'm afraid I can't help you," he said.

"Oh, but you can," said Weego, walking slowly towards them. Sparpole looked on with caution. "If you'll remember, back when we made our deal, you offered me whatever I wanted in exchange. I disposed of the other River Keepers—my own kind, and the last of them at that—to give you free rein. But I didn't get nothing you promised. Instead, I spent years in exile, watching over your thankless brood." Rufus listened as the creature spoke. He was a traitor. Rufus looked at him with even more revulsion. Weego, as if feeling Rufus's disgust, turned to him and smiled. "Well, Georgie," he said, pulling his cane up under his arm and straightening his jacket. "What I want now is to die."

Sparpole's face was impossible to read, partially because of the waves underneath his watery skin. Slowly, the figure cracked a smile. He began shaking his head.

"You're too important, Weego. I could use you."

"You already have, Georgie. You already have." He again turned to Rufus. Reaching into his coat, he produced a knife. "You dropped this, Rufus." With a wink, he threw the knife at Rufus, which stuck into the near his leg.

In the next second, the watery bonds had left Rufus and moved on to Gideon. At first, Rufus didn't know what was happening, but Weego's face made it clear that he was in control. The torrent of water wrapped around Gideon and slammed him to the floor. He screamed out in pain as Weego manhandled him. Though he wanted to, Rufus found himself unable to react.

But Weego's assault was short-lived, as Sparpole sent a cannon volley of water to blast the tiny creature. It was relentless, a thunderous force of water. It went on longer than it should have, time seeming to stretch as Sparpole made to finish him off.

Finally, the torrent slowed to a trickle. Rufus wasn't even sure that there would be anything left of the creature. However, when the water stopped, there was the little oxman, bruised and beaten, but alive. He looked right at Rufus and smiled before Sparpole sent one final torrent which wrapped around him. Weego's body was like a limp doll as he was lifted off the floor. Then, with a violent thrust, Weego was flung through the wall and into the strange alternate world beyond.

As Sparpole turned back to him, Rufus reached for the knife. However, he was too late, as a jet of water pulled it away. More watery ropes came to pin him to the floor.

"He couldn't kill you, boy," Sparpole said to Gideon as he collected himself on the floor. "That was a part of his blood oath with me. But I bet it hurt like the dickens." Gideon was soaked, but up on his feet in seconds. In fact, he looked more charged up than ever.

"I'm fine," he said, snorting. "I'm ready for this."

"Good," said Sparpole. "We have something to finish. Gideon, take this." With that, the knife rose on an arm of water. Gideon looked at it for a moment, eyes wild, before grasping it in his hands. "I remember that blade all too well," said Sparpole. "It was planted in my back by none other than my dear old ma." A grin crept over Sparpole's face. He motioned to Rufus. "It's his fault she's dead now, ain't it?"

Something seemed to have taken control of Gideon. He was no longer himself. His eyes swam with bizarre colors that morphed and changed with each step he took.

"What are you doing to him?" shouted Rufus, still unable to move.

"Nothing that he ain't willing to do himself," said Sparpole. "He wants this, Rufus. I can feel it burning inside him." He turned back to Gideon. "Now go on, boy. Bring me back, then we can pass through these doors together."

"Gideon, no!" he shouted, but his brother's face was vacant.

"This is what you are, boy!" yelled Sparpole. "You were born for this."

Gideon took a step towards Rufus, knife poised.

"What are you doing, Giddy?"

"You killed her," shouted Gideon in an unnatural voice. A storm began to rage in the world beyond the walls. Loud cracks of thunder rang out. Rain blew in from the portions of walls that had been ripped away.

"Go on, son," said Sparpole. "You'll know what it is to be someone powerful, someone respected."

"You never thought we'd find him," said Gideon, looking

Rufus in the eyes. "But I knew it. I knew we would." His voice was hysterical, the hate in his eyes suffocating.

"Why do you think he needs us?" shouted Rufus. "You're being fooled, Giddy. He's gonna kill us both!"

But his words seemed to evaporate into the air. Gideon knelt down on the floor next to him, knife held high above his head. Rufus looked in his brother's eyes. They were maniacal, enraged, scared.

"I have to," said Gideon.

Rufus pulled in breaths. For a moment he was empty, not even graced with the comfort of a final thought or memory to see him to the finish of his life. But then a fire deep inside him began to burn. Rufus again felt control.

As his brother thrust the knife down, a barrier of water slid between Rufus and the blade, stopping it inches from his heart. Gideon looked surprised but remained determined. He lifted the blade again. However, as he made to bring the blade down, his arm began to seep water. At first, it looked as if he were sweating profusely. But it began to leak faster until it started to evaporate before his very eyes. Gideon screamed out in pain as his right arm disappeared completely.

As Gideon fell to the floor, so did the knife. Rufus picked it up and looked at it for a moment as he stood. Rufus felt a control that was complete. He held the knife out to his brother.

"You never cared about me!" shouted Rufus. His head spun. His entire childhood played out in front of him. Every let down, every broken promise was laid out before him. For once, his brother looked like a weakling. Gideon wasn't the one who was going to get to walk away from this fight, and that made Rufus feel good. "You were going to kill me!" Rufus walked closer, pointing the knife at his brother's neck. "All this is as much your fault as is mine. I should have cast you off a long time ago."

"Boy," said Sparpole, a strange smirk on his swishing face. "You're the one that I want by my side. You've got the Pinhook spirit." Sparpole approached them. "Look at him, Rufus, moaning on the ground. He's pushed you around all your life, ain't he? I remember even when you two was young 'uns, he was always too much for you, always made you cry."

Rufus looked at Gideon. All of his brother's deceptions—his lies and betrayals—came flooding back to him as he walked across the parlor towards his brother. Gideon stammered and spit, unable to free himself from the watery bonds Sparpole had covered him with. The more Gideon fought the emptier Rufus felt—all of his fury had begun to burn off.

"Go ahead, boy," said Sparpole. "Take your place next to me. Finish it. Then maybe together we can even bring back your grandmother." At the mention of Grandma Jezebel, he could only think of the last time he saw her; her face filled with fear, her last words being to take care of family. Rufus turned back to the watery figure—their father.

"I won't," said Rufus.

"Mongrel," snarled Sparpole, drawing his sword from its sheath. He moved toward Gideon, pinned down on the floor. The anger in his brother's eyes swiftly turned to fear as their father held the sword over him. Dark water bubbled from little sores in his watery skin.

"Get away from him!" said Rufus, pointing the knife at him. Sparpole only laughed.

"You can't cut me, boy. I ain't flesh and bone...yet."

Rufus tried to use his anger to call the water, but this had moved far beyond anger. Sparpole lifted the sword high above his head and swung vigorously. As the blade met Rufus's meager knife, the sword shattered into thousands of tiny droplets that floated through the air like a spring mist. A look of shock spread across Sparpole's face.

Rufus swiped at him, landing the blade across Sparpole's arm. The figure shrieked as a dark liquid spilled out. It was not blood, but some sort of murky life force. It oozed out of him like dingy river water.

"No, Rufus!" he shouted. "I'm your daddy!"

"You'd have killed us both!" Rufus shouted. He swiped again, landing it across Sparpole's chest. The apparition slunk backwards, his color quickly fading. He tried desperately to keep the life in him as waves rippled under his skin. There was true fear in his eyes as he began losing his human shape.

"Son," said the apparition, reaching out to him.

Rufus's pause was unexpected. Something held him back. He remembered Grandma Jezebel's words before she fell. He looked down at his brother, trembling, crying, clutching at his missing arm. Rufus had found him, but the damage had already been done. He began to circle Sparpole.

"You're the reason our family is shattered," said Rufus. "You destroyed everything around you. It's because of you that Grandma Jezebel is dead." The words came out so easily, and he was surprisingly calm as he spoke.

Sparpole laughed.

"I remember when you were born," he spat, sinking lower and lower. "I looked you in the eye and I knew I had you sized up. I told your mama right then and there that you were nothing, and that you'd always be nothing. You're a poor excuse for a Pinhook!"

Rufus fought back a flash of rage. This had to be done

without anger.

"I get to decide what I am from here on out," said Rufus as he drove the dagger into Sparpole's watery chest. Rufus looked deep into his father's eyes, could see the fear that spread through his pallid face. Sparpole tried to cling to whatever strange lifeforce sustained him, but soon his whole body began to rumble. Rufus took a step back as the rumbling became more violent, shaking the form of his father until it was unrecognizable. Then a flash of light erupted from within, blowing Rufus back across the room as his father spilled like a shattered glass of water. In the flash—as he was blown across the room—he saw his grandmother's face. His first thought was that he was dead. But then he landed on the far side of the room where they had entered. He was dazed, but alive.

He gathered himself. There was only an inky stain on the floor where Sparpole had been. The remaining dark liquid seeped into the floorboards as if sucked through a straw and the room was again calm.

He saw Gideon rising to his feet, staggering towards the doors that Sparpole intended to take them through.

"Gideon!" shouted Rufus, too dazed to stop him. "Don't!"

"I have to find him!" shouted Gideon.

"He's gone, Giddy! There's nothing to find!"

"No!" Gideon's scream was from a different part of his soul, a place of desolation. It sent the hairs on Rufus's neck standing up straight.

"Gideon!" Rufus's voice broke as his brother neared the set of doors. With his one remaining arm, Gideon grabbed hold of the ornate handle and turned it.

"I'm sorry, Rufus." With that, he opened the door. Everything seemed to slow as hundreds of skeletal figures charged forth.

Rufus met his brother's eyes for only a moment. He saw the fear in them, the sorrow, but then Gideon was overwhelmed by the mob of frenzied ghosts.

The figures ran at Rufus like feral dogs let loose on a rabbit. There was no escape. He could only close his eyes as the call of the water washed over him completely.

It took a moment, but he finally managed to open his eyes. All around him were the black-eyed spirits, some adorned with top hats, some with fine gowns. Their faces were soulless, their bones fleshless. But Rufus was no longer scared. A wall of water had encircled him, forming a partition that kept the marauding spirits at bay. The ghosts could only glare at him.

But then a scream ripped through the air. It was the Specter Steamer's whistle—the boat was leaving.

"Gideon!" shouted Rufus, but there was no answer. More figures began filling the room as the boat lurched forward. If Rufus stayed much longer, he'd be trapped. Reluctantly, he turned and ran down the stairs and onto the deck, his watery shield parting the spirits like curtains.

As he reached the deck, the bow plunged below the surface. Rufus ran along the outside walkway towards the giant paddlewheel at the back of the boat. Everything tilted at a sharp angle as the boat began to submerge. Rufus leapt and prayed.

29

A Home

Rufus felt the water all around him, but he no longer struggled. With barely a thought, the water pulled him to the surface. He emerged onto the banks without so much as a drop on him.

Winesap sat by the burning plant, now just a few smoldering coals. Blood ran from a gash on her forehead. She stared at the embers, looking distant and forlorn. Josie emerged from the graveyard, carrying a few plants she'd collected.

Winesap looked surprised when she saw him.

"Is he gone?" she asked, her voice dry and defeated. Rufus didn't know if she was speaking of his brother or Sparpole, but the answer was the same. He nodded. She looked out to the river.

"I killed Sparpole with this knife," he said, staring at the blade still stained with dark liquid. He looked back up at Winesap.

"You probably want to kill me next, don't you?" said Winesap. Josie dropped her plants and stared Rufus hard in the face.

"I don't want to kill anybody. I'm not like *him*. I'm surprised you don't know that by now." He looked back at his knife.

Twice now it had been used on his father. It was a heinous heirloom. He casually tossed it into the water. There was a look of shock in Winesap's eyes, but she said nothing. He turned back to her. "Why did you do it?"

Winesap took a long, deep breath.

"Mud magic can blind you," she said as she turned to him. "Don't think you won't be tempted by it." Rufus looked back out over the water. Mud magic had overtaken Gideon so fully that Rufus didn't recognize him. Almost as if reading his mind, Winesap spoke again. "And Gideon?"

"He's still on the boat. The ghosts…" he said, but lost his voice as the sickening faces flashed back into his mind.

Winesap nodded.

"The Specter Steamer collects roaming spirits," she said. "They stand watch over the pilot house, which is occupied by Winslow Pinhook, the father of mud magic."

Rufus didn't want to ask the next question, but it charged from his mouth anyhow.

"Is Giddy dead?"

Sympathy filled her eyes.

"No," she said. "The spirits wanted him *because* he was alive. It's possible they'll keep him that way, though he might eventually become one of them."

Rufus turned back to the river. It ran dark and calm as if nothing had happened. Beyond them, through a rare opening in the ceiling of trees, a thunderhead filled the sky. It seemed to stretch for miles, shooting bolts of lightning in all directions. Gideon was out there, alongside unimaginable horrors.

"And what about Jasper?" asked Rufus, still staring out at the water.

"He followed you into the water," she said. "I didn't see him come back." She paused for a moment as the reality of it sank in. "Some part of him must have escaped Sparpole's grip. Some part of him still wanted to save his grandsons."

"That's it then," said Rufus. "My whole family. There's nothing left." He sat down in the dirt.

Winesap looked out toward the gravestones, towards the large one that held the remains of George Pinhook.

"Your father was dead long before your grandmother put that knife in him," she said. Just then Josie started to smear a mashed concoction of the plants she'd collected into Winesap's cut. She winced but continued. "I sought you out because I knew that you could be more powerful than Sparpole ever was. He'd been consumed by the power of mud magic. It has a toxic effect." She paused for a moment. "Rage feeds it most." She turned back to Rufus. "What you make of your name is up to you now."

"Are all the other mages dead?"

Winesap nodded and looked at the dirt.

"I'd known some of them since they were children. They were like family to me." She turned to Josie, who quietly continued her work dressing Winesap's wound. "I won't be going back to the showboat with you."

"No!" shouted Josie, standing quickly. "Why not?"

"The minks knew our business," she said. "Word will spread. The authorities will learn that I tried to bring Sparpole back. They'll come for me."

"Are they going to come for me as well?" asked Rufus.

"Not likely," she said. "But I can offer you a way out if you want it."

"What do you mean?" said Rufus.

"I can send you home," she said. "Out of the Oxbow. You

see, I'm the one who finally discovered how to open the path between the worlds after all these years. The Specter Steamer leaves a trail of its magic wherever goes. Mud magic becomes even more powerful in its presence." She looked out to the water still covered with a glowing red fog. "I could send you back, but you must decide right now."

Images of flat, barren fields flooded his mind. The sounds of bugs, the heat of summer radiating through the thin floorboards of the houseboat, the constant weight of boredom. That had been his life. He looked back up to Winesap.

"You say that Gideon could still be alive?"

"It's possible," she said, though she had the unmistakable look of a parent trying to temper an eager child's expectations. "But maybe not."

"Then I'm staying." He let the words sink in.

"I don't know if you'll ever have a chance to get back," she said. "You could be stuck here."

"There's nothing to go back to," he said. "And if there's a chance that my brother's still here, I'm staying."

"Very well," she said, getting up to her feet. "But now I have to go."

Josie stood quickly.

"I'm going with you," she said. "You can't just leave me."

"It's too dangerous where I'm going," said Winesap. "I'd do well to survive myself. Plus, I need you to go with Rufus."

Josie held back the urge to plead, but it was clear that she was distraught.

"But how are we supposed to do the show? What will *I* do?"

Winesap grabbed her shoulder.

"You left the Oxbow with the meanest bunch of bounty hunters there is and came out without a scratch. You survived an oxman riot, navigated the Mink Market, and tried to take on Sparpole himself. You don't need any help." Winesap looked at Rufus. "Just tell Otto Modest that Rufus is a river mage. He'll help with the show."

Rufus looked up.

"Help with what?" he asked.

"Rufus, you need to learn your craft. There's no better place to do it. Otto Modest is a tyrant, but it's a home. I think you need one of those about now." She motioned to one of the rafts pulled up on the banks. "Get in. Take this back to the showboat before the river trap wears off."

"It was you that set the river trap for The Otto Modest, wasn't it?" asked Josie.

The sly look on her face was answer enough.

Rufus boarded the little raft, but Josie lingered for a moment.

"When are you coming back?" she asked Winesap.

"I don't know that I will," she said, putting a hand on Josie's head. "Take care of my show." Josie could only nod. "Now get going." Josie reluctantly stepped into the boat, which moved of its own volition. Winesap watched them from the graveyard as they made their way into the dark of the swamp.

It was a long, tedious trip back. They sat in quiet as the boat cut its path through the sludge lining the top of the water. Neither of them wanted to speak; neither was able to sleep. They both sat lost in their thoughts. Lightning from the thunderhead provided occasional glimpses of light through the thick canopy of the swamp, though no rain fell.

The first light of morning was breaking as they reached the mouth of the swamp. Where there had been a city of mink boats lashed together the day before, now there was only empty water. They continued upriver for a time until the silhouette of The Otto Modest came into view.

Their raft ran right up alongside the stationary showboat. It hadn't moved since they'd passed it the day before. Considering the earliness of the hour, the boat was already a flurry of activity. Something seemed to be happening. Rufus jumped out first, and made to help Josie, but she insisted on stepping aboard herself. They walked together to the bow, where most of the crew were gathered.

As they walked to the front to see what all the commotion was, a large figure stepped out in front of them. It was the man whose portrait was painted on the side; it was Otto Modest.

"Where's Winesap?" shouted Otto. He was draped in a huge, multicolored bathrobe. Rufus reckoned that if it were hoisted on a ship it would be big enough to act as a sail. "We need to break this river trap. We've got some special guests."

"Winesap is gone," said Josie. "She's not coming back."

The gargantuan man let out a noise like an enraged bear before he turned his sights on Rufus.

"Who's this?" he said.

"This is Rufus," she said. "He's a river mage. Winesap said that he's going to help with the show now."

"Did she now?" he asked.

The man clamped a hand around Rufus's neck and began to drag him to the side of the boat. Before Rufus could even think, a column of water knocked the man down to the deck.

Everyone on board stopped what they were doing. The man climbed to his elbows.

"Alright, river mage," said Otto as he pulled himself up. "Not bad. Let's see if you can prove your worth. We have special cargo and need to get moving." From behind a stack of crates emerged none other than Tatum and, behind her, tightly bound with all manner of ropes and chains, Weego. Almost instantly, the color drained from Rufus's face.

"No," said Rufus. He couldn't believe it. The last time he'd seen the creature, Sparpole had tossed him so violently that he was sure he'd be dead.

"Don't worry about him," said Otto. "His bindings are treated with fox flower so that he can't work his magic. Tatum caught him in the swamp last night. We're going to split the reward as she lost her boat in the fight."

Tatum's beady eyes zeroed in on Rufus.

"You," said Tatum. "I remember you. That river mage paid good money for you. You gave my boys a good wallop with your mud magic. If I'd've known you was a stinkin' mage I'd have gutted you myself."

She rushed forward.

"Hold on there," said Otto, putting his full weight in front of Rufus. "We ain't on your boat now, remember? You need me to take you to the army outpost." He patted Rufus's head roughly. "This one's mine. He's apparently running my show now and he's going to get this boat free of the river trap." He looked back at Rufus. "Of course, if he can't free this boat, then he's all yours." Tatum sneered.

Otto pushed him forward. With a bit of hesitation, Rufus went over to the edge of the boat. "Go on, boy. Tell that river that I've got business needs attending. Set us loose!" yelled Otto impatiently. Most of the crew had come in behind him, watching eagerly.

Rufus put his hands into the water and closed his eyes. For a moment he felt nothing, but soon another sensation overtook him: he felt anger pulsing through him—not his, but the river's. He could feel himself fighting against the will of the river, and the river was winning. Exhausted, Rufus finally pulled his hands free and fell back onto the deck.

"I don't think I can..." he started, but a scream of the steam whistle cut him off.

"We're moving!" yelled a deckhand.

"He did it!" said Otto. "Somebody pick him up. Good job boy!" As two deckhands hoisted Rufus back to his feet, Otto leaned in. "If I was you, I wouldn't go messing around with the likes of Tatum. She was reared on razor blades and broken glass as a baby, and she nursed off of rattlesnakes and cottonmouths. You ought to thank me for keeping her off you. I'll consider you in my debt." With a swoop of his gargantuan robe, he was off, leaving Rufus at the foot of the stairs. "Let's get moving," he yelled.

Tatum walked over to him.

"My crew..." she started.

"They're dead," said Rufus. "Mud walkers." He was battle-worn and weary, but he no longer feared her. "They tried to use me as bait. It didn't work out so well." Tatum began to rock back and forth, lifting a finger to him. However, she said nothing, but simply spun and stormed away.

It was then that he saw Weego again. In the split second before Tatum yanked him away, he gave Rufus a wink.

He looked around. Josie was nowhere to be seen. Not knowing what else to do, he walked to the front of the boat and sat down, watching the water as they steamed ahead.

Within an hour they'd made it to the little military outpost called Groat's Landing. It was a ratty place, looking more like an occupied war zone than a city. Battlements stood disused and broken; slumping walls seemed held together by the creeping vines and ivy that covered them. The fort was not much better, though it did, at least, look occupied. The steam whistle began howling, a piercing arrow through the silence—Otto wanted every wretched soul in Groat's Landing to know about his catch.

As they pulled into the docks, two gaunt soldiers in tattered uniforms—neither of them much older than Rufus—approached, looking confused.

"Excuse me, boys," shouted Otto as the stage plank swung over to the banks. "But I was wondering if we could get this here creature hanged this morning?" Two deckhands dragged Weego out from behind him.

The soldiers nearly tripped over each other as they ran back down the docks. A man with a bold mustache and wild hair soon emerged, clad in his long pajamas. Otto didn't delay getting to the business at hand.

"Morning, Captain!" he shouted. "This here is Weego, last Keeper of the Oxbow, wanted for grand treason against the People's Government of the Oxbow Territories." Rufus reckoned that Otto had never looked so proud. The captain looked astounded. He put his glasses on and studied Weego before turning back to his men.

"I'll be…" he said. He turned to one of the young men next to him. "Send word to Oxalis that we've found the Keeper."

"Don't forget who found him," said Otto. "One Gwendolyn Tatum and the famous Mr. Otto Modest. Do you need help spelling my name?"

"It's on the side of your boat, sir," said the captain, pointing to the large letters.

"Oh, right," said Otto. "Just how long before we hang him?"

"Hang him?" asked the captain. "He's wanted in Oxalis. They'll want to make a big show of it down in the capital."

Otto looked perturbed.

"Let me tell you something," said Otto, taking a large step towards the man. "There ain't a more dangerous creature in all the land. You give him a moment and he'll close your eyelids for good. We hang him now."

The captain looked at Weego, who seemed intoxicated with all the talk of his death.

"He's right, sir," said one of the young men. "All the cells are rotted out. The ones we do got are filled with oxfolk from that riot in Wagtail."

The captain set to thinking. His eyes moved in small circles, his brain no doubt working through each possible scenario. He looked at Weego, who gave him another big smile, then back to their shoddy, crumbling fort.

"Alright," said the captain. "He hangs this morning."

Otto turned back to his crew.

"String him up, boys!" he shouted.

Masses piled off the boat, following Weego on his final march. But Rufus stood leaning against the wall of the lower deck, taking in deep breaths of the morning air.

"Hey, boy," said a voice behind him. It was an old man with pipe-cleaner legs and caterpillar-like eyebrows. "Are you sure that you don't want to see this? Most youngsters get excited about a good hangin'."

"No," said Rufus. "There's enough pain in the world. I don't need to go seeking it out."

The man turned to him and nodded. He seemed impressed.

"Agreed," he said. "Anyways, when you get to be my age, the only death you get excited about is your own." With that, he turned back around and disappeared inside the boat.

Rufus turned to follow him, but then something tugged at

him, some feeling deep down. While he was a traitor and a pest, Weego had helped him. Somehow, Rufus couldn't help but feel sorry for the wretched creature. At the very least, he figured he ought to see whatever sort of show he was about to put on. With a sigh, Rufus took off along the muddy trail toward the center of town.

It had taken only minutes for word to spread. Along the main drag—a wagon-rutted mess of mud that ran alongside the river—stood the gallows. A large crowd had already gathered, many still wearing their nightclothes, all eager to see the hanging.

The gallows were as ramshackle as everything else in town—one of the young soldiers' feet went right through the first step, eaten through by rot. But they recovered, and after a short inspection it seemed that the stage of the gallows was solid enough for another hanging.

The crowd looked on, seeking death as flowers seek light.

Wasting no time, the noose was slipped over Weego's neck. He smiled a most ill-timed smile, looking directly at Rufus.

"Any last words?"

"Yes, actually." The crowd was silent, rapt in their attention. "It's my duty as a Keeper of the Oxbow River to inform you that the plague of the Pinhooks is still upon us." There were gasps from the crowd. Rufus himself stood frozen. A flicker of rage welled up inside him. "One of them has come to the Oxbow and will wreak great havoc." Weego's eyes went right to Rufus. For a moment, Rufus considered using the water to stop him, but then he realized what Weego was doing: giving him another chance to kill him. Rufus wouldn't indulge him. Rufus smiled back at Weego. "Get it over with then."

"May the Oxbow have mercy on your soul," said a soldier

as the stool was kicked out from under Weego. However, just as the line went taut—when there should have been a body writhing as the life escaped it—there was instead a splash of water, as if someone had just dumped a bucket. Weego the River Keeper was gone.

The crowd erupted into an excited chatter.

Otto ran onto the stage, knocking one of the young soldiers off in the process. He was so red he looked as though he would bleed through his pores. He ran up to the empty noose and studied it.

"Where is he?" he shouted, enraged. He dropped to his knees, running his hands through the puddles where Weego's body should have been, the body that surely would have made him one of the richest people in the Oxbow. Though Rufus had his reasons for wanting to see Weego dead, it was a fine consolation that Otto Modest would be losing a fortune. As Otto stood, he fell through the rotting wood stage, becoming trapped up to his bulging gut. The assembled crowd broke out into laughter. The two scrawny guards attempted to help pull him up, but it was no use—they'd have to disassemble the gallows to free the huge man.

As Rufus looked on, a moxbug landed on his shoulder. He took the little creature in his hand and looked back to the boat. On the bow he could see a number of the blue lights. He left the crowd and made his way back to the boat where he saw Josie studying a few of the bugs in her palm.

"Did they kill him?" she asked without even looking up.

"Only a Pinhook can kill him," he said.

She turned to look at him. Her face was unreadable.

"And did you?" asked Josie.

"No. But who knows what I'll have to do to get out of here."

"You aim to ruin things just like a Pinhook, and then just leave?"

"Listen," said Rufus. "I know that my family was…is…terrible, but I'm not." He paused. "At least I don't think I am." He wondered if it was true. Josie picked up another moxbug.

"I was going to leave you hanging there," she said, staring forward. Rufus knew she was talking about what had happened in the swamp. She looked up at him. "You grow up around here and things like other people's pain just start to matter less and less. You realize you've got to fight for your own life. And when I heard you were a Pinhook…" She took a deep breath. "I'm sorry I lied to you, stole from you."

Rufus didn't know how to respond. He hadn't lived the same life as her, hadn't grown up in the same way. For her it made sense to do what she had done.

"Do you think Winesap is coming back?" he asked.

She looked up, bleary eyed.

"I don't know," she said. "She's always seemed on the verge of deserting me."

"I'm sorry about that," he said.

She looked up at him.

"What about you?" she asked.

Rufus thought about it.

"I don't have anywhere else to be," he said. He looked at her, saw the strain in her eyes. He knew that she wanted to mourn Winesap, but was embarrassed to show Rufus. "I'll need help though," he said. "I don't know anything about running a show. Maybe we could use some of your bugs."

She thought for a second.

"No," she said. "It doesn't need my bugs. I think it needs you." She turned back to him. "Wait here a second." She went inside the boat. Moments later she reemerged holding a fiddle. "I know that it's not New Orleans or wherever it was that you were talking about, but you could still play."

He looked at the fiddle.

"I don't know what to say."

"If I were you, I'd just let the fiddle do the talking."

Rufus cracked a grin, his first in some time.

"Thanks for this."

They sat in silence for a moment, looking out at the sun rising over the river before she again spoke.

"I need to go check on my bugs," she said, turning to leave. However, she stopped after only a few steps. "Rufus," she said. But she stopped short of completing her sentence. With a warm smile, she turned and disappeared into the boat.

Rufus looked out onto the water again. Though the pain for his grandmother still felt raw and total, he realized he had never wanted to go back to his old life, even if he'd had the chance. Here he was, a fiddle in his hand, living on the river like he'd always hoped he would. It wasn't his river, but it was becoming so. The sound of the giant paddlewheel chopping through the water soothed him. Moving felt right.

He placed the fiddle onto his shoulder and dragged the bow across the strings. The sound echoed out over the water. As the first few bars of a song rang out, Rufus found himself strangely at peace. His grandmother was there in the music.

The Oxbow, for now at least, was home.

* * *

Epilogue

He emerged from the water, staggering up onto the banks as the last of the evening light faded. The steamboat behind him traced its pattern through the current, though its paddlewheel left no wake. Indeed, it did not even disturb the surface as it left its trail of red fog hanging in the sky like the distant lights of some big, bright city.

Collapsing into the mud, he clutched what remained of his right arm. The pain was searing—had been for some immeasurable amount of time. The fog seemed to mix with his pain to put him into a new state of delirium. He wanted only to lay here, to sleep forever in this mud, the gentle sound of the river lapping up against the banks.

But after a few moments, he managed to lift his head high enough to see his surroundings. An old city of stone lay in ruins before him. A great wall ran around it, though large portions had been reduced to rubble. Inside, its streets were dark and deserted. It was unlike any city he'd ever seen, almost like some ancient, overgrown place out of the storybooks he'd read as a child. He looked back to the river, where a set of colossal towers loomed in the distance. They must have been as tall as skyscrapers. It appeared to be a dam, though it looked more like a giant gate spreading the width of the river.

The sound of footsteps over the rubble drew his attention back to the city. From the crumbled wall emerged two figures, both wearing red robes with hoods that covered their faces. His breathing quickened. He was defenseless. At this point, any horror they could inflict on him would surely be a mercy.

The two figures walked down to the banks.

Still favoring his missing right arm, he managed to use his left to pull himself onto his back. He would at least see their faces.

One of the hooded figures stepped forward—face still concealed by the hood—and walked a slow circle around him.

A deep breath.

The hooded figure knelt down next to him, pointing at the missing arm.

His pulse quickened. Another pain shot through his phantom limb.

The hooded figure reached for his missing arm. With one hand on his right shoulder, the figure put his other hand directly on the wound.

He expected agony, but after a moment, a cool sensation replaced the pain. He looked down to see water emerging from his wound, almost as if the figure was coaxing it out of him. But instead of splashing into the mud, the water held its shape: the shape of an arm.

Soon the full form of a hand and five fingers completed the figure's work.

He was too overwhelmed to speak. His pain had subsided fully; he could now move his watery arm and each finger as though they had always been there, though he could hardly believe that he was able to see straight through them.

After a moment, the figure finally pulled back the hood to reveal a man with a thick beard and warm smile.

"Welcome, Gideon," he said, his voice kind and consoling.

"My name is Mofran." The bearded figure then motioned to his accomplice. "You may already know my companion, Ms. Winesap."

At this, she pulled back her hood.

"It's good to see you again, Gideon. We have a lot of work to do."

Glossary of The Oxbow

- **Bottle Trees**: A popular tradition in the South, bottle trees are made by placing bottles on ends of tree branches. They are said to ward off bad luck or trap evil spirits.
- **Children of Oxum**: A group of people devoted to the practice of mud magic and the mysterious Oxum, a group of ancient beings who control the River Realms. The Children of Oxum must practice in secret, as they are outlawed by the government of the Oxbow.
- **Flame Flower**: A flower native to the Thorn Forest that enhances the potency of mud magic.
- **Flatboat**: A rectangular boat with a flat bottom used for the movement of cargo or other goods.
- **Fox Flower**: A mossy flower found in the Glamorris Highlands that decreases the potency of mud magic.
- **Keelboat**: A small, river-going vessel with a fin protruding beneath the water to act as a counterbalance. Usually propelled by a long pole or oars.
- **Mink**: One of a river-going people who rarely have a permanent home. Instead, they can often be found traveling up and down the river selling wares such as mink butter.
- **Mink Market**: A semi-annual gathering of minks held at different locations along the river. The market is formed

by lashing together hundreds of flatboats and is usually accompanied by a special celebration, *The Night of the Minks*.

- **Moxbug**: An insect native to the Oxbow, known for its bright blue light. It also produces a glittering dust, which is traded illegally and known for increasing magical ability.

- **Mud Magic**: A form of magic particular to the Oxbow. This magic is typically derived from the river itself and mostly revolves around water, though there are many facets of the practice that are yet unknown. The government of the Oxbow has made such practice illegal, though most authorities will turn a blind eye to it.

- **Mud Walker**: A deadly species of magical creatures known to move through mud. When they emerge from the mud, they can stand as high as ten feet tall. They live mainly in the swamp regions of the Oxbow. No one knows who first encountered a mud walker, as they didn't likely survive the experience.

- **The Otto Modest**: A showboat famous for its terrifying and otherworldly productions which are aided by mud magic. The boat is named after its newest owner, Otto Modest.

- **Oxalis**: The capitol and largest city in the Oxbow.

- **Oxbow River**: This is the biggest river in the Oxbow. Known for its unexpected changes and bizarre behavior, the Oxbow River is famous for being the only river of its kind to have no true end and no true beginning. It runs in a large circle through the entirety of the Oxbow. As such, it and its many tributaries are the main source of transportation for residents of the Oxbow.

- **Oxman**: Also known as oxfolk, this term encompasses

a wide array of creatures native to the Oxbow, including River Keepers, Dortha Giants, and a number of other races.

- **Reelfoot**: A game that consists of cards enchanted with mud magic. The cards typically reflect important events, people, and creatures of the Oxbow. Gameplay takes place through apparitions that emerge from the cards. These apparitions can do battle, compromise, or trick each other depending on which mixture of cards is played.
- **River Mage**: A dedicated practitioner of mud magic.
- **River Trap**: A hazard of traveling on the rivers of the Oxbow, a river trap occurs when a river-going vessel is frozen in place on the river, almost as if locked in ice on the river. River traps have been known to last for months and even years in some cases. They usually result from angering the river—perhaps by boating at night—but can also be put into place by a powerful river mage.
- **Snake ropes**: Snake ropes are simply a regular rope enchanted with mud magic so that they may move of their own volition. Often used in trapping and bounty hunting.
- **The Sorrows**: Commonly referred to as the time period encompassing Sparpole's War, when the government of the Oxbow had to fight against the powerful river mage, Sparpole, and his allied forces of minks and river pirates from the cave rivers in the east. There were many innocent casualties, as Sparpole inflicted his terror not just on the army, but against whole towns and villages.
- **Specter Steamer**: A mysterious steamboat said to be piloted by Winslow Pinhook, the most powerful human river mage the Oxbow has ever known. The Specter Steamer is accompanied by a deep red fog that usually

turns the water itself the color of blood. Many say that it accompanies souls to the heart of the river.

About the Author

Raised in a small Missouri town, Ross Martin grew up hearing tales about his riverboat-faring ancestors. He holds a Master's degree in Creative Writing from Royal Holloway, University of London and is also a founding member of the experimental music outfit, Lowlegs. He writes about the world of the Oxbow from his home in Austin, Texas. To learn more about the creatures, people, and places in The Oxbow, visit:

www.rossmartinbooks.com

You can connect with me on:
- https://fb.me/therossbow
- https://www.instagram.com/therossbow